MARY & ETHEL
... and Mikey Who?

Available from Moreclacke Publishing

Books by Sherman Yellen

Spotless: Memories of a New York Childhood

Cousin Bella — The Whore of Minsk

December Fools and Other Plays

Book by Paul Ford

*Lord Knows, At Least I Was There:
Working with Stephen Sondheim*

Books by Robert Armin

The Flash of Midnight

*The Used and Abused:
Fyodor Dostoyevsky's The Insulted and Injured Retold*

Book by Stephen Cole

MARY & ETHEL... and Mikey Who?

Book by Larry Moore

Annabelle and Thatch

Rediscovery Series

Why They Married
by James Montgomery Flagg

MARY & ETHEL
...and Mikey Who?

Stephen Cole

MORECLACKE PUBLISHING
New York City

Copyright © 2024 Stephen Cole
All rights reserved.

For information, contact Moreclacke Publishing at
info@moreclacke.com
or
Moreclacke Publishing
325 West 45th Street, Suite 609
New York, NY 10036-0075

Copying from this book in whole or in part is strictly forbidden by law. No part of this book may be reproduced, stored in a retrieval system, or transmitted in any form, by any means, now known or yet to be invented, including digital, mechanical, electronic, photocopying, recording, streaming, video, or otherwise, without the prior written permission of the author.

This is a work of fiction. Although many of the characters herein are inspired by and share names with real individuals whose lives and exploits are part of entertainment lore, most of what follows is a work of creative imagination by an author who was not actually transported back through time.

Cover design by Robert Armin

Printed in the United States of America
Moreclacke Publishing, New York, NY

Library of Congress Control Number: 2023909406

First Hardcover Edition

ISBN-13: 979-8-9859344-5-8

ELLA
I do all my shopping there with Mary and Ethel.

THIRD WOMAN
Mary and Ethel who?

ELLA
Mary Schwartz and Ethel Hotchkiss.

"Drop That Name" from *Bells Are Ringing*
by Betty Comden & Adolph Green, 1956

Dedicated to Peter Rinaldi

Special thanks to Jocelyn Weston for reading every draft and Robert Armin for publishing the best version.

A Who's Who? guide to the celebrity names dropped herein appears at the back of this book.

Prologue

Munching On a Foxtrot
Brooklyn, NY, August 1983

"Mikey Minkus! You turn that music down this instant!"

In defiance of his mother, twenty-five-year-old Michael Marvin Minkus of Brooklyn, New York, turned his stereo up louder. Michael had not been called Michael since fourth grade, when his mother dubbed him Mikey because he was so adorable. Despite being less than adorable nowadays, the name stuck. Sometimes Mikey wished it had not.

From the revolving ten-inch record, Ethel Merman munched on a foxtrot, while Mary Martin yodeled contrapuntally. Michael sang along with both singers.

"Picture you upon my... when I'm calling you-oo-oo-oo... will you answer... two for tea alone!"

"Do you hear me?" screamed the voice from upstairs. "Don't make me come down those stairs."

He heard her. How could he not hear that piercing shriek?

"My bursitis is killing me and if I burst a blood vessel and bleed all over my new housedress, I will never let you forget it. Turn that down or I'm gonna give you such a lam in the jaw!"

A lamb in the jaw. This was something Mikey never understood. How could she even lift a lamb to hit him in the jaw? And where, in all of Brooklyn, would she even find such a farm animal? This was exactly why Mikey moved down to the half-finished basement and lived next to the washer and dryer that ran constantly. To get away from her *mishogos*. Mikey's mother ran a clean ship and she liked clean clothes, thus the constant whir of the Maytag had to be drowned out by his music. Only Ethel and Mary could make him forget he was living in a *fakocta* Jewish laundromat.

At twenty-five, Mikey had started to resemble his mother. Unlike his late and bald father, Morris, at the same age (or so his mother said), Mikey still had his hair and wore it a bit long. His mother straightened *her* hair, but Mikey kept *his* fulsome wave and enjoyed brushing it to the side with no part. Unfortunately, he also had his mother's Russian plow-woman build with short, solid legs and a barrel chest. Still, he *was* "cute," a word he detested with "handsome" still in the dictionary, but never used on him. "Shrinking Violet" was never an expression for Mikey either, except when his mother was around.

"Mikey!"

Just as the dulcet tones of Mary Martin traded with the brass of Merman and sang "Tea for Two" while Merman caressed "Stormy Weather," Mrs. Minkus, in all her glory, appeared.

Rifka Minkus was a short, solid… let's face it, lumpy… woman who wore her hair in a stylish (stylish for 1965, thought Mikey – this was 1983 for Lord's sake) beehive and since she had just come from the beauty parlor, that beehive was higher than ever and already wrapped in toilet paper in preparation for her nap.

"Mom, not with the toilet paper again. Why do you wear toilet paper on your head anyway? Is it some Chassidic ritual? Anyway, it's really scary."

"You should be scared," barked Mrs. Minkus, ignoring his toilet paper remark. "I know I am. A grown twenty-five-year-old boy listening to two *alta kockers* shrieking on the Victrola. Why don't you get a job?"

Just then Rifka looked up at the walls. The walls that were covered from floor to ceiling with posters, photos, and record covers. All of them featuring "that loudmouth" Ethel Merman. Mrs. Minkus noticed a new one.

"Another poster? Where did you get this one and what the hell is *Straight, Place and Show*? I never heard of such a movie."

"It's from 1938 and it starred the Ritz Brothers."

"Oooh," softened Mrs. Minkus. "They were very funny. I remember seeing them at the Brooklyn Paramount with your father. We laughed our *tuchases* off."

"No, they were not funny. They were second rate imitations of the Marx Brothers. I only have the poster because it featured…"

"I know. I know. It featured your girlfriend, Miss Loudmouth. Why, if I can be so bold to ask, would you put that *punim* all over your walls? I mean, you don't even know her."

Mikey bristled at this. This was his mother's constant cry: "You don't even know her."

"Yes, I do!"

Mikey knew that you didn't have to know people to love them; to love their talent, their drive, their whole career and life. In any case, Mikey felt that he did know Ethel Merman. Hadn't he met her when she signed her memoirs at Korvettes? Hadn't she smiled at him in that way? Well, he was the youngest one there. And then when her disco album came out, wasn't he first in line to get her to autograph that, even though he hated disco?

He knew her. And he knew that she had to remember him.

And as for being gainfully employed, Mikey liked to think of himself as "between jobs." He hated the temp work his mother *kvetched* him into. Yes, he could type and yes, he was personable at the front desk, but this was not the life he wanted. He just didn't see himself as Suzie McNamara.

"Who is Suzie McNamara?" his mother demanded.

"Oh, Mom! Ann Sothern? Don't you remember? She was on TV and we used to watch the reruns… and please put your teeth in."

In fact, Rifka had actually taken out her choppers and polished them with the hem of her housedress while Mikey berated her. She shrugged and put them back in.

"Thank you. In any case, a private secretary is not what I want to be. It's no life."

"Well then, what do you want?" his mother asked, as she always did when he would whine about going to the City to take another typing test.

That was the question of the year. What did he want? To really know Ethel Merman. That would be the highlight of his third decade on Earth. To have a meal with her. To ask her about Cole Porter and Irving Berlin and Josh Logan and George Abbott. And Gershwin. All the heroes of his *Theatre World* collection.

His mother interrupted his thoughts again.

"Ya know, I was just reading about your girlfriend."

"Where?" asked Mikey, suspiciously.

"In the *Enquirer*."

"That rag? What are they saying now?"

Mikey didn't usually read those scandalous articles, but even if he did, they were mostly about TV and movie stars. Seldom was there anything about Broadway.

"It's a whole article about why she didn't appear on the *Oscars*."

Mikey and Rifka waited in vain back in March. The *TV Guide* had highlighted her appearance. She was supposed to sing in honor of her late friend Irving Berlin, but for some reason she didn't appear.

"She had a stroke."

"What?"

Mikey almost fell over. He didn't want to believe his mother or *The National Enquirer*, but one thing Rifka Minkus was not was a liar. Mikey scrambled as quickly as his stubby little legs could go up the stairs to read the paper for himself. His mother with the toilet paper on her head trailed behind him in a more relaxed fashion, so as not to lose one square of Charmin from her head.

Up in the apartment proper, Mikey went straight to the kitchen table, covered in oil cloth and newspapers, and found the *Enquirer*. The headline screamed out to him:

"MERMAN FELLED BY INOPERABLE BRAIN TUMOR."

Mikey scanned the article without reading every word, but when he got to the part about Ethel being cared for by her son at her apartment at the Surrey Hotel in Manhattan, he knew what he had to do.

He had to see her! Today!

Behind the closed door at the Surrey Hotel at 20 East 76th Street, right off Fifth Avenue near Central Park, was a small bedroom, not the master bedroom where "Merman the Broadway Star" slept, but a dimly lit converted den with a bariatric hospital bed and old-fashioned TV on which a handwritten sign was Scotch taped: "Do Not Change the Channel!" The only remnant of Ethel's old bedroom was the small toy crib containing the miniature Muppets that Kermit the Frog's creator, Jim Henson, had given to Merman after she had appeared on *The Muppet Show*. Ethel loved her bite-sized Miss Piggy and Kermie and Fozzie Bear. They comforted her in these, the darkest days of her life. This dark sanctuary was the room where the 1983 Ethel Merman now resided twenty-four-hours-a-day.

Ethel's nurse was named Mary. The few people who came to visit in the last month were amused by this. Ethel and Mary together again. Of course, this Mary was not blonde and not a singer. She was a practical African-American woman who went home each night to Harlem, where she lived with her daughter. At first, Ethel, when she could get it out, called her Black Mary, while Bobby, Ethel's son, called her Mary2. Luckily, Mary2 stuck.

Mary2 was just putting the finishing touches on Ethel's eyebrows. Ethel had plucked out her real eyebrows years before and expertly painted them on when she did her makeup each day or for a show, but now Mary2 was drawing them in and, as Ethel began to fidget, Mary2's hand slipped and

Ethel's right eyebrow shot up onto her forehead making her look like she was wildly suspicious of something. Mary2 wondered if she should make the other eyebrow match. But then Ethel would have a permanent look of surprise. She giggled a bit. Ethel spoke out of the side of her mouth, like some old time gangster, the lasting result of the brain tumor which manifested itself as a stroke some four months earlier.

"What the fuck?"

"Miss Merman! Please!"

Mary2, like Mary1, could not stand profanity.

"I told you, Miss M! The Lord is watching. And listening. And he don't like no filthy talk."

With her good right hand, Ethel just swatted the air. Ethel knew that Mary2's conversion to religion was a fairly recent event and that she knew more curse words than Ethel and the naval fleet put together. Ethel didn't care who liked her cursing or not. If "what the fuck?" came out of her mouth, she felt lucky. Lucky to get any words out at all.

Mary2 fixed Ethel's eyebrows and straightened the ill-fitting red wig that sat perched on her head. Ethel was sitting up in her hospital chair, her now thin legs dangling over and barely reaching the floor. She wore a loose housecoat that did not disguise how much weight she had lost.

"You look fine, just fine."

Ethel's fake eyebrows shot up as if to say, "Bullshit, Mary, bullshit!"

Although her son, Bobby, who came to live with her during her recovery, decreed that mirrors must be kept away from her, Ethel knew she did not look her best.

"Mom," Bobby lied, "you look twenty years younger. There's not a wrinkle on your face."

Ethel could feel it. Bobby was not really lying. There were no wrinkles on her seventy-five-year-old face because the cortisone injections had stretched her skin over a bloated and puffed-out mug.

He was a good boy, Bobby. A surprising son.

Merman had always been the perfect daughter. She cared for her aging parents until they died in their nineties. Ethel, though, never expected her children to be like her. After all, she reasoned, they were not raised, as she was, in middle-class, Germanic republican flats in Queens. Reared in Manhattan penthouses overlooking the Park or Denver mansions with backyards and barbecues, Ethel's kids grew up among the privileged and did not have to go to work as stenographers right out of High School, as she did while waiting for her Show Biz break. Ethel was fond of jesting that her son Bobby, unlike Mary's son Larry (who was now the toast of nighttime serials), never worked.

But now, here he was, an only child since his sister's death, taking care of his mother in her greatest time of need. The perfect son of the perfect daughter, leaving San Francisco and "his hippy dippy life," as Ethel called it, and moving in with her at the Surrey Hotel and, even though Ethel had her stove taken out of the kitchen (literally removed) and there was a hole where the oven used to be, Bobby somehow kept his mom fed and as healthy as can be, under the circumstances.

And the circumstances were not good.

At first, they thought it was a stroke but Ethel knew that her mind was still working, even as half of her body went numb, and she went crashing to the ground that morning in March. That morning she was scheduled to leave for Hollywood to be on the *Oscars* and sing "There's No Business Like Show Business" in honor of her friend Irving Berlin who died that year at 101 years old.

Ethel had not actually seen Irving for several years. He had become a virtual recluse inside his Beekman Place townhouse. But he called and they spoke on the phone once a week. That sweet little scratchy wisp of a voice would come through her line, "Ethel? Is it really you? Sing something loud for me!" And Ethel would hit a nice big note making Irving laugh and say (and he said it every time), "I always told everyone, you better write a good lyric for Ethel 'cause they're gonna hear it in the second balcony!"

And Ethel did intend to belt the song to the second balcony of heaven, so that Irving could hear it. Costume designer Bob Mackie had created a new sparkly dress for her appearance ("Bob, can you split the seam some on the left side? I wanna show some leg!") and Ethel had had her hair done and sprayed within an inch of its life. She always made fun of Ann Miller and her huge, lacquered wigs, but she got her friend Annie (when they were speaking) to tell her about her secret stash of super-hold spray net. She had carefully wrapped her head in toilet paper to keep the hold and gracefully slept on her satin pillowcase so as not to put a dent in her do.

Ethel woke up the next morning and got ready to haul her butt down to the lobby where her car would be waiting to take her to JFK for her flight to Los Angeles. The next thing she remembered was falling. Falling and falling and falling. Oh fuck, she thought, a stroke.

The Merm was made of steel, right? This couldn't be happening. She remembered using every bit of steel to drag herself to the house phone. Ethel loved living in hotels (her apartment at the Surrey was as grand as any Park Avenue abode would be) because of those extra amenities, not the least the house phone that allowed the front desk to screen her calls (when you got Merman on her personal line, you would first hear a gruff-sounding, deep-toned masculine voice say "Hello!" and then after Ethel knew who you were, her normal tone would resume). Now, with half of her body dead to her, that house phone came in handy. With all of what was left of her control, Ethel pulled the wire and the phone came crashing down to the floor. The receiver fell off of its cradle.

"Hello? Hello? Miss Merman? Are you there?"

The LL train (HELL HELL to its riders) clunked along above ground for about a half-hour of the tedious one-hour trip into the city. It was hot as hell and the open windows did nothing to help the situation. Still, as Mikey read the *Enquirer* article for the third time, he ignored the heat and overlooked the dangerous neighborhoods the train went through. He even forgave the train when it went underground, and he could only see blackness through the filthy windows. He paid all the horrors of the New York subway system no heed. Not today. Today the LL train, the last of the strap-hanging, straw-seated monstrosities with no air-conditioning, was his galloping steed charging to his heroine's bedside.

Surely, *The National Enquirer* could not be totally right. Ethel Merman was not dying. How could that be? No, Michael would see her and find out that she was recovering and would soon be back on the boards singing again. This was his mantra going past New Lots Avenue, Livonia and Broadway Junction. As he recited it over and over: "Ethel will not die, Ethel will not die," the LL train went into a tunnel, stalled, and all the lights went out.

"Ethel will not die," Mikey said out loud to the dark.

The reason for the Merman makeover was Mary Martin. Mary Martin, who was surrounded by Ethel Merman. Literally. As the elegantly clad Mary sat on the overstuffed and very floral couch, she saw images of Ethel on every wall of Merman's apartment in the Surrey: paintings, photos, costume sketches. A huge portrait of Merman as Panama Hattie dominated the space.

There was Ethel in her 1940s hair with those incredibly wide shoulder-pads that made Joan Crawford jealous.

Mary, with the perfect taste she inherited from her husband Richard, felt that there was perhaps just a touch too much ego in this room.

Mary fished into her purse and pulled out her compact to look at her face. She dabbed some powder on her nose, although it was far from shiny. She thought about applying a fresh coat of her peachy-pink lipstick but decided against it. The coat she had applied ten minutes ago was still moist. She closed the compact and surveyed herself in the large mirror over the fireplace.

At almost 70, Mary had kept her boyish *Peter Pan* figure and wisely let her blonde hair go a becoming silvery white. She fluffed her hair a bit. She wisely kept it short, though not as short as when she was "washing that man right out of her hair" eight times a week in *South Pacific*. Once a habitué of the great couturier Mainbocher, now that Mary's late husband Richard Halliday was no longer around to dictate her styles, she preferred simple, easy-to-pack permanent-press pantsuits that appeared crisp and clean and still chic. She always carried a good-sized Hermès bag that contained one or more needlepoint patterns in progress so that her fingers were seldom idle.

Today though, Mary's fingers shook as she pulled out the piece of needlepoint she was working on. It was to be a rug. Another rug that she would gift to a friend or relative back in Weatherford, Texas, where she grew up. Mary had needle-pointed enough rugs to fill a warehouse the size of Texas. Her eyelid twitched involuntarily as she steadied her hand and began to stitch.

She had not seen nor spoken to Merman for over a year. Not since Merman appeared on Mary's PBS TV show *Over Easy*, a show that celebrated aging. As if that were something to celebrate, thought Mary. That last dual performance still lived on in Mary's nightmares. Not that she hadn't been warned. Benay Venuta, Ethel's oldest friend, and a Broadway performer one or two rungs lower than Merman or Martin, called Mary to tip her off.

"Ethel told me that she was going to sing on your show with you," Benay bellowed in her own Mermanesque voice. "…and she said, 'I'm NOT holding back!'"

And when the time came for them to sing Irving Berlin's challenge duet from *Annie Get Your Gun*, Ethel did *not* hold back. Mary shuddered at the memory. After the show, the two First Ladies of the American Musical Theatre walked off the set and never spoke again.

Mary looked around at the small, framed photographs on the crowded side table and smiled to herself. A tiny Gauguin, a miniature Renoir, a pint-sized Toulouse-Lautrec. The last time Mary had visited, she was astounded by these cheaply framed items.

"Ethel, why do you have *photographs* of these paintings so nicely framed?" she asked.

Ethel responded, "I cut them out of magazines and put them in frames. They're just as good as the originals."

Mary just smiled and rolled her eyes at the memory.

Now, Mary picked up a photograph in a fancy gold frame and looked at the glossy color image of Ethel with the Queen Mother. This was real. There they were, two small, frumpy ladies, Ethel with her big teased and hair-sprayed hair and gaudy gown, and the Queen Mother looking more… Queenly. It was inscribed in ink, "To Ethel, fondly Elizabeth R." Mary had, in fact, sung for the Queen and the Queen Mother and *all* the royals. They all came to the Theatre Royal Drury Lane to see her, first in 1946 when she did that awful Noël Coward operetta, *Pacific 1860*, and then when she triumphed in *South Pacific* in 1953. They all came again when she was Dolly in *Hello, Dolly!* in that very same theatre. But Mary didn't have an autograph from any Elizabeth! Not even Taylor!

"Mary Virginia," she could hear her mother Juanita saying in that Texas twang she herself had inherited, "stop coveting thy friend's autograph!"

Mary looked at the two ceramic dogs guarding Ethel's non-functional fireplace ("I love those dogs. You don't have to walk 'em," Ethel had declared) and then gazed back at the closed door and wondered if Ethel would even want to see her.

When the subway lights came back on, the train was on the other side of the East River just getting into the First Avenue station in Manhattan. Before switching at the Union Square stop for the Uptown Lexington Avenue line, Mikey started to re-read the article in the *Enquirer* for the fourth time. He had snatched it away from his mother's messy table despite her protest of not having finished it. He had to study what had happened to Ethel. The article described that horrible morning before she even got to leave for Los Angeles; how she fell and managed to call the front desk, and then her son, Robert Leavitt Jr. was quoted:

"'When the front desk got the call and there were just garbled sounds of words coming through the receiver,' said Mr. Leavitt, Merman's only surviving child, 'they knew something was very wrong. So, they rushed up and rang Mom's bell. Then they knocked and knocked, knowing she had to be in there. Finally, they started to use their pass key to get in, but Mom, as usual had bolted the door from the inside and securely fastened the three chains on the door. She was always super-careful since her jewels got robbed back in the '70s. I guess Mom heard the attempts to open the door and although her whole left side was paralyzed, she crawled the length of the living room, all the way to the entrance way… and she somehow got the strength to unchain the chains and unlock the door.'"

The conductor said something unintelligible over a scratchy and impossibly loud public address system as the train roared to a screeching halt at Union Square. Mikey looked at the note he had written in the margin of the paper. It was the address of the Surrey Hotel, 20 East 76th Street. He knew he could get off at 77th and Lexington and walk three big blocks west. How he would get past the front desk and up to Ethel Merman's apartment was another story. One thing at a time, Mikey. One thing at a time.

Mary Martin's mind was not on her needlepoint and she dropped several stitches. Her fingers would just not cooperate. She carefully folded it up and put it back in her bag and stared at the closed door. She had no idea what to expect when it opened. She fished in her purse and took out her compact again. "You just did that, Mary," she told herself as she put it back. On the phone weeks earlier, Ethel's son, Bobby, kept telling her that Ethel was doing well. But when she pressed him, he reluctantly told her that Ethel was not doing well at all and, in fact, the doctors gave her months to live.

When Mary, still in Palm Springs, heard this, she gasped, as she recalled her own touch with death just five months earlier. Mary felt lucky to remember as little as she did of the taxicab accident in San Francisco. The last thing she remembered was joking and playing with the cab driver's long hair. Then there was a crash and she blacked out.

Her dear pal Janet Gaynor was still suffering in the hospital with injuries and, worst of all, Mary lost her "Uncle" Ben Washer, the man who took over from her late husband, Richard, and took care of her everyday needs and wants and managed her career. Someone at the hospital told Mary that the cab driver with the long hair was dead too. But as bad as Mary's injuries were, she, with the steely determination that kept her a top Broadway star, was released from the hospital in two weeks. She knew that Merman had at least as much fortitude and grit (if not more) and would also get through this terrible ordeal.

As Bette Davis loved to say, "Old age is not for sissies!"

The door to the den opened and Mary2 came out.

"She's ready, Miss Martin," Mary2 told Mary1.

"Well, that's great! The question is, am I?"

Just then, the doorbell rang.

Mikey was shocked at how easy it was. He arrived at the Surrey at 12:45 PM and presented himself at the front desk. In his arms were a bouquet of flowers he had picked up at a corner grocery on Lexington and 77th Street, and a shopping bag containing a box of chocolates he had brought from home. He hoped that Ethel liked the same chewy caramels his Mom did.

"Excuse me, but I'm here to see Miss Merman and I…"

Before Mikey could tell the lie he had concocted, the bored looking concierge pointed him to the elevator bank to the right of the desk.

"24-D," said the concierge without so much as a smile. "Mary is expecting you."

"Mary?"

Mikey hid his shock, confusion, and joy.

"That's right."

"They must think I'm someone else," Mikey thought. Before the concierge could change his mind, Mickey bolted for the elevator banks and pushed the button four times. Ten seconds later, the elevator landed in the lobby and the doors opened. Mikey was greeted by a uniformed elevator operator, one of the last of a dying breed in automated New York. He confidently entered the plush, mirrored elevator, careful not to give too much of his emotion away.

"Twenty-four please!"

As the elevator smoothly ascended, Mikey hummed the same foxtrot that Ethel was munching on earlier, singing the words in his head.

"We will raise a family, a boy for you, a girl for me… can't you see…"

"Twenty-four. Miss Merman's apartment is just to the left."

"… how happy we will be!"

"It's about time! Lordy, you white boys can be so slow."

The shiny mahogany door was open and before him stood Mary2, hands on hips, tapping her foot to some inner rhythm. Mikey had hesitated to knock on the plush door with the ornate knocker and elegant-looking bell. Choosing the knocker seemed less pushy, but the bell would be louder, so the bell it was. A smoother and more melodious "ding-dong" Mikey had never heard. Back in Brooklyn, the doorbell could wake the dead, but here on New York's chic Upper East Side, the bells were like music by Jerome Kern. In fact, the notes of this one matched the first four notes of "All the Things You Are." Mikey poked his head into the apartment.

"Come on," commanded Mary2 as she strode back toward the living room with her arm in the air and her fingers snapping. "Don't dawdle."

Mikey giggled and Mary2 turned back and saw the flowers. She strode back to the boy and grabbed them out of his hands.

"Flowers are verboten!"

Mikey looked blankly at her.

"Can't have 'em. Not one dainty little rose or pansy," Mary2 proclaimed as she dropped them into a large waste basket. "Miss M is allergic. But then how could you know that?"

Mikey smote his forehead. He did know that. How could he have forgotten? He read it in her memoirs. He read how when Irving Berlin wanted to give her flowers on the opening night of the Lincoln Center revival of *Annie Get Your Gun*, he gave her tin roses and a note saying, "a metal petal for Etel."

"Keep moving," came Mary2's directive.

Mikey followed the woman in white into the apartment. Was she the maid? No, she looked more like a nurse.

The grand foyer leading to the living room was bigger than Rifka's whole apartment and certainly larger than his tiny basement bedroom. Mikey glanced up at the crystal chandelier that reminded him of his mother's dangling earrings from some distant Saturday night when she and his Dad would be going out on the town to a Brooklyn nightclub like Ben Maksik's, where they once actually saw Judy Garland sing. His gaze then took him down to the marble floor, which was so highly polished that Mikey could actually see himself in the shiny surface. He grimaced at his clear reflection and wished he had taken the time to get a haircut. But with Ethel Merman on her deathbed, time was slipping away. He spit on his hand, smoothed down a cowlick, and followed.

"Are those your tools in that bag?"

Before a confused Mikey could respond, they were in the large sunny living room with windows overlooking Central Park. Mikey could not believe he was seeing this room in person, the room he had read about and seen in photographs in *Architectural Digest Magazine*. There were the ceramic dogs guarding the fireplace. There was the massive portrait of Merman as Panama Hattie and the Benay Venuta painting of Merman as Rose in *Gypsy*.

And there, sitting demurely on the floral couch in front of him was Mary Martin. His mouth fell open.

Mikey religiously watched Mary's PBS TV series, *Over Easy*. He even taped every episode with his new VHS machine. He tried to get his mother Rifka to watch, but she said, "That's a show for old people. Not my cup of tea."

But, although Mikey had been watching the older Mary Martin on TV for a year now, in his mind's eye she was still Peter Pan in black-and-white on his Motorola TV. Because he always thought of her as "youth and joy and freedom," Mikey was slightly shocked to see the little old lady in a white pants suit, sitting on the couch. Was this the Mary who was expecting him? Expecting him to do what?

"Mary," said Mary1 to Mary2, "May I see her now?" Mary Martin noticed Mikey and, with her polite Southern upbringing, stood and put her hand out to greet him. "Oh, hello, I'm Mary too... Mary Martin."

"I know who you are," Mikey excitedly exclaimed as if Mary Martin were an idiot.

"Well, good," said Mary1 with a deep gurgling laugh that stood her well on stage. "I'm glad that's settled."

Mary2 took charge, pointing Mikey to a chair near the fireplace. "You sit right here," she barked. "I'll be back in a minute." Mikey did as he was told and Mary2 turned to Mary1 and escorted her over to the room containing Ethel Merman. "Right this way, Miss Martin."

"It was nice meeting you, young man."

Mikey sat down and blushed at the thought of Peter Pan finding it nice to meet him.

As Mary entered the dimly lit room, she took a second to let her eyes adjust to the gloom. She looked around and saw a small, shockingly thin woman seated in a chair with her shriveled legs dangling a foot from the floor. Her bloated face was made up like a clown and on her head was perched an ill-fitting red wig. The woman's painted-on eyebrows shot up even higher in surprise to see Mary. Mary stared into the eyes of the woman in the chair.

"Ethel? Is that you?"

The door gently, but firmly, shut behind Mary Martin, leaving Mary2 and Mikey alone in the vast living room.

"Wow! I could not be more shocked," Mikey said to no one in particular. "Mary Martin visiting Ethel Merman. I thought they were archrivals."

Mikey was so used to being alone in his basement with his idols' images lining the walls, that talking out loud to those very walls was second nature to him. He didn't even notice that Mary2 was hovering behind him as he sat on the couch.

"There's more to it than you think," Mary2 interjected.

"More to what?"

"More to a friendship."

"They're friends? Didn't I read about Ethel blasting Mary off the soundstage on her TV show and Mary storming off the set and the two of them never talking to each other again?"

"They're sure talking now… well, at least Miss Martin is," Mary2 said looking over at the closed door. "Listen, kiddo…"

"Mikey," he interrupted.

"Mikey?"

"Short for Michael Marvin Minkus."

"I get it! Well… Mikey Marvin Minkus… these ladies go way back. Before you were a twinkle in your daddy's eye. I was there. I know. Now," Mary2 said, getting down to brass tacks, "let's talk about the bed."

"Excuse me?"

"You look a little young for this job."

"I'm twenty-five years old."

"Well, you look younger. That's good, though. Guess how old I am."

"I couldn't." Mikey blushed all kinds of pink. "Really, I couldn't"

"Okay, I'll tell you. I am just a little older than Miss Martin. Seventy. Seven-O! Bet you would never believe it."

"No. Never."

Mary2 stared right at Mikey with a straight face.

"Well, black don't crack!"

After a moment, Mary2 burst into a loud guffaw of a laugh.

"The look on your face, Mikey Marvin," Mary2 said through her laughter. "You look like you mighta thought I was trying to get you into my bed." Mary2 laughed even louder at her own joke. Then she spoke again.

"You know I'm talking about Miss Merman's bed, right?"

Mikey was both appalled and intrigued at the same time.

"You want me to get into her bed?"

"Don't be a fool! I want you to fix it! That dang bariatric bed keeps going up and down without anyone pressing the button. Miss Merman is going nuts and cursing up a storm outta the side of her mouth."

"So, have you known Miss Merman and Miss Martin a long time?"

"I was there when they met. I was a dresser back then for the great Sophie Tucker. Bet you don't remember her."

Mikey didn't know what to do. Should he tell this woman in white the truth and risk being thrown out before he even got to meet his idol? Or should he just shut up and pretend he can fix a bed so that he can get nearer to the star behind door number one? Despite being raised by "Rifka the Mouth," as half the neighborhood called her, Mikey decided to stay silent and see how far that might get him. But two seconds after vowing not to speak, his vow was broken and his curiosity satisfied.

"I have one thousand records in my collection," said Mikey with a mix of pride and embarrassment, "so of course I know who Sophie Tucker was. She was known as 'the last of the red hot mamas' and sang 'Some of These Days' and wound up doing bawdy records where she kind of talk-sang the songs."

"Smart kid. I worked for Miss Tucker back in 1938 and 1939 when she was starring in a Cole Porter musical called *Leave It to Me*. I was there the night Mary Martin was about to leave *Leave It to Me* and head to Hollywood. That's the night she met Ethel Merman for the first time. Oh, you shoulda been there," Mary2 exclaimed with a dirty laugh that denied all her bible-totin' ways.

Mikey silently agreed. "Oh, I shoulda been there."

Just as he settled in on the couch, sure that he was about to hear the best bedtime story of his life, Mary2 abruptly got up, let out a huge burp, and left the room.

"People come and go so quickly around here," Mikey thought, almost forgetting that it was a line from *The Wizard of Oz*.

With Mary1 in with Ethel and Mary2 nowhere to be seen, Mikey took the opportunity to get up to examine some of the fabulous artifacts in this Merman museum. He noticed the same autographed photo of Ethel and the Queen Mother that Mary Martin had held just moments before. He held each of the miniature Muppets, carefully replacing them in their crib so no one would notice. He also spied a door with a silver sequin star hung on it. A fanciful thing for a star to have put on what he assumed was a closet. The door was slightly ajar. Mikey, who could never resist prying (the legacy of Rifka!), gingerly pushed open the door.

It was a closet. A huge walk-in closet that seemed roomier than any in his mother's apartment and almost larger than his entire basement bedroom. As the door opened, a soft, flattering light automatically switched on from overhead. Other tiny stage lights illuminated as he took a few steps in.

The closet was filled with clothes – no, costumes – hanging on hangers and hooks, each illuminated by its own tiny, pink-gelled theatre light. On the floor neatly arranged, were dozens of pairs of women's shoes in different styles, some dating back to the 1920s. High heels, low heels, spike heels, no heels, Joan Crawford Fuck-me Pumps, flats, clogs. All organized, it seemed, by the height of the heel. All polished and glittering, as if they were so many ruby slippers ready to be heel-clicked. On the shelves above were awards: the Tonys, the Donaldsons, the Critics' Circles, the Golden Globes, some statuettes, some boxes, some plaques.

As Mikey moved further into the seemingly endless closet, all the light suddenly went out and darkness surrounded him. He instinctively started to feel his way around, first feeling the soft luxurious fur that was hanging on a hook, which led him further into another part of the closet. Mikey was feeling nervous and disoriented. Did he hear the door click and lock behind him or was it just his imagination? He had no idea which way was in and which was out at this point. Where was the door? He began to sweat. Was the air-conditioning off as well? Had the city been plunged into another of those summer blackouts? This whole adventure reminded Mikey of the time he had gone to a funhouse in Rockaway and gotten locked in a room with no doors or windows. He had to scream to have the attendant let him out.

But today, Mikey was not afraid, as he had been back then. Now, Mikey had a strange impulse to continue forward and further into the closet, despite the dark and the heat and disorientation.

Mikey wondered, "How far did it actually go?" Then he found out as he pushed against what he thought was a wall and came out into yet another closet.

A closet in a dressing room at the Imperial Theatre.

In 1939.

Chapter One
Just a Perfect Blendship
New York City, May 1939

"Michael Marvin Minkus!"

The loud, husky, baritone voice belonged to a large, bulky woman mechanically applying mascara with the tip of a safety pin to her already long beaded lashes. As Mikey's eyes adjusted to the glare of the multitude of bare bulbs surrounding the makeup mirror, he recognized the round face framed by golden curls reflected in the grimy glass.

"Sophie Tucker?"

"Aunt Soph to you, my boy. What were you doing in that closet for so long? Did you find my corsage? Not the small one, mind you, but one that can be seen from the last row of the balcony when I bounce it on my bosom. Come on, give it here."

Mikey looked down at his hand and found that he was, in fact, holding a very large fake corsage with a huge pin attached to the back.

"I don't have all night. I don't want to wear it for Act Two. I need it for my entrance. Mary! Mary! Help this helpless child to pin this on my costume. Mary! Where the hell are you?"

"No need to curse like a drunken sailor, Miss Tucker," Mary cooed as she entered the tiny dressing room. Mikey recognized her as Ethel Merman's nurse in white, but now she was dressed in a starched maid's outfit with a blindingly white apron and cap on top of her tight black hairdo, punctuated by a bun in the back. Didn't she just tell him that she had worked for Sophie Tucker? Was this a dream?

Mary took the corsage from Mikey's hand and efficiently pinned it to the lapel of Sophie Tucker's costume. The corsage was so full and long that it almost covered one of Miss Tucker's ample breasts.

"There! Thank you, Mary. What would I do without you? And you, my boy, the ticket is by the door."

"Ticket?" inquired Mikey with a confused air.

"Technically a house seat. I wouldn't want my sister's little boy to sit with the *hoi polloi*. Usually, your Aunt Soph sells her house seats to the highest bidder, but tonight, I bit the bullet and paid the box office the exorbitant price of five dollars! So, you had better stay awake for everything, including when Aunt Sophie is off taking a leak. Now be off with ya and don't forget to applaud my entrance."

Mary stood at the door holding out the ticket for Mikey. He took it from her hand, all the while looking her in the face. Was this the same Mary2 who worked for Miss Merman? She certainly looked the same, if a bit younger. And wait a minute, wasn't Sophie Tucker dead? What was going on? As Mary2 relinquished the ticket, she winked at Mikey. Just a friendly wink, but a wink, nonetheless. Did she know? But know what?

Aunt Sophie, who doted on her nephew as if he were her own son, yelled after him. "Put on your jacket and tie. A gentleman never enters a public place in shirtsleeves. Didn't your mother teach you anything?"

Mary2 held out the jacket and pre-tied tie and waited for Mikey to put them on. Miraculously, the jacket fit.

"Don't forget to say *merde* one last time to your girlfriend Mary," Mary2 proclaimed with a laugh.

"Mary? Aren't you Mary?"

"I am Mary the second. Mary the first is *Miss* Martin to you, Mikey Marvin. *Miss* Mary Martin to you."

Mikey took the ticket and left the dressing room, hearing the door slam behind him and a peel of laughter emanating from over the transom.

Three steep flights above, twenty-five-year-old Mary Virginia Martin, like Sophie Tucker and every other performer in the Imperial Theatre, was doing her makeup. Mary Martin took special care tonight, because she knew it would be her last time with her now beloved company of *Leave It to Me*. When the show opened eight months earlier, Mary had been a complete unknown, but now here she was, her life completely changed. From a Texas hick to the cover of *LIFE Magazine* and now on her way back to Hollywood with a signed Paramount contract in her pocket. Wouldn't Daddy have been proud? Daddy, Mary mused as she applied a fresh coat of Tangee lipstick to her already shiny red lips. "My Heart Belongs to Daddy" was the song that propelled her to fame, all the while keeping her from her real Daddy when he was dying.

"Enough wallowing, Mary Virginia," Mary could hear her mother scolding. "Life goes on and you will too."

"But Mama," Mary said when she got the phone call, "I have to be there now. For you. For Lukey. For…"

"Your Daddy would not want you to miss your shows. He died proud, but he died. I have Luke right here where he belongs, and *you* belong on that stage singing your song. There is no such thing as guilt, Mary Virginia, so do not wallow in something that does not exist. Think about Daddy when you mention him to that big audience, honey."

"I do," wept Mary. "I do think about him every night. But I want to come home now."

"No, darlin'. Without your Daddy, there's no home here. Luke and I are gonna move to Los Angeles."

"But that's even further than Weatherford. How will I see my little boy?"

"It's showtime, Mary. Put on your makeup and do what God put you on this Earth to do. I will take care of your son."

And Mary did put on her makeup, and she did go on and on. But now, with her mother and son in Los Angeles and a piece of paper that would, God willing, lead to movie stardom, Mary could make things right with her little boy. Maybe Mama was right. Maybe Daddy was smiling down.

Just as Mary finished her eyebrows, she heard a knock on her door.

"Come in."

The door barely opened a crack and Mikey put his shy face in between the door and the frame. Mary's face brightened as her Texas accent kicked into gear.

"Ah said to come on in, Sugar."

Mikey pushed open the door all the way and slowly entered Mary's dressing room. There were several other makeup mirrors on either side of hers indicating to Mikey that Mary shared this room with at least two others, but no other girls were to be seen.

"Where is everybody?"

"Who? Oh, the other girls? Well, when the show first opened, they were here alright, but now they're all squeezed into the dressing room next door. After the reviews and the *LIFE Magazine* cover came out, my new agent Louis Shurr renegotiated for me. Don't you love that word, 'renegotiated?' Well, honey, Ah didn't get a dressing room downstairs near the stage, but Ah got ma privacy. Ah gotta say, sometimes it gets dang lonely. That's why Ah'm glad when you visit your Aunt Sophie and come up and see me. Are you gonna watch the show tonight?"

"I have a house seat."

"Well, you better. This is my last venture on Broadway. Next time you see me it'll be up on the silver screen at the Paramount on Broadway and 43rd."

There was another knock on the door followed immediately by a loud voice from the other side.

"Fifteen minutes, Miss Martin."

"Thank you, Stanley! Will you be there after the show at the Rainbow Room?"

"You bet, Miss Martin," came the voice from the other side of the door.

"You'll be there of course, right, Mikey? I mean at least you are closer to my age than your Aunt and Billy Gaxton and Victor Moore. It'll be fun."

"Sure. I would love to be there. I mean, I've got nowhere else to go."

"Well, you better go and sit in your fancy house seat before the Overture starts. Hurry."

"Okay." Mikey was nothing if not obedient. His mother Rifka made sure of that. He hustled his way to the door, stopped only by the honeyed twang of Mary's sigh.

"No *merde*?"

"What's *merde*?"

"Literally? Well, it's a word I never use... but think of what a horse leaves on the street. Kerplop! But you know to us show folk it's good luck."

Mikey vaguely recalled reading about that tradition.

"Well," he muttered as he left the dressing room, "*merde*."

As the door closed behind Mikey, he heard the deep gurgling laugh of Mary Martin and thought he must have said it wrong.

"Shit," thought Mikey as he hurried down the stairs.

Merman was pissed, literally and figuratively. She had put everything she had into her latest musical, *Stars in Your Eyes*. "You would think," Merman said to anyone who would listen, "that between me and Durante we would run more than three goddamned months!" And for this she returned from Hollywood!

Now, here she was in May of 1939 sitting in the audience... in the AUDIENCE! And some kid was asking her to stand up so he could get to his seat.

"Excuse me, but that's my seat," whispered Mikey, pointing to the one empty chair two seats in as the first bars of the Overture sounded.

Mikey had had to run around the corner after exiting the stage door on West 46th Street to get to the theatre entrance on 45th, so he was out of breath and sweaty and had no time to do much more than get his ticket torn, get a *Playbill* (he wanted to buy a souvenir program, but had no time. How much that would be worth back in 1983 danced in his head) and be directed to his seat by a bored usherette. Now that he was trying to squeeze his way into the row, he was blinded by the light reflecting off the conductor's bald head and had no idea whom he was making stand.

"Pardon me!"

"Fuck! Cole! Get up. The kid needs to pass."

With much effort, Cole Porter (who had been reveling in the experience of hearing his music), rose from his seat, leaning heavily on one of his canes. Ethel looked at the kid with daggers. It had only been a little over a year earlier that that damned horse had gotten spooked, reared up, and fallen on Cole's legs, shattering them both. Ethel knew that he was in constant pain.

"I'm so sorry," Mikey whimpered as he squeezed his body between the seats in front of Merman and Porter. Finally, as the Overture segued from the romantic strains of "From Now On" to the raucous "Most Gentlemen Don't Like Love," Mikey, Merman and Porter were seated, and Cole was back to being entranced by his own tunes. It was only when the Overture switched gears to the sultry ballad "Get Out of Town" that Mikey started to realize with whom he was seated. It was then he remembered what the lady next to him had said.

"Cole!"

Mikey's head whipped around to the man in the seat on the aisle.

"Cole Porter, of course," Mikey thought. And the woman with the loud voice next to him wearing so much perfume and covered in jewels and furs? How dumb could he be?

Mikey made himself remember what she had looked like when she was young and still in her 30s. The face, the hair… the voice. There was no mistaking that voice. She looked exactly the way she did on the *Straight, Place and Show* poster with those horrible Ritz Brothers. Mikey almost fainted to realize he was close enough to touch Ethel Merman. He could hardly pay attention to the show, and he wanted to remember every second of it. After all, hadn't this been his dream? A time machine to take him back to see all the fabulous musicals he had missed because he had not been born yet. He fantasized about seeing all the Porter and Gershwin and Berlin musicals. And now here he was seeing a show that didn't even have a complete cast recording, *Leave It to Me*.

Concentrate Mikey, concentrate! But how could he concentrate with Ethel Merman and Cole Porter sitting right next to him?

Somehow Mikey knew to applaud for his Aunt Sophie's entrance (he was starting to accept this time period, despite his confusion as to how he got there) and began to enjoy the show, still aware of the reactions coming from the two aisle seats next to him. Cole cheered at every song and laughed at every joke. Merman merely grunted and her applause was half-hearted at best, especially when Mary Martin appeared in her duet with William Gaxton. Ethel looked at the pretty young blonde with what his mother would call "the fisheye."

When the lights clicked on in the theatre for intermission, Ethel turned to Cole and said, "Come on! I need a drink."

Mikey looked over to see Cole Porter shaking his head negatively and pointing to his legs, first his left and then his right.

"No, Ethel, Geraldine is being a psychopathic bitch tonight and her sister Josephine is not that far behind."

Wow, thought Mikey. He's so rich and famous that he has names for his legs.

"I'll just sit here," Cole continued, "and let them battle it out for who can hurt me more."

"But damn it, Cole, you know that they won't let a lady into a bar unescorted."

"Well, then it's a good thing you are not a lady."

Mikey was perplexed enough to interrupt their conversation.

"Ladies can't drink alone?"

Merman responded. "They can if they buy a bottle and sit at home."

"But that's ridiculous," Mikey said, wishing he could tell Ethel that it would change one day.

"That's what I think too."

"I'll escort you."

It took Ethel a full fifteen seconds to respond.

"Sure. Why not? Let's go, kid. But you're buying!"

Cole shifted Geraldine and Josephine a bit and both Merman and Mikey slid by him with some effort. Ethel hustled up the aisle of the Imperial with Mikey following as quickly as he could.

"Well, girls," Cole Porter told his legs as he popped a pill, "why don't you just take a wee nap during the interval and leave me in peace."

Merman and Mikey got to Downey's, just around the corner from the Imperial on Eighth Avenue and 44th Street, just in time to beat the intermission crowd, which now filled the place to the brim. Before he could say a word, Merman had ordered a champagne cocktail for herself.

"And a Coke for the kid. He's driving me back to the theatre."

As Mikey sipped his Coke, Merman held court on a high stool near the bar.

"Hi, Helen! How's tricks, Larry? Jerry! How ya doin'? Where's Eva? In the can?"

Mikey recognized the owlish looking man with the wireless glasses. That was Jerome Kern!

"Sorry about your show closing so fast, but you know how it is," Kern said, offhandedly.

"If Durante and me couldn't make a go of it, then it must be the Depression or something. Although between us, I blame that fucking World's Fair. They're charging nothing for strippers over there in Queens, so who the hell wants to come to see us for four-forty?"

Jerome Kern didn't look amused and left his perch at the bar with a polite goodbye. Ethel, with no one left to schmooze turned to Mikey.

"So how did you wind up in house seats, kid?"

"My Aunt Sophie."

"Oh," cooed Ethel, "you're Tucker's nephew. The one she always brags about. She says you're smart and you know every piece of show biz trivia there is to know."

"Well..."

"Do you know that new kid in the show? That Texas babe? Mary Martin?"

"Yes... and..."

"I haven't seen a star rising that fast since... since..."

"Since you burst on the scene at the Alvin in 1930 in *Girl Crazy*?"

"Your Aunt is right. You are smart."

"Would you like to meet Miss Martin?"

"You know her?"

"I told her *merde* before the show."

"What's that mean?"

"I haven't a clue."

Ethel looked at the watch she had pinned as a brooch to her breast.

"Shit! We gotta hustle our asses back for Act Two. Cole is gonna kill us if we miss the Entr'acte."

"My doctor said, 'No sex!' Can you imagine?" Cole Porter said to the handsome male usher who stood towering over the seated composer. "Well, I'm learning to channel it all into my work."

"All?"

"Well, maybe not all," Cole responded salaciously, as he looked up into the baby blue eyes of the usher.

Just as Cole wrote down his phone number for the handsome young man, Ethel and Mikey rushed back to their seats and made Cole move Geraldine and Josephine over to get into the tight row.

"Glad you could make it back, Miss Merman," Cole intoned sarcastically, as the usher returned to his ushering.

"I wouldn't miss the second act for the world. Isn't this where the new kid sings your filthy song in a fur coat? By the way, steer clear of that usher, he has the clap."

Porter gave her a look that could kill but chose not to comment.

"That's right, Ethel. And Miss Martin made the cover of *LIFE Magazine* in that coat. I don't recall you ever being on their cover."

"Clare Booth Luce hates my guts cause I flirted with her husband once."

The lights flashed and the conductor took his place.

The Entr'acte played while Ethel applied a new coat of Tangee lipstick. Cole Porter shifted a bit in his seat, knocking his heavy metal leg brace against Ethel's leg. On purpose.

"Ow! Jesus, Cole, that's my leg."

"And that," Cole replied, "is my music playing."

Mikey fell right back into his show-watching trance, ignoring everything around him, including Ethel's snorts and snores during the first quarter of Act Two.

Then the curtain parted and Mikey felt Merman sitting up a little taller. The scene was a Siberian train station. And there, like a still photo come to life from one of Mikey's Broadway musical books, was Mary Martin perched on top of a steamer trunk wearing a short fur coat, hat and muffler. But for the first time the scene was in color.

Cole nudged Ethel and rather unsubtly pointed to his *Playbill* where the next song was listed.

"MY HEART BELONGS TO DADDY."

Mikey's heart beat faster as he knew he was about to see one of the great moments in musical theatre history. He had a record of Mary Martin singing this song and he had seen a sanitized version of it in the movie about Cole Porter. Oh my God, Mikey thought, that movie *Night and Day* was about the guy sitting two seats away from him. Not for the first and certainly not for the last time, Mikey shook his head and wondered, how was this really happening?

A trumpet from the orchestra pit growled and Mikey almost fell out of his seat. Cole merrily mouthed the words and Merman… well, Merman watched and would later describe it perfectly to her parents in Astoria: "The double entendres dripped out of the dame's mouth like Southern Comfort and voom voom voom, the coat was off and underneath, well… nothing but a goddamned teddy. Sorry, Mom… She tore off her game of golf and didn't mind if some guy dined on her fine finnan haddie (fish to you, Pop!) and still her heart belonged to…"

"Daddy," murmured Cole, lightly singing along. "Wait a minute," muttered Merman to Mikey, "the kid is stripping!"

Cole smiled that Cheshire Cat smile of his as he patted Ethel's hand. He knew this was the dirtiest song he had ever written, but the combination of the witty filth and the naive Texas girl singing it – Ethel was sure that dame had no clue what it was about – made for a showstopper. Of course, Merman had to admit, this Martin kid really did have a great voice too. Damn!

Why, Ethel wondered, had Cole really brought her tonight? Was it about that new show he had mentioned to her? Something about Madame du Barry. Would he now want this Martin gal in it? As Ethel worried about the new competition, Mikey was, as his mother Rifka liked to put it, in hog heaven. And Cole Porter, tapping his two canes in rhythm, enjoyed immensely every word and note that he had written.

When the curtain fell, the regular customers ran out to hail cabs, but those in the know knew it was Mary Martin's last night to play Dolly Winslow in *Leave It to Me*. Those folk all flocked around the corner to 46th Street where the stage doorman let them backstage to congratulate and say goodbye to Broadway's newest sensation.

Mikey, Cole and Merman were escorted by the house manager through a small, hidden door near the stage that led to a thin, dark passageway. Mikey and Merman led the way with Cole carefully holding up the rear on his two canes. Finally, they reached Sophie Tucker's dressing room where Sophie was already holding court. Merman uncharacteristically held back in the corner watching shyly.

"Mary, darling," Sophie announced, "a toast to the toast of Broadway! I remember when I first saw you rehearsing Cole's dirty little song..."

Cole merrily pushed his way into the dressing room and interrupted Sophie in his soft slightly effeminate but securely continental voice, "Be careful, Miss Tucker, or we might have to cut 'Most Gentlemen Don't Like Love.'"

"Sorry about that, Cole. Didn't know you were in the house."

William Gaxton, the dark-haired, slightly aging leading man who had co-starred with Merman in Cole Porter's *Anything Goes*, chimed in. "I did! I heard extra applause after every song coming from Row D on the aisle... and no laughs!"

A blushing Mary Martin noticed Mikey right away and called him over as Sophie continued to wax lyrical.

"Well? Was I good?" Mary whispered.

"You were amazing," Mikey responded in a cracked bar mitzvah voice that made him sound years younger. "I never thought I would ever be witness to such an historic performance."

"You make me sound as old as Marilyn Miller's mother" Mary said with a laugh.

"Sorry."

"...and Mary has always been humble. I taught her that..." Sophie droned on.

"Was that THE Ethel Merman you came in with?" Mary hungrily asked.

Mikey suddenly knew why he was here. Why that closet had led him to this place at this very moment. He was destined to introduce Mary Martin and Ethel Merman to each other. All his life he had read about history and now he was in a position to actually make some.

Suddenly, he remembered Mary2 telling him, "I was there." And there she was, watching from the other side of the dressing room.

"Miss Merman!" Mikey called.

Cole Porter watched as Mikey introduced the two ladies, one an established star of the stage and screen and the other an up-and-comer. Cole felt both possessive and protective. It had been his idea for this to happen tonight. It was why he brought Merman to see his new discovery. Oh, sure, he was also playing a game. A game called "tease the Merm." Porter knew that Mary Martin was off to Hollywood and not available for his new show, not that her type of innocent blonde was right for the role of Madame du Barry. No, that role of the sluttish naïf was Merman to the core. But wasn't it fun to make La Merm just a little bit nervous, especially after her first almost flop. Yes, in the long run, maybe this meeting of the divas was a good thing for all.

As Sophie droned on, everyone's eyes turned toward Merman, so powerful was her attraction as a star. What they saw was Merman and Martin silently taking each other in with nervous smiles.

William Gaxton went over to hug his former co-star.

"Careful, Billy!" Ethel said. "Don't crush my family jewels," referring to the diamond-encrusted lavalier that rested on her ample bosom.

An undaunted Sophie plowed ahead, ignoring the interruption.

"Back to Mary... Mary, when I first heard you singing that... charming song about your Daddy... I knew you didn't know what the hell you were singing about. Do you remember?"

Mary smiled and raised her eyebrows indicating that she remembered. She then gave Ethel a secret smile, telling her that they must indulge Miss Tucker. Ethel warily smiled back.

"Well, I told you that anytime you get something you think is a little naughty," Sophie continued, "just raise your eyes to heaven and belt it out. And you took my advice and sailed all the way to stardom. I'm proud of you, my girl, and I expect my commission check in the mail. Also, I want a royalty for that record you made of my song, 'Most Gentlemen Don't Like Love.'"

Cole Porter chimed in. "I think it's *my* song, Sophie."

"It was until I sang it into a hit."

Everyone laughed as Sophie raised her glass to Mary. "Ladies and gentlemen, let's all drink a toast to our girl from Weatherford, Texas, Little Mary Martin. To her future in the woods of Holly. Although they never knew what to do with the Last of the Red Hot Mamas, I am sure they will know what to do with you. But come back to us soon, Mary. We'll be right here at the Imperial."

"Hear! Hear!"

"Drink up! But no seconds in my dressing room," proclaimed Sophie as she started to shove everyone out. "Miss Tucker needs to get out of her girdle and into a dry martini."

Her toast completed, Sophie, with the help of Mary2, handily ushered the assorted throng out of her dressing room and slammed the door behind them.

In the hallway, Ethel said, "Well, I guess Sophie needs her privacy."

Victor Moore, another *Anything Goes* veteran who was playing Tucker's husband in the current show, laughed and, with his impeccable timing and whiny voice declared, "She takes about an hour to get out of her corset. And then, watch out!"

Mary grabbed Mikey's hand.

"Mikey, I gotta go put some cold cream on this face or I won't have any kind of complexion for Technicolor. Give me five minutes and then be a lamb and bring Miss Merman up to see me."

Mikey looked at Mary and then back at Ethel.

"I have a better idea. Why doesn't Miss Merman get Mr. Porter to have his driver take us all to the Rainbow Room, where you two can really gab."

"Why, Michael Marvin Minkus," Mary responded, "you are brilliant!"

"As Cole loves to say," Ethel added, "'let's all go out and drink ourselves to death.'"

As Mikey led Ethel Merman toward the stage door and the waiting limo, the door to Sophie Tucker's dressing room opened and a smiling Mary2 emerged. Mikey stole a glance back at her and saw her displaying her toothy white grin.

Mikey had never been to the Rainbow Room before or any room remotely like it. Brooklyn boys who lived in the basements of their mothers' homes seldom saw anything like the plum-colored plush Art Deco walls framing a carpeted revolving dance floor, surrounded by tiers of elegantly set tables and banquets facing floor-to-ceiling windows, with modernistic electric shades (also in deep plum) that, when activated, opened to reveal a 360-degree view of a magical metropolis only told of in books.

Mikey had, of course, been to the Radio City Music Hall (taken by Rifka as a tot), just a block up from this fairy tale tower, so he had an idea of its plush splendor. Between the movie and stage show, Mikey would exit the five-thousand seat auditorium and enter the majestic lobby where he could imagine living in the palace of dreams, walking down the grand staircase underneath the magnificent chandeliers, and then entering a Men's Room that he would gladly trade for his basement room, if only he could. Mr. John

D. Rockefeller sure must have wanted the peasants to have a great day of fantasy for popular prices, thought Mikey. But if the Music Hall was Rockefeller's gift to the *hoi polloi*, the Rainbow Room was his grand bequest to the upper crust who could afford more than dreams, those who could afford to dance in the clouds among the stars.

Of all her companions that night, Mary Martin was most at home in the not quite five-year-old Rainbow Room. She had, after all, moonlighted here after performances of her show for months at a time. And now, on the bandstand was her conductor, Eddy Duchin. The very same Duchin who had accompanied her on her hit recording of "My Heart Belongs To Daddy."

Now, as they exited the elevator and walked through the gallery guarded on the east end by a stately Maître d', the two elegantly appointed staircases down into the Rainbow Room loomed before them.

"So," asked Ethel in her usual no-nonsense way, "who goes in first?"

"Why, Ethel," Mary responded in her unusually innocent honeysuckle tones, "you're the bigger star. You should go in first."

"Well, yes, but if I go in first and the band plays 'I Got Rhythm,' the crowd's gonna give me a nice hand."

"Of course, they will."

"Yeah, but then when you come in and Duchin strikes up your 'Daddy' tune, they're gonna scream and jump outta their seats. So, you go first."

"I don't see why they wouldn't play 'I Get a Kick Out of You'" muttered Porter under his breath.

"That's a ballad, Cole. And ballads ain't good for entrance music. So, Mary and your filthy tune go first."

"I think I have to use the Ladies' Room. I'll meet y'all inside," cooed Mary.

"Oh, no you don't. I'm not fallin' for that trick. I invented it back in 1930. Just ask Ginger Rogers. And anyway, I need to hit the loo too."

Neither Mary nor Ethel budged. Mikey was amused by this unsubtle game of Mexican Standoff, Broadway Style.

"Since there are two staircases, why not walk in together?" Mikey reasonably suggested. Both ladies whipped around to look at him. Neither smiled, but four eyebrows were raised. Mikey went on.

"Ethel will look like the magnanimous star giving the new toast of the town a loving send-off to Hollywood. And Mary will seem respectful to a more established Broadway luminary. Everybody wins."

Ethel looked at Mary and Mary looked right back at her.

"But what music will they play?"

Cole, who had been seated through the whole debate, perked up. "I have just the song. I just finished it, in fact. It's going to be the eleven o'clock spot for Bert Lahr and whoever gets to play Madame du Barry."

With that, Cole pulled from his lapel pocket a folded piece of manuscript paper with some chicken-scratch scrawls penned in ink. He handed it to Mikey

"Hand this to Duchin and tell him to fill in the chords and give it a hillbilly swing."

Mikey read the lyric aloud.

"If you're ever in a…" He stumbled when he could not read the next word. "Jab?"

"Jam," Porter corrected.

"Here I am! If you're ever in a mess, S.O.S. Hey, I know this song!"

"You can't know it. I just wrote it in the limo while waiting for all of you to exit the Imperial."

Mikey caught himself. "I mean, I know this song is going to be known by everyone. A showstopper and a classic."

"I like this boy."

"What's the song called, Cole?" Merman inquired.

"'Friendship.' Just 'Friendship.'"

"What could be more perfect for your dual entrance?" offered Mikey.

Mary thought for a second.

"'Friendship.' All right."

"All right," Ethel agreed.

The ladies shook on it. Cole rolled his eyes.

"But I still have to tinkle," Mary said.

"What the hell does that mean?"

Cole rolled his eyes again. "Pee, Ethel. The child has to pee."

"Well, why the hell didn't you say so? Come on. I'm not letting you outta my sight."

As the two musical comedy divas linked arms and headed back down the hall past the elevator banks to the lavish Rainbow Room john, Ethel could be heard to inquire, "So when do you leave for Hollywood?"

"Tuesday."

"Let me know if you need help packing."

With the ladies now safely ensconced in the Ladies' Room, Cole sang out for Mikey's entertainment in his fey but pitch perfect singing voice, "Just a perfect blendship."

Mikey couldn't help himself and continued the song. "When other friendships have been forgot... Ours will still be hot!"

Cole was bemused. "You're a quick study."

From behind stalls three and four came two simultaneous flushes. After a moment, both doors swung open revealing Ethel and Mary. "Come on," commanded Ethel. "If we're gonna make a grand entrance, we better do some repair work and re-plaster our foundations."

Perched on delicate velvet stools of deep plum, both ladies looked at their faces in the mirror and started with their eyebrows. Ethel, having just returned from Hollywood not that long before, had tweezed most of her natural brows out and replaced them with a delicate Jean Harlow-esque brow that gave her that Tinseltown tootsie look she wished she could perfect.

"My real German brows keep growing back and, of course, the blonde rinse is almost gone. Is yours real?"

"Of course, it is," said Mary indignantly. "With a little help from Mr. Kenneth's bottle."

Mary began that deep low chuckle and it spread like wildfire to Merman who guffawed like the Queens stenographer she used to be. The ice was broken.

"That Mikey kid is pretty smart. I can't believe he's related to Sophie Tucker."

"I tell you, Ethel, that boy has been a lifesaver to me. He hasn't been around much, but just the little bit he has... well, he's made this lonely little mama a little less lonely."

"You've got a kid?"

"Oh, yes," answered Mary with a mixture of pride and regret. "Luke... I call him Luke, but his real name is Larry. He's almost nine."

Ethel gave the young-looking Mary a look.

"I know, I know. I was only seventeen when I had him." Now Mary giggled and confided her embarrassment. "It's so hillbilly!"

"Are you married?"

"Of course not. But I was back then. You don't think my little boy is a... well, he's not. My mama takes care of Lukey now. They're waiting for me in Los Angeles. What about you, Ethel?"

"What about me?" a paranoid Merman snapped.

Mary ignored Ethel's outburst and quietly asked, "You ever wanna have kids?"

"Oh sure. But I wanna be married first. And, well, I got the guy, but the guy's not the marrying kind."

"Why not?"

"His wife won't let him."

Ethel's perfect timing made Mary guffaw just as she was applying a new coat of Drumstick Lipstick.

"Now you made me ruin my mouth. You are bad, Ethel. Just bad! But I have a feeling all those wisecracks cover up a vulnerable woman. And knowing Ethel Merman… well, I can't imagine her standing for a married man."

"Oh, I don't stand for him. Most of the time, we're lying down."

And with that perfectly timed zinger, Mary ruined her lipstick for the second time. They were both laughing now and didn't hear or see the woman coming up behind them.

"Do you two need some help?"

"Mary!" cried Mary noticing Sophie Tucker's dresser, now in a completely different uniform of plum. "What are you doing here?"

"Well, working for Miss Tucker is an honor, but she's a little bit, well… you know…"

Ethel chimed in. "Cheap!"

"That's the word!"

"So, *this* Mary needs to moonlight in the Ladies' Lounge. Don't forget to leave me a tip on the way out…. oh, and I am told by my friend Marcel, the Maître d', that Mikey and Mr. Porter are gettin' a little antsy out there."

"Let 'em wait! Miss Martin and I are bonding. Can we get a drink served in here?"

"Ethel!"

"Sorry, Miss Merman, the Rainbow Room don't have waiter service in the loo. But if you're really thirsty…"

Mary2 looked around to make sure no one else was looking and hiked up her skirt, revealing a handy hip flask strapped to her ample thigh.

"I hope you like Scotch. It's not too old, but being it's been between my legs all night, it's agin' fast."

"Oh, plop," Mary gulped.

Mary2 professionally removed the flask from her garter and poured out three shots in the glasses which she conveniently had hidden under the skirted vanity where the ladies sat. Both Ethel and Mary2 grabbed a glass. Mary Martin just looked at hers. Ethel was appalled.

"Don't tell me you're a teetotaler."

"Don't be silly," said Mary, daintily holding her glass and assuming her best Texas twang. "Ah've been drinking moonshine since I was twelve." She proved it by taking a slug and not choking. Ethel and Mary2 followed suit.

"So," Mary2 said as she sat down, "you two are becomin' pals. Have you told each other your deepest, darkest secret yet?"

Both Ethel and Mary looked blankly at Mary2, who went on.

"If you are really gonna be friends, you gotta share the deep and the dark. So, each of you needs to tell the other your deepest, darkest secret. Ain't you never heard of that before?"

"Secrets, huh?" mused Merman.

"Secrets," murmured Martin.

"Who are you?"

Cole Porter looked into Mikey's squinty, brown eyes with his own wide-as-saucers peepers and with all innocence, but the deep inquisitiveness that made him a great lyricist, asked again, "Who are you?"

Sitting next to this great genius near the entrance to the Rainbow Room, Mikey started to sweat. He had no idea how to answer the question. Was he twenty-five-year-old Michael Marvin Minkus, an unemployed boy living in his mother's basement in Brooklyn in 1983? Was he Sophie Tucker's nephew living on his wits in 1939? Was he really someone hobnobbing with his idols? And who and what would he be tomorrow? And when would it be? Would he ever get back to his own time? Did he even want to?

"There are people," said Porter, "who transcend time. People who can be whoever you want them to be, when you need them to be. Sometimes these people are forgotten by history. But they make a difference without making a sound. Maybe you are one of those people."

Mikey listened closely.

"Those two talents keeping us waiting… and remember this, my boy, real talents, as exasperating as they are, are allowed to keep us waiting… Those two are becoming friends, unlikely as that might have seemed two hours ago. And I think you are to blame. The question is now, how will it all play out?"

Before that question could be answered, having reapplied their war paint and fortified themselves for whatever was down those Rainbow Room steps, Ethel Merman and Mary Martin came striding down the promenade arm in arm.

"Mikey," slurred Mary, "go tell Mr. Duchin that we're ready for our entrances."

Mikey had never had such an important assignment. Things like this never happened at Rifka's house in Brooklyn. To be the musical messenger helping to facilitate the premiere appearance of this new two-headed monster – a sacred monster to be sure – Merman 'n' Martin, joined at the spotlight, coming down their dual staircases to a new Cole Porter tune. This was heady stuff.

Mikey suddenly remembered seeing this happen before. His memory though was not of the past, but of the future. An older Merman 'n' Martin coming down dual staircases, forty years from now, this time in matching red Dolly gowns. Mikey remembered seeing them from the next to last row of the balcony in 1977, but now he wondered if he was somehow also backstage at the same time.

Mikey's head began to throb. There was only so much a boy could take and Mikey's poor noggin, whose brain resided in the past and the future at the same time, was about to burst with dreams and memories. But now, he had to concentrate on the one task at hand. Porter handed him the music and Mikey happily slipped into the Rainbow Room.

"Well, Ethel," Mary asked Merman, "shall we?"

"Yes," said smiling Cole Porter as he slowly stood, leaning heavily on his canes. "You two go make your grand entrance. I'll be right behind you. Then we'll see who gets the most applause."

"Psst."

Mikey was hunting for the Men's Room when he heard what sounded like one of the broken steam pipes in the boiler room near where he slept.

"Psssssst. Mikey Marvin."

Finally, he noticed a crack in the Ladies' Room door and saw a brown hand with a crooked finger beckoning him. He cautiously approached the room with the ornate "L" and the door opened wider, revealing Mary2. She grabbed his arm and pulled him into the women's lounge. Mikey was appalled.

"Mary! I can't be in here. This is the Ladies' Room!"

"Technically this is the ante room. You know, where all the aunties fix their makeup. The toilets are in there."

Mary2, with surprising strength, pushed him down onto the very seat that just an hour before had cushioned Merman's behind.

Mikey turned a bright pink and tears came to his eyes. His embarrassment was at fever pitch. Mikey's phobia about Ladies' Rooms came naturally from being Rifka's boy. Rifka, who never closed the door when using the facility. Rifka, who, since he was a little boy and right up to the present, demanded that Mikey come in and sit on the tub while she continued her conversation, which was only interrupted by the sound of a delicate tinkle and occasional plop hitting the water beneath her. Rifka, who treated the loo as a salon, where the latest gossip could flow.

Now, here he was, trapped in one of New York's most elite Ladies Lounges, even if this was only the ante room. Mikey did not want to know what horrors were poised behind the inner sanctum doors.

"How did their entrances go? And even more, how are they doing now?" Mary2 asked.

"Fine," Mikey responded, as he tried to pull himself up off the seat to no avail. "Why don't you just come and see for yourself."

"You're kidding, right? I can't go into the Rainbow Room."

"Why not?"

"I know that you're a stranger here, little boy, but here in 1939 New York, a colored woman can work in the backstage of a theatre, in the kitchen of a restaurant, or in the loo, but she don't get to go inside places like the Rainbow Room. I thought that since you knew how to fix beds, you were smarter than that."

"What? What do you mean fix beds?" Mikey was shocked to think that this Mary2 could be the same as the Mary2 who let him into Ethel Merman's apartment... When? This morning? Forty-five years from now?

Mary2 smiled her secret smile, ignored Mikey's confusion, and stopped holding him down.

"Did you know that there's a secret passageway from the Ladies' Room to the kitchen?"

"How would I know that? I've never been in the Ladies' Room or the kitchen."

"Aren't you curious about it?"

"Not really."

"Oh, Mikey Marvin, there are more things in heaven and earth than you ever dreamed in your little basement room."

"What? How do you know about my basement room?"

Mary2 ignored him again and just plowed on.

"Well, I am famished. So, I'm going to take a teensy break and get something to eat. You don't mind manning the Ladies' Room for a bit, do you?"

"What are you talking about? I can't…"

By this time Mary2 had pushed through the secret door near the real door to the stalls and passed into a dark passageway. The door slammed behind her and to Mikey's eyes it looked like there had never been a door there at all, just a wall. Mikey was alone in the Ladies' Room and he was beginning to panic.

"Mary! Mary! Where are you?"

He started to put his palm on the wall where she had disappeared and suddenly it gave way and opened. Mikey stepped into a dark passage and the door closed behind him, leaving him in blackness.

Mikey meekly called, "Mary? Mary?"

Chapter Two

Letters to a Runaway Bride
Hollywood, April 1942

"Did you find the box of letters?"

Mikey could hear the faint voice from the other end of the passageway. The voice sounded male and not at all like Mary2. Mikey started to walk more swiftly toward the sound. The more he walked in the darkness, the more frightened he became. Once again, his mind flashed back to when he was a little boy and had gone to that fun house in a Rockaway amusement park near the beach in Queens. He was excited to go in at first but after entering through the mouth of a clown, he found himself in a small dark room, and when the large door behind him shut, it shut out the light. Mikey remembered panicking as he stumbled around in the dark, trying desperately to find what he knew should be an exit into the next part of the fun house. He walked into walls and banged and yelled and eventually started to scream and cry so loudly that the proprietor came to find him and let him back out the front entrance. Mikey remembered being in tears when he finally saw the light of day again. Ever since that day, he hated small dark places. Now, in desperation, he pushed against a wall and, just as he had when he was a little boy, he fell out onto the floor, into the light and back to safety.

Standing over him was a tall, willowy man in a dressing gown (at least that's what they were called when Noël Coward wore them) with his hair slightly disheveled. The man's face was a mixture of fear and anger.

"Well? Where are they?"

The gruffly demanding, but cultured, mid-Atlantic-sounding voice belonged to Richard Halliday. Mikey recognized him from pictures in Mary Martin's memoir. Halliday had been Mary's second husband. Mikey also smelled liquor on his breath.

"Where are what?" Mikey innocently asked.

"The box of letters I asked you to retrieve. Oh… why Mary keeps you around, I don't know. You're useless. A useless little twit of a… well, useless."

Halliday went over to the dresser and picked up the almost empty tumbler of bourbon and slugged it back in one gulp.

"Don't just stand there looking at me. Go look for them again," he ordered.

Mikey was loath to re-enter the dark closet and told Halliday so.

"It's dark in there."

"Well, then, twit… turn on the light."

Halliday opened the door and found a switch and flicked it on.

"Voila… and God said let there be light for your closet. Of course, my closet has had a little too much light perhaps."

Mikey was confused but happy that the closet was lit and did not look as deep as when he had emerged from it a few minutes before.

"Now find the letters. Mary keeps all her letters and whatever the hell else Texas shit in boxes, instead of filing them like an organized woman."

"There are lots of boxes in here," called Mikey from inside the closet.

"She loves baby blue. Look for baby blue."

Mikey emerged with a baby blue box.

"Is this it?"

Halliday grabbed the box from Mikey's hands and frantically opened it, tearing the ribbons that kept it sealed. Halliday's hands were still damp from his glass and he dropped the box which then exploded, sending letters flying all over the room.

Halliday pointed to the letters at his feet.

"You take half and I'll take half. The task at hand is to find out where Mary went."

"But… how?"

"If I knew the answer to that I wouldn't be looking for clues, now would I?"

"But when did she leave… why?"

Halliday gave him a look that shot daggers, scooped up a bunch of envelopes and staggered out of the room, leaving Mikey with the rest of them on the floor.

Mikey pulled the first letter out of its envelope. It was undated, but after seeing who the author was, Mikey devoured it.

Cole Porter
Waldorf Towers
Park Avenue
New York City, New York

Mary darling!

I was thrilled to get the announcement about your nuptials. Mr. Halliday sounds like a gentleman and a scholar and you, of course, deserve no less. Enclosed is a small token of my joy at your marriage. It's a painting for you to hang over your mantel or your toilet in your new home. I have discovered a simply brilliant artist who calls herself Grandma Moses. Can you imagine? She really is a charming old lady who paints in her barn. I literally flipped over her work (well, maybe not literally). So primitive and yet so inspiring. I have bought everything she would sell me so that I can share her with friends I love. I hope this Grandma Moses rooster will bring luck and prosperity to your new union.

Now, on to the dirt! La Merman has finally ditched Sherman Billingsley and all at the Cub Room are aghast. Sailors walking by 58th Street fell into a faint overhearing the Great Ethel hurling her unprintable insults at the poor man. Well, he did deserve it. You did know they have been an item for years, no? Well, they have. Of course, Mrs. Billingsley was never too pleased about it, but what could she do? As for me, I hope it's over for good for selfish reasons. I want La Merm to concentrate on playing a whore instead of being one. By that I mean Hattie from Panama. We are banking a lot on starring her solo, without a Lahr, Gaxton or Durante. This is the fourth show that we have done together, and I think I am finally getting it right. I understand how long she can hold a note (longer than the Chase Manhattan Bank) and what words sit best for her. She can make "terrific" terrific by holding the middle F and continuing her breathing. I once asked Ethel what she breathes from? She answered, "From necessity!" You are a beautifully trained singer, Mary, but she is just a freak of nature.

Sometimes (all the time), I long for your brilliance to return to the Broadway fold, but I do understand the lure of the silver screen. I love Hollywood too, but for different reasons (or are they the same?). My reasons being the freedom it affords me to indulge in being myself, not to mention the lovely big checks from Metro!

Now, down to business. You wrote me that you ran away from home. Mary, Mary, Mary. Marriage is not easy. Look at Linda and me. We've been together now for almost twenty years. Nothing is easy. Take Hollywood. I love it and Linda hates it. So, to keep my marriage alive, we compromise. I live where Linda wants me to. Listen to Uncle Cole and find some way to compromise.

You blame yourself for not being "a good enough housekeeper," but Mary, darling, Richard's mother cannot be part of your marriage and if deals must be struck, well strike them, but do not run away to Weatherford again. You are a top Hollywood star now and Weatherford, Texas would not know what to do with you.

Speaking of top stars of the Hollywood firmament, how is the elusive Jean Arthur? Next to Garbo, she is Hollywood's reigning mystery woman. No one knows a thing about her... except you...so spill, Mrs. Halliday. What is the secret behind that scratchy voice? Will she leave pictures and come to Broadway? Is it true that you both were seen at a costume party dressed as dueling Peter Pans? Give Cole the dirt. I won't tell anyone but Elsa Maxwell, who will whisper it to her 10,000 most intimate friends.

So, my Mary-Wary-Martin... please keep me informed of all the Hollywood dirt that your friend Hedda won't print and I will send you a cup of Broadway bile as often as I can put pen to paper. Rehearsals for "Panama Hattie" start next week, and I have already gone over my songs with La Merm. I play and sing them, she tries them out and changes notes and rhythms and I say, "Do it anyway you like, darling. Just stop the show!" Saves on the ulcers and I can yell at the musical director later.

Best love from the 46th Street Theatre on 67th Street.

Devotedly,
Cole

Well, thought Mikey, Cole Porter deemed Mr. Halliday a gentleman. I guess he never met him when he was drunk and agitated. Mikey put the letter carefully back into the embossed envelope and tried to piece together what was actually going on. Mr. Porter made a big thing about Mary running away before and now it seems, from Mr. Halliday's remark, that she had run away again. But why?

Mikey opened up the next envelope embossed with an EAM on the outside. There were two letters inside. The first one Mikey pulled out was a carbon copy of the letter Mary Martin wrote to EAM aka Ethel Merman.

Mary Martin
Paramount Pictures
Los Angeles, California

November 20, 1940

Dearest Ethel,

I read in Hedda's column that congratulations are in order. The woman who was married to Broadway finally got hitched to a guy! Welcome to my world! How does it feel, Mrs. Smith?

By now you should have gotten the little token of our affection. Of course, Richard picked it out and shipped it off while I was working at the studio, so we know it's tasteful and suitably expensive. Do let me know what we sent you.

Also, how does it feel to be the toast of Broadway? Two hit shows in one season! I bet your mama and daddy are proud.

Now, tell me all about your fella. The photo of him carrying you across the threshold was sweet and he looks handsome (and strong). You, of course, look radiant. Is it true that you married and then went on that very night as Panama Hattie and did two shows the day after your wedding night? Nothing keeps us gals off the stage, does it?

Speaking of that, how I long to be in front of a real audience. I never realized how dull making movies would be. Now I know why you left Hollywood! Singing to a playback of my own voice is so spooky. And there is such a sense of disconnect for me. No energy coming back from real live people. Just a faceless movie crew watching without a sound or even a breath. And to top it off, I am constantly exhausted working from dawn to dusk. I am not sure how long I can stand it.

Marriage is funny, isn't it? You just dive in and learn along the way. And marriage to Richard is so different from how my marriage to Ben was. Ben expected me to be a good Texas wife: cook (!) and clean and sit there and wait for him to come home from the office. I would twiddle my thumbs all day. Richard knows that my career is important to me, and he makes it important for <u>US</u>. In Weatherford, I was expected to decorate the house and make a home. Out here, I have not only Richard and his impeccable taste, but Mammy as well – that's what we call his mother, can you believe it? Richard does most of the decorating (he even chooses my clothes!) but Mammy is a big help with antiques (how the Hallidays love their antiques), which bore me to tears. In fact, I have to admit that I ran away. Yes, Ethel, I upped and left Richard and Mammy for a whole week. I left a note saying I was not good enough to keep his house and that I also didn't care if Paramount fired me. Can you imagine? I went all the way back to Weatherford to see where I actually came from. And once I got there, I realized that you really can't go home.

Of course, my mother and little Luke were out in Los Angeles and the big house was empty. I had a nice visit with Sister and her husband, and over a big lunch of fried foods my friend Bessie Mae put the fear of God into me and told me to go right back to my husband and my career. She drove me all the way to Dallas and put me on the train back to Hollywood. Lucky for me Richard understood. He seems to know me inside and out. But sometimes I don't think I know anything about him.

But back to you, oh mighty Merm! I fondly recall our last (and first) encounter. That night in the Ladies' Room at the Rainbow Room was magic. I hope we can make that happen all over again when and if I get back to little ol' New York, preferably in the Spring. Meanwhile, enjoy whatever it is we sent you as a gift and I hope your marriage to Mr. Smith is as great as your marriage to Broadway.

> Your best Buddy,
> (and no, I won't record "Let's Be Buddies")
> Mary

Mikey felt a kind of warmth while reading Mary's letter. As if he could feel her writing it. The sincerity leapt off each handwritten word. He also felt sorry for her. She really didn't know her husband at all. That seemed the clearest message he took from this letter. And she really didn't like it out there in Hollywood. Is that why she ran away that time? Was Richard keeping her there or was it that Paramount contract? In the same envelope was a cleanly typed note from Merman. Of course, it was perfectly typed. Ethel had been a stenographer, hadn't she? Mikey took it out and read:

> Ethel Merman ~~Smith~~
> The ~~Pierre~~ Century
> NY, 36, NY
>
> December 15, 1941

Dear Mrs. Halliday,

I know! I know! I am the world's worst correspondent, but let me be among the first to congratulate you on giving birth (how did I know? I heard it on Louella's radio show, how else?) and you can congratulate me on getting married again. That's right. Out with the old and in with the new. As you probably heard from Cole (yes, I know he writes to you and fills you in on the dirt) my marriage to Mr. Smith went phtttt. I haven't even had the time to get new stationery, so forgive the above. Bill and I felt it would be better for us both if he lived in L.A. and I lived here. The only casualty of the divorce was the gorgeous apartment at the Pierre that my pal Dorothy Fields decorated specially for us. Oh well. Now I'm at the Century and my parents live downstairs. As some young gal singer used to sing, who could ask for anything more?

My new guy's name is Robert Leavitt and he's in the newspaper game. And guess what? When we met, he had never seen any of my shows. I quickly got him a pass to

"Panama Hattie," which by the way continues to run and run and run. I think he liked it. He never said, the son of... oops, I forgot you hate profanity. But he is a looker and we have a swell time together. Bob is also of Jewish extraction, meaning I guess that if Hitler comes over here, we're doomed. Everyone always thinks I'm a Jewish dame, anyway, never guessing that I'm Episcopalian. I suppose they think that because I'm from New York and loud I'm a Yid! Well, now I guess I'm Jewish by injection.

So, Mary, I guess the Depression really is over. My feeling is that business is booming again here because of the war in Europe. I also have a bad feeling we're going to get into it too. Well, lucky for us that has nothing to do with Broadway or Hollywood, right? I really do appreciate your newsy letters and just because I never write back, please don't let that stop you. Who knows, when Hattie finally closes, maybe Bob and I will take a trip out to the Coast and visit you and Richard (and your new kid) and see how the real movie stars live. Or maybe, if the studio lets you get away for a weekend, you could come see me.

love,
Ethel

PS: There is a nice gift on the way (and no, it's not my Decca "Panama Hattie" records) for the kid.

PPS: If you run into Bill Smith, don't say you know me!

Mikey's face broke into a smile. So, Mary and Richard had a baby. Leave it to Ethel to not even mention if it was a boy or girl. But where was the baby if Mary was missing? And what year had he jumped to anyway? Mikey got up off the floor to look on Mary's desk. He found a date book there and saw that Mary's next to last entry was on Wednesday, April 15, 1942: TAX DAY! The next day was marked "KMH-Bing." Mikey knew that Thursday nights were when Mary appeared on Bing Crosby's Kraft Music Hall on the radio. He had a book of radio logs that he studied as if they were the Talmud. After that the dates were blank, except for a red circle around April 17th. Mikey had a strong hunch that this was Mary's D-day... today! It seemed clear to him that she was planning this escape. Mikey now worried about Mary. Where did she go and why?

In the next room, Halliday was drinking and reading letters from Mary's best friend in Texas. He was worried as well.

At that very moment, Mary was in a taxi heading toward Burbank, where Los Angeles had its only airport. She had never flown before, but if ever there was a time to get out of town fast, this was it. Richard always said that she was not organized enough to run her own life, but now, by golly, she was going to prove him wrong. Why she even cared to prove anything to him was a mystery to Mary. But even as she was running away, she felt under Richard's thumb.

Just last night, even though he wasn't there at NBC's Sunset and Vine Studios to pick her up as usual, she had stayed to sign all those autographs, Richard's instructions ringing in her ears:

"Always be gracious and sign everything, Mary. Keep practicing using the pen with the white gloves on. And never give them any cause to think you are not a lady. A beautiful lady without any flaws. Keep your head up high and show that swan-like neck to its best advantage."

Mary hated her neck, it was too long. And she knew she was not beautiful. She was moderately attractive and had good legs. She knew that she wore clothes well, clothes that Richard picked out for her, just as he styled her hair. She used to love wearing it down and long, but Richard preferred it upswept and more sophisticated.

She was lucky that her figure came right back after giving birth to Heller. But she told herself no more, not one more child! Why, Lukey was already twelve. Soon he would be a man. Little Heller was still teething and crying all the time. And Richard kept at Mary day and night, when he wasn't drinking. There were records to make and radio shows to rehearse and, of course, even though she was between pictures (a nice way of saying it), Paramount owned her and demanded she come in to take more cheesecake photos. And what about that war bond drive? And don't you want to sing at Lockheed in Burbank? Don't bend over to sign the autograph, Mary Virginia, that man is looking right down your front.

Then there was her mother, Juanita Presley Martin. Well, thank God for Mama. What would Mary even do with Larry? She couldn't handle a twelve-year-old boy. No one could. No one except Juanita. She somehow handled him well and they adored each other. There were times when Mary was jealous of their relationship. It was so much more than a boy and his Grandma. Sometimes, she felt the way her sister Geraldine must have felt when Mary was dubbed the favorite child. And she was still a child – Richard's child.

Well, no more. Not after what she had witnessed this afternoon.

Mikey was just starting to read the next letter from Ethel when an even drunker Halliday stormed into the room.

"She has not run off to Weatherford this time. This time I'm sure it's New York."

"How do you know?" Mikey asked.

"This last letter from her cockamamie friend Bessie Mae Ella Sue Yaeger. That Weatherford harpy actually advised Mary where to go if she ever needs to escape. It's right here in black and white... Well Bessie Mae likes red ink, so I guess in red and white... Read it yourself."

Halliday shoved the letter at Mikey and went to fix himself another drink. Mikey started to read the letter, but Halliday screamed from across the room, "Don't waste your time on the cordialities, just look at page two, four lines down." Mikey obeyed and flipped over the note paper.

"...and darlin' if you ever have that urge to run away again, Weatherford is not the place to run to. Honey, you know best that it's the place you ran FROM. After our long talk, I know that New York is the place for Mary Virginia. So, make it work with Richard, but honeychile... make it work in New York."

By the time Mikey finished that section of the letter, Halliday was back across the room with his drink and yanked the paper out of his hands.

"Am I right? Of course, I am. She's been talking of nothing but Broadway again, even though she owes the studio a dozen more pictures. And of course, she thinks nothing about *my* career. I have a job at Paramount too, but it's always 'Ah miss the stage. Ah hate makin' movies.'"

Halliday's impersonation of Mary's Texas accent was cruel, but accurate, thought Mikey.

"You," Halliday commanded with a sweeping gesture of his arm, "will go to New York and bring her back. There's no time for the train. You're going to fly."

"On a plane? But I've never flown."

Halliday ignored Mikey's whining and went into one of the dresser drawers and pulled out a wad of bills. "Here. This ought to be more than enough to get you there and a few sundries. Once you find Mary, cable me and let me know she's alright."

"Forgive me for asking, but why did she leave?"

"Never mind. That's none of your concern. Have Louis drive you to Burbank and book a flight. Louis!" Halliday called. "Louis, come in here."

A very handsome man of about twenty-five entered, buttoning up his shirt and tucking it into the pants of his uniform.

"Louis, drive this boy to the Burbank airport and make sure he gets on the next flight to New York. Wait and see that he is in the air. I don't care how long you have to wait. Just make sure he is airborne."

"Yes, Mr. Halliday. Of course, Mr. Halliday."

Halliday made another dramatically sweeping gesture toward the door and fell into the bed. Mikey scooped up the letters, put them back in the box and, without Halliday noticing, took them along with him. As Mikey and Louis left the room, Mikey could hear Halliday sobbing.

TWA had four flights a day, but if her driver would just hit the gas, Mary was sure she could make the last one at 6:45 PM out of Lockheed Air Terminal in Burbank. Before she left the house, she had called ahead to reserve a seat and was told it might be sold out. That's when Mary Martin, Weatherford Wife, turned into Mary Martin, Hollywood Star. Using a bit of what Richard taught her ("Mommy, you're a star now, use your influence."), she called an acquaintance she met at a party at her best friend Jean Arthur's home. The new owner of TWA, Howard Hughes.

"Hi, Howard," Mary cooed in her best "heart belongs to daddy" voice. "I just have to get to New York quick as a bunny. Do you think you could help a gal singer get the heck out of Dodge?"

Howard Hughes, who could never resist a woman's pleas, told Mary that there were always two unsold seats on his flights reserved for emergencies or if he wanted to go somewhere.

"Just like house seats in the theatre," Mary declared.

Mr. Hughes told her that she was welcome to them, and Mary thanked him kindly and sincerely.

Now, she just had to make that flight.

Mikey sat in the back seat while Louis the chauffeur went way over the Los Angeles speed limit in order to get them to Burbank in time for the last plane to New York. Louis always did what Mr. Halliday ordered and Mr. Halliday wanted the boy on his wife's tail. Mikey held on tightly to the box of letters and prayed that they would not get into an accident as seat belts hadn't been invented yet and he was sure to be thrown from the car and die on the side of a highway. His mother, Rifka, told him that was what used to happen in the old days all the time. Rifka also told him that flying wasn't safe either. This was to be a day of days for Rifka's scared little boy.

"Did you read about that accident TWA had back in January?" Louis asked, trying to make small talk with Mikey.

"What?!"

"Seven people dead in the desert."

Mikey was apoplectic. "Why are you telling me this?"

"Just making small talk. You're not scared of flying, are you?"

"No," Mikey lied. "I've just never done it."

"Oh. Well, here's some of Mr. H's sedatives," Louis calmly said as he passed a bottle of pills back to Mikey. "He always leaves a stash in the car and then forgets about them. If you need to, take one at the beginning of the flight and then in about 5 hours, another."

"Five hours? How long is this flight?"

"About eleven hours I think."

"Oh, my God."

Rifka's words rang in his ears. "Never go on a plane or you will die."

Well, Mikey thought, before I die I'll have lots of time to pour over these letters and learn what I missed since last seeing Mary in 1939. Just then, Lockheed came into sight. When Louis drove the car up to the terminal, Mikey could see the blindingly shiny silver aircraft, like nothing he had ever seen before, except maybe in a sci-fi film. Even the propellers (propellers?!) were reflective and silver and caught the rays of the late afternoon sunlight as they twirled in preparation for flight. TWA was emblazoned on the side of the aircraft in bold red letters and the plane even had a name stenciled on its nose: The Stratoliner. Even the name sounded futuristic, which, despite his fears, Mikey found secretly amusing.

All this would be enough to fill Mikey with wonder, but then he saw something he did not expect to see. There before him was Mary Martin, dressed in a chic blue-and-black suit with matching hat and handbag, and she was boarding the plane. As Mary disappeared through the door and onto the plane, Mikey realized with some relief that he would not be following her and trying to find her in the crowds of wartime New York. They would be flying on the same flight. Mikey hopped out of the car, said goodbye to Louis and, with his box of letters clutched to his chest, ran to catch the TWA Stratoliner to New York. In his head he was singing the title song of one of his favorite Broadway musicals, which was yet to be written and produced, *On the Twentieth Century*.

"New York in eleven hours… anything can happen in eleven hours."

This calmed Mikey as he climbed the gangway and entered the plane. As usual, Broadway to the rescue.

Chapter Three

Eleven Hours to Broadway
TWA Stratoliner, 1942

"New York in eleven hours…"

Even with the jaunty and optimistic Cy Coleman tune in his head, as Michael Marvin Minkus entered the sleekly modern plane his knees nearly buckled with the fear his mother had instilled in him. The smiling and elegantly costumed stewardess wanted to show him to his seat, but Mikey was peering past the other passengers, looking for Mary Martin. Finally, he saw her. Mary looked more at ease than most of the other passengers, who seemed a bit nervous, but then Mary had done this flight before. In fact, her first cross-country flight two years prior was filmed by Paramount and shown as a short between features. Mary's calm also revealed that she was an actress, for deep down inside she was breaking apart. Mikey wanted to go over to Mary to say hello and also find out why she was running away, if in fact she was, but the stewardess gently but firmly guided him to his seat, telling him the plane was about to taxi and take off.

Although Mikey had never been on a modern jet, he knew that it could never be as noisy as this 1942 propeller plane. The sound inside the cabin was deafening and certainly not conducive to conversation. Mikey sat in the very first row in a window seat and turned around to see that Mary Martin was two rows behind him on the aisle. She had her eyes closed now and had taken her hat off and placed it neatly in her lap. The stewardess sternly pointed to Mikey's lap and Mikey turned his body forward and fastened his seatbelt. He held tightly to the box as the plane began to taxi toward the runway.

Mary was not asleep as the plane smoothly took off into the air; she was quietly meditating. But her mantra ("daddy daddy") was not working. All Mary could think about was what she witnessed today.

Mikey, who learned from Rifka that religion and prayer were a bunch of hooey ("if there was a God would I have so many *fakocta* wrinkles?"), was so scared as the plane bumpily ascended, that he prayed anyway. As the plane leveled off, both Mikey and Mary, in their separate seats in their separate rows, found solace in the constant whirring noise of the propellers, which Mary thought was as cooling and comforting as an electric fan. Mikey decided to take out one of the letters from the box and find out more about what he had missed in the last three years.

The first letter he took out was a flimsy carbon copy dated May 1940.

Mary Martin
Paramount Pictures
Los Angeles, California

May 1940

Dear Ethel,

Hold the presses! I've got really big news! I am sure you have heard about my new movie to be, "Rhythm on the River." No? Well, who cares about that...except that I am going to be opposite Bing. The big news is I'm no longer to be "married to Hollywood." I am actually getting hitched, as we say in Texas. They also say the second time is the charm. And if they don't say that, well, they should. His name is Richard Halliday (doesn't that name alone sound grand?) and he works at Paramount, too. No, he's not an actor, he's a story editor! I haven't a clue what he does, but he sure is elegant and refined. What he sees in a little hick like me I will never know. Still we're getting married in May and for my honeymoon I get to sing with our Bing. In other words, the studio is giving me one day off to get hitched and then back under the Technicolor lights. What could be better?

In a strange kind of telepathic symbiosis, Mary, in her seat two rows behind Mikey, was remembering how she first met Richard Halliday one month before writing that letter to Ethel Merman. She had made her first film, returned to the stage as a full-fledged star in an out-of-town disaster that didn't make it out of Philly, and was just back at Paramount with her tail between her legs, when she was summoned to the front office for a meeting with Y. Frank Freeman, Paramount's head-of-production. Mary remembered what she wore, of all things. She only remembered it because it was described by gossip columnist Hedda Hopper in her column the next day: "a tailored suit with a periwinkle blue frilly ruffled blouse." Mary wore it because it made her feel more feminine.

Although the meeting started out cheerfully and Mary was happy to hear from his accent that Mr. Freeman was a fellow Southerner, things turned darker as the conversation got more specific. She could still hear the poisoned honey dripping out of his mouth.

"So, Mary, I don't want to beat around the bush. I like to cut to the chase, as they used to say in the silent days. All of us at Paramount would like to see you happy and settled out here, now that your return to the stage didn't quite pan out."

Mary winced as she remembered Freeman's cobra-like smile when he said that. She was so embarrassed about the Ralph Rainger-Leo Robin out-of-town flop *Nice Goin'* but was determined not to let it show. She knew that Paramount now owned her.

"Be careful what you wish for," her mother Juanita always said. And now she was a movie star… she had gotten her wish and wished she'd never gotten it. Mary Martin Movie Star! She remembered how Mr. Freeman said those words to her.

"Being a movie star, Mary has — how shall I put it — obligations. You not only sign a contract with the studio, but you make a kind of pact with the public, to be everything that they want you to be. And you, Miss Martin… you have it all… talent, looks, charm. We tend to try to overlook liabilities, like your divorce and child. We can keep all that in the background, as it were."

Then, Mary recalled, Freeman sprang it on her. Two years ago seemed like yesterday to Mary.

"But… we think you should… settle down and get married, Mary."

And just like that, Mary's world began to change. She was introduced to a man, a man whom she had previously met at a party at her friend Jean Arthur's house but had forgotten about. A man who worked for the studio as a story editor. Richard Halliday.

Richard, tall, willowy, and impeccably dressed, seemed like the perfect gentleman. The opposite of her ex-husband Mr. Hagman. Richard wooed her in the proper fashion… flowers, candy, compliments… but something about him screamed "not the marrying kind." Still, the studio sent them to premieres and parties and promoted them in the columns as an up-and-coming romantic couple with "stars in their eyes and matrimony on their minds." So, it was not a total surprise when Richard popped the question one night at Ciro's. Mary remembered feeling both flattered and slightly sick to her stomach. She also remembered Richard's reaction to her son, Larry.

"Military school. It will toughen him up and make him a man."

Mary shook her head now to even think that she could allow it. Where was she? What was she thinking?

She remembered looking up from the table at Halliday's patrician face, for he had proposed to her standing, rather than kneeling. That face, so unlike the face and form of the burly Texan Ben Hagman, the man who lusted after her and finally wore her down, causing all sorts of calamities from marriage to little Larry and then to divorce. Lust did that. Sexual energy that Mary knew that she needed to conserve for her performances. Because that is what she gave out with when she sang, pure unadulterated combustible sexual energy. Mary felt that if she spent her lust unwisely on another person, what would she then have left? She knew that if she was ever to be coupled again, it would be best if lust was not a big part of the deal.

Mary cringed now when she thought of the deal she had made with the devil. As the plane engines roared in counterpoint to the propellers, Mary mouthed the words she had said that night at Ciro's. "Sure, I'll marry you."

Feeling disgusted with herself, Mary was glad no one was sitting next to her when she repeated one of Richard's aphorisms whenever she did something outrageous or wrongheaded: "Well, you sure put your foot in that one, Mommy."

As the plane bumped its way over the Rocky Mountains, Mikey continued reading, as much for the information as to keep his mind off the certain doom of this flight. Mary's letter to Ethel continued:

I ran into Billy and Madeline Gaxton out here and Billy told me that Cole has written you a whale of a new score for "Panama Hattie." I have to admit that I'm just a little bit jealous. I just heard one of the songs I'm going to sing in "Rhythm on the River" (that's what they're calling the movie I'm about to make with Bing... at least for now) and it's called "Ain't it a Shame about Mame." A little bit Daddy-ish, but then that's what the studio bought. I hope they don't expect me to show my legs! I also hope I get a nice duet with Bing.

My mother and Larry are doing fine and after I finish this movie, I expect Richard – I keep wanting to call him Mr. Halliday – and I will take a proper honeymoon. That is unless Paramount has another picture lined up for me. Well, it's been a tornado of work and romance out here. And they say the weather is supposed to be better on the Coast.

Write to me soon, Ethel, and let me know how rehearsals are going.

Your everlovin' Bing-bonger,
Mary

Mikey was happy to read about Billy Gaxton, whom he met backstage at the Imperial and again in the Rainbow Room. Gaxton had been kind to a very nervous Mikey, who, to quote a Mary Martin song as yet unwritten, felt like "a stranger here myself." Mikey was also thrilled to read about Merman doing *Panama Hattie*. Back in Brooklyn, he owned the 78 rpm set of the songs. But as he thought about Merman as Hattie, he realized that that was two years ago (according to his current time). Mikey didn't remember how long the show ran and wondered what Merman was up to now. He hoped that he would get to see her when they were in New York.

But in reading between the lines of this letter, it was clear that Mary's marriage to Mr. Halliday was not all hearts and flowers. Maybe, thought Mikey, that's why she was fleeing.

Interrupting his reverie was a terrible bump. As the airplane flew further over the Rockies, the inevitable bumps and choppy air grew worse. Mikey was totally unprepared for each new change in air pressure. His ears popped in rhythm, and he almost flew out of his seat several times. As his fear reached fever pitch, he remembered the vial of pills that Louis had given him. Sedatives he called them. Something to calm his nerves. Mikey found them in his pocket and tried to open the lid, but the turbulence was so extreme that when he did get it open, the pills flew up in the air and onto the floor of the cabin. As the pilot tried to find less choppy air, he ascended to a higher altitude taking the nose of the plane up first. The pills that fell on the floor were now out of Mikey's seat-belted reach as they all rolled back under the seats. Mary happened to be looking down when a bunch of sedatives cascaded from under the seat in front of hers, as if trying to escape.

Mary empathized with the pills.

As the plane straightened and the flight smoothed out a bit, Mary bent down and picked up one of the familiar pills and looked at it, as if she were looking into her past. For two years now, she had watched Richard take at least two of these little blue wonders a night. And that was after having many drinks. The drinks sometimes transformed her husband (oh, that word) into someone else. An angry, judgmental and sometimes abusive *doppelgänger*.

If one of the servants did not set the table just to his liking, if the salad fork was missing or there was a fingerprint on his wine glass, the screaming would commence. Mary was usually spared a direct assault, but since she was always there, across the table, she could not avoid hearing Richard's volcanic eruptions. The language that spewed from his mouth like lava sometimes made Mary, who never used any language bluer than "plop," cover her ears.

As the evenings wore on and more drinks were imbibed, Richard would mellow a bit, but his bitterness was always there, just beneath the surface. Finally at about eleven, he would give up the ghost, take a couple of "blue babies," as he called them, and sleep. That was when Mary felt safest.

After the baby was born, Richard drank less, but never entirely stopped. He seemed to adore their little girl almost as much as he disliked Mary's son, who was living with her mother on the other side of Los Angeles. Mary's mother was a Godsend, especially today when she had to leave her one-year-old baby girl with her for a while. Juanita looked at her distraught daughter and asked no questions.

Now, Mary looked at the little blue pill in her hand and tried to clear her head for the long flight ahead.

As the plane found its way out of the turbulence and leveled out, Mikey held his nose and popped his clogged-up ears. Then he quickly unbuckled his seatbelt and started to scurry up the aisle in search of the errant sedatives. Seeing the pills, Mikey got down on all fours and started collecting them, bumping into the feet and shins of passengers.

"Excuse me… pardon… sorry… excuse me."

"Michael!"

Mikey looked up and there was Mary Martin holding one of the pills. She looked very stern, like his high school gym teacher when Mikey refused to climb the ropes.

"What are you doing on this aeroplane?"

Mikey was speechless, but muttered, "flying?"

Just then the stewardess came hurtling down the aisle on her wobbly high heels.

"Sir, you must take your seat and buckle up. You never know when we are going to hit another rough patch of air."

Mikey stood up with his hand full of pills and looked confused. Mary motioned to the seat next to her, the vacant one reserved for Howard Hughes, who was obviously not going to be using it.

"Sit down, Michael."

Mikey, who was used to being told what to do by Rifka, sat down in the seat next to Mary.

"What are you doing here?" Mary demanded. "Did Mr. Halliday send you to follow me?"

Mikey looked sheepish and blushed red.

"I thought so. He cannot stand being out of control."

Mikey didn't know what to say so he started to put all the pills he picked up from the floor back into their vial. Mary looked at the bottle of sedatives and then at the pill in her hand and made a decision. She pushed the call button that summoned the stewardess.

"May I have a glass of water, please."

The stewardess brought Mary the water and Mary took the pill.

"If it works on me the way it works on Richard, I'll be out like a light."

Mary, unused to any kind of medication or liquor, thought the little pill would take effect immediately and put her out so that she didn't have to think anymore. She waited for the drowsiness to hit her. Richard was always out like a light by this time. Instead of getting drowsy, Mary just felt relaxed. So relaxed in fact that she decided to kick her shoes off. When she looked down at her stocking feet, Mary giggled one of those deep gurgling, slightly naughty sounding, giggles that Mikey remembered from her dressing room at the Imperial all those... hours ago.

"Did he tell you?"

Mikey looked perplexed. "Tell me what?"

"No, of course he wouldn't. Well, settle down, my lad. Since there's nowhere to go for about ten hours, not counting layovers to refuel..." And now Mary's voice started to get both more Southern and just a little slurred..."Little Mary's gwinna tell ya a story."

Mikey shoved the vial of pills into his pants pocket and gave Mary his full attention, but before she could start her story, she took his face in her right hand and looked him directly in the eyes, as if to make sure she could trust him.

"We've been together a long time, haven't we, Michael."

Mikey had no answer but guessed at it.

"Four years?"

"Ever since I was in *Leave It to Me*. I never thought I would be the type to have an assistant, but when you offered to fly out to Hollywood with me... It filled an empty space in me. I felt just a little less scared and lonely. You know, I think I can trust you more than I can trust anyone, except maybe my momma… but even she reports back to Richard now."

Mikey's face was still in Mary's hand when a tear formed in his eye. Mary wiped it with her small, dainty handkerchief. She knew now she could really trust him. She let go of his face and started her tale.

"Well, you know how it is at the studio when I'm between pictures. They never like to waste their precious properties on silly things like rest or vacations, so today I was called in to shoot cheesecake for every holiday they could think of. First up was Thanksgiving. Me as a pilgrim holding a rifle but showing my sexy gams… Me as Santa holding a sack full of goodies in a very short skirt showing what no Santa ever showed… Me as the Easter bunny showing off, what else, my legs. And my cute fluffy tail. Finally, it was getting to be lunch time and I had had it. I just didn't want to see what kind of skimpy outfit they would come up with for Arbor Day. I just walked off the set, tossed off my bunny suit and hitched a ride home with one of the grips. Louis was scheduled to pick me up in the car at five, and when I had called home to get him to come sooner, there was no answer."

Mary grew silent and by now was looking straight ahead into the expanse of the plane, as if she were reliving this. The silence lasted perhaps a minute, but to Mikey it seemed like hours. Mikey prodded her. He wanted to say, "Earth to Mary," but instead said, "So you hitched a ride with a grip…" Mary returned to the plane, if not Earth, and the story.

"Yes. And when I got back to Bel Air, I went into the house. I knew Heller would still be out with my mother and Larry. She always took her on Thursdays because that's the nanny's day off. It was your day off too. I was so exhausted from changing those skimpy costumes all day and from the hot lights of the camera… they were taking color shots and you know how much light they need for that… well, anyway, I decided to just conk out for an hour or two before Richard got home. I walked through the living room and straight upstairs to hit the bed. When I opened the bedroom door it was pitch black. The lights were all out and the shades were drawn, which I found a little odd as we never pull them down during the day. Richard likes to come home to a bright house. Not thinking much of it, I just switched on the light and there they were. Richard and Louis."

Mikey's mouth literally fell open, but Mary just went on.

"They were too entangled in each other's arms to cover up quickly enough. There was a gasp and I heard Richard call my name in an almost stern way. As if he was angry at me for barging in."

"What did you do?" Mikey managed to ask.

By now Mary had tears in her eyes. "I shut the light off and ran out of the room. I left the house and walked all over Bel Air for hours. I must have looked like a lunatic. No one walks in Bel Air! Then I decided to leave. Now that I've gone, I have no idea where I'm goin'."

Mikey had the answer and blurted it out.

"Ethel Merman."

"Ethel?"

"Yes, Ethel will know what you should do next."

"But why? How will she know? She's not the Wizard of Oz. And isn't she on marriage number two herself?"

"I don't know. I just have a feeling about it."

"Well, feelings are important, Michael. And Ethel IS the Wizard of Broadway. She told me so herself."

As she said it, Mary let out a big unladylike yawn and lapsed into a very sleepy Texas accent.

"Ah think the seckative is clickin' in and…"

Before she could finish her Southern-fried sentence, Mary's head dropped to her chest and small but very distinct snores came from deep within her and out of her peachy pink mouth. Mikey closed his eyes too, but without the help of Richard's miracle pill, found it hard to sleep. He looked down at the pills and grabbed what was left of Mary's water and downed two of them. Immediately Mikey's mind started to drift and before too long he didn't know if he was asleep or in that blue/gray twilight time that brought so many of his favorite fantasies alive.

"Mikey! Mikey!" a voice he knew was calling but his eyes were closed and his body was in a paralyzed state, so he couldn't answer.

"You are gonna love New York in 1942. Spring is here, baby, and ooo-eee, the shows you can see."

Mikey opened one eye and saw the stewardess talking to him, but instead of the polished and shiny blonde woman that greeted him when he got on board, she looked an awful lot like Mary2 stuffed into a stewardess costume. Mary had gained some weight since he last saw her pushing her way through the secret passageway from the Ladies' Room to the kitchen of the Rainbow Room.

"Remember those books, those *Theatre World* annuals you loved lookin' at in the library? You were always late for dinner and your mama would whoop ya, right? Well, think back, Mikey Marvin, to the spring of 1942. Or should I say think forward?"

Mikey, in his dream state, did think back and remember how he used to dream he could put his finger on any entry of any season in those books and magically be whisked to the box office to buy a ticket. Was his fantasy coming true?

"Wait till you see Ray Bolger in *By Jupiter*," Mary2 cooed in his ear, as if offering him a candy too delicious to even swallow.

"And the revival of *Porgy and Bess*... I know you love that one from the record you play all the time."

Mary2, the stewardess, was right. Mikey was almost salivating.

"And what about those bombs?" Now Mary2 sounded like a TV drug dealer offering bags of crack to an addict.

"Oh, baby boy... *The Lady Comes Across* and what about *Beat the Band*? I can get you some hot seats."

Mikey instinctively put his hands out as if to pull in all those Christmas goodies. Before he could feel those tickets in his hands, Mary2 magically turned into Richard Halliday, also dressed as a stewardess. Halliday adjusted the little stewardess cap on his head so that it was at a jaunty angle. Halliday always knew how to wear clothes, Mikey thought, although he had just met him that afternoon. Halliday was brusque and businesslike.

"Forget all that nonsense. Stow your tray table and bring your seat to its upright position," Halliday ordered. Then he turned on his heels, but not before one last order emerged from his ridiculously lipsticked mouth.

"Bring Mary back home!"

Chapter Four
Four Bars and Out
New York City, April 1942

Ethel Merman wondered if every woman in her fifth month threw up and blew up as wide as a barn door. Not that Ethel had ever seen a barn door. They didn't have those in her section of Queens. The closest Ethel came to nature was the park across the street. Central Park. These days, even during the coldness of winter, she enjoyed leaving her apartment at the Century and walking across Central Park West at 62nd Street into the cold, clear expanse of leafless trees and frost covered earth that used to be grass. Now that April was here and buds were budding, Ethel went out even more. She liked to sit on a bench near the carousel a few blocks up and east on 65th Street and remember when her Pop would bring her to the city from Astoria and place her on a towering wooden horse. Sometimes, now that she was a grown up star, she would meet her pal Dorothy there. Over on Broadway, Dorothy was Dorothy Fields, daughter of vaudevillian Lew Fields, and sister of playwrights Joseph Fields and Herbert Fields (the latter of whom had been her favorite collaborator). The Fields family ruled show biz by night, but by day Dorothy was just Mrs. Eli Lahm, mother of a one-year-old and friend to "Mermsie."

"Mermsie! Herbie and I have a great idea for your next Cole Porter show," Dorothy said, as she rocked the huge perambulator containing a screaming baby.

"Dorothy, do you remember what it was like to give birth?"

"No. This lumpy thing in the carriage is my laundry."

"I don't know when I'm going to be ready to shake my can and sing on a stage."

"Mermsie, I give you three months alone with a screaming brat and you'll be begging for Bert Lahr to pinch your ass."

"So, what's the pitch? What's the story you and Herb came up with?"

"Okay! I read about this woman in a magazine. It seems that she could receive radio transmissions through the fillings of her teeth, and she started to get enemy radio messages… in German! Lucky for her she took high school

German, so she got in touch with the Army authorities and they intercepted some enemy plot and saved our boys overseas."

"That's funny! But is it a musical?"

"When Herbie, Cole and I get through with it, it will be!"

"Well, Dorothy, you and Herbie just write what you think is best and if I can't do the show, you can change the sex and give it to Danny Kaye."

"He's more of a lady than you are, Mermsie!"

The two friends doubled up laughing.

"You're lucky you can still laugh like that," Dorothy added. "Wait till you get to your ninth month. You'll be laughing out of your ass. Literally."

"No fart jokes!"

And this made them laugh even harder, waking the baby, forcing Dorothy to rock the pram even harder as she put her head in to soothe her screaming little boy. Ethel also "coochie-cooed" through her laughter in her attempt to stop the baby from crying. Suddenly, both ladies heard another voice.

"Well, I'm glad that someone is havin' fun."

They looked up to see the rather incongruous sight of Mary Martin in a full-length fur coat that matched her blonde hair.

"Mary," Merman proclaimed. "What the hell are you doing in Central Park?"

Dorothy stood up and ran her hands over Mary's fur.

"I love the coat."

"Ethel! You're pregnant," exclaimed Mary with some shock in her voice.

"Yeah," Ethel responded with a hint of embarrassment. "Just a little."

"She's been running for five months," Dorothy quipped. "Four more and she's in profit."

"Thank you, Dorothy... And don't start counting on your fingers, Mary. The important thing is I'm married. But forget about me, how did you find us here?"

"My assistant Michael knows everything. When we couldn't find you at the Century, he remembered reading that you loved to sit here in the Park whenever you weren't doing a show."

"I remember Mikey. Where is he now?"

"Off to see a matinee."

Dorothy noticed that Mary looked uncomfortable in her heels and slid over on the bench to make room. "Well, sit down, Mary, and take a load off."

Ethel and Dorothy began grilling Mary.

"So, are you in New York for a publicity tour?"

"No."
"To take in some shows?"
"No."
"Seeing the sights?"
"No."
"Is this gonna be twenty questions? Cause I gotta hit the can."
"I ran away from Halliday, Heller, and Hollywood."
"That sounds like a law firm."
"Shit!" Merman proclaimed. "She's doing the runaway bride bit again."
Dorothy looked puzzled.
"When Mary gets upset, she tends to bolt," Ethel explained as she pulled her expanding body up from the bench with Mary's help. "Come on, kid. Let's go somewhere where I can pee and we can get a drink and talk."
"May I suggest the Stork Club?" Dorothy remarked."
"Go to hell, Dorothy!"
"But Sherman Billingsley misses you so." Dorothy laughed throatily and got ready to depart. "And on that note, I am going to take my little boy for a walk near the lake."
"Good! If he starts to cry again, push him in."
As she glided the carriage toward the lake, Dorothy Fields looked over her shoulder for a final quip. "You're going to make a wonderful mother, Mermsie. Second only to Medea. Lovely seeing you, Mary."
"Okay, Mary, get a move on! The Merm's gotta pee!"

Mikey looked up at the Shubert Theatre on West 44th Street as he gripped his ticket tightly. There in lights on the marquee (although it was only 1:35 in the afternoon and the bulbs were not lit) were the words:

RAY BOLGER IN BY JUPITER
SONGS BY RODGERS AND HART

Mikey was pretty sure that what he experienced on the plane had all been a dream or hallucination brought on by Richard Halliday's sedatives, but "dream" Mary2 had been right. This show was at the top of Mikey's 1942 wish list.

Before he entered the small vestibule where the swamped and harried box office staff and the efficient ticket takers worked, Mikey looked across

Shubert Alley toward West 45th Street and to his immediate right where the glorious Astor Hotel towered above him. He had been here before, but it was in the future after the Hotel had been razed. His father had taken him to see *Promises, Promises* when Mikey was only twelve years old. It was the last time he and his Dad had done anything together. It seemed so odd to think of something that seemed a memory, as something that was yet to happen.

"Poochie," his Dad had said, using his infant nickname for the first time in years, "I hear this show is so good, we might have to see it twice."

It was 1970 and just before the diagnosis and death sentence came down from the doctors on high at Mount Sinai. Cancer. Mikey knew that word too well, even though it was only whispered in his presence by Rifka.

"Look up there," Mikey remembered his father saying, as he pointed above the main entrance way to the Shubert. "Do you see that carved angel holding a plaque? Well, that plaque has the signature of the architect of this theatre, Henry B. Herts, 1913. And now it's sixty years later. He built something that will last. A temple for art. And he signed it, can you imagine? In cement! So that it will be there forever. Like you and me, Poochie. Like you and me."

Mikey looked up at that very same plaque in May of 1942. It looked a little cleaner, but it was just the same. He thought of his Dad as he handed over his single orchestra seat ticket, fifth row center on the aisle. When he got to the usherette who would be showing him to his seat, Mikey was interrupted by someone whom he later found out was the house manager.

"Mr. Minkus?"

Mikey could not imagine who was calling his name.

"Mr. Minkus. If you would follow me, please. There's a long-distance phone call for you in my office."

"For me?"

"You are Michael Minkus, are you not?"

"Yes."

"Well, then follow me."

Mikey did as he was told and was taken to a small office just off the lobby where a heavy black receiver had been removed from its phone cradle and placed on a desk.

"Please make yourself comfortable, Mr. Minkus."

Mikey sat down and put the receiver to his ear.

"Michael! What are you doing at the theatre? Why aren't you with my wife?"

It was Richard Halliday.

"But how did you know I was here?"

"Never mind. I have eyes and ears all over the Shubert's empire. Now, before you sit down to watch a musical, tell me where my wife is!"

"There's nothing like peeing at the Pierre," Ethel quipped from inside her stall as a very nervous Mary Martin checked her makeup in the mirror and waited for Merman to finish her business. The Pierre Hotel stood majestically on Fifth Avenue overlooking the east side of Central Park at 61st Street. Ethel chose it because of its proximity to where they were and because she knew exactly where the Ladies' Room was. Ethel also knew the staff, which had been helpful in the good old bad old days of "no unescorted ladies allowed." Now, of course with America officially part of the European war and so many American boys off fighting, no bar or restaurant could afford to enforce that antiquated rule.

"Peeing at the Pierre… I tried to sell that title to Cole Porter for a lyric, but even he thought it was too shocking to sing. When I lived here with Bill…"

"Bill?"

"My ex-husband. When we had the apartment here, sometimes I couldn't make it to the 43rd floor fast enough and I would settle in with my *Collier's* magazine right here in this very stall."

Mary heard the flush and knew that it was time. She would have to tell her story. When Ethel emerged from the stall, Mary blurted out, "I can't live this lie one more second!"

"Ixnay on the i-lay," Ethel whispered looking under the stalls, "You never know where Winchell has spies."

After Ethel tipped the matron who turned on the tap and handed her a towel, she and Mary hightailed it out of the Ladies' Room and entered the elegantly appointed rotunda where little tables beautifully covered by crisp white tablecloths daintily sat waiting for them. Mary took note that each table had a vase of fresh flowers. Richard believed in fresh flowers in every home.

After they were seated by the Maître d', the waiter came to Ethel and Mary's table and Ethel cleared her throat to stop Mary from spilling any beans that the waiter might catch and dish up to the nearest gossip columnist.

"May I take your order?"

"Two Scotches on the rocks. And what'll you have, Mary?"

"Ethel, you're pregnant!"

"You're right. Add a little soda… on the side."

"I'll just have a lemon Coke."

The waiter took the order and left the ladies to themselves. Ethel looked around the empty bar at the Pierre, making sure no one was listening in, and then smiled at Mary.

"Looks like the coast is clear. So?"

"So?"

"You can't keep doing this deer in the headlights bit, Mary. You're too slick for this gig."

"Ethel. I didn't know where else to go or who else would even understand. It was Michael who said *you* would have the answers for me. I did all this wrong once already, I just can't do it again."

"What are you talking about?"

"Marriage and a child and a career. I feel like it's all *déjà vu*. Is that the right word?"

"I think so. But I was never good at Spanish."

The waiter served the drinks and Mary helped herself to one of Ethel's Scotches, knocking it back like a pro. Ethel watched in astonishment as Mary daintily wiped her mouth on the silk serviette and went on.

"Oh, Ethel, you have so many friends on Broadway."

Ethel looked at Mary seriously and replied, "Honey, I have lots of fair-weather friends and a few real ones. Let me tell you, the real ones I knew from Astoria will always outlast the ones on Broadway. Like my pal, Josie Traeger."

"I have a real pal too. Back in Weatherford. Bessie Mae Ella Sue Yaeger."

"That's a mouthful!"

Mary giggled. "I know… Oh, Ethel, I just thought of something. Our two best friends rhyme! Traeger and Yaeger. Can you imagine? It's a sign!"

"Yeah," Ethel agreed, "but of what?"

"I haven't the foggiest." The two ladies laughed and Mary knew that she could probably trust Ethel.

"I know Richard isn't Ben. Ben is a man's man. He hunts and shoots and fishes. Richard does my hair."

"It looks great."

"Thank you. The studio likes it on the blonde side."

"For once they're right."

"Ethel, I feel like this marriage was forced on me."

"By who?"

"I think it's by whom."

"Okay. By whom?"

"By the studio, that's who!"

Mary eyed Ethel's second drink and Ethel pushed it over to her side of the table. Mary took a swig.

"I mean I hardly know him."

"Who... I mean whom?"

"Richard. And here I am with another baby and what am I doing to her? Oh, I know Heller is not Larry. Larry got the short end of the stick for sure, but how do I avoid making the same mistakes with her?"

With that question, Mary finished Ethel's second drink. A well-dressed couple in their fifties entered the room and, although there were many empty tables, sat down right near Ethel and Mary. They seemed poised to listen right in. Ethel flagged down their waiter.

"Waiter. She'll take the check."

"Where are we going?"

"Don't worry. I know exactly where she is," Mikey told the officious man on the other end of the phone. "And we chose a spot to meet later on." Mikey crossed his fingers behind his back as he placated Mr. Halliday enough to get him to hang up so that he would not miss the Overture.

"You'd better not louse this up," the usherette told Mikey as she sat him in his seat.

"What?"

Mikey looked up, fully expecting to see Mary2 holding a stack of *Playbills*, but what he saw was a sweet little lady with dyed-red hair telling him to please take his seat and enjoy the show.

"I think I'm going out of my mind," Mikey said out loud to no one at all, as the lights dimmed and a spot hit the conductor. As the first bar of the Richard Rodgers Overture sounded, Mikey thought that if he WAS out of his mind, he didn't mind it in the least.

The Sherry-Netherland Hotel was only a couple of blocks down from the Pierre on Fifth Avenue, but Ethel hailed a cab, nevertheless. The doorman welcomed the Broadway star and Hollywood's newest blonde. He was a theatre maven (as most doormen are apt to be in New York) and remembered Mary from her fabulous turn in *Leave It to Me*. Last season he saw Merman in both *DuBarry Was a Lady* and *Panama Hattie* and even stayed to get her autograph.

"Welcome to the Sherry-Netherland, Miss Merman… Miss Martin."

"Hi, Ralph. Point us to the bar!"

Ralph's smile broadened when Ethel remembered his name. Truth be told she was his favorite Broadway star since he first saw her in *Red, Hot and Blue* with Durante and Bob Hope. As he looked at the pregnant Merman, he remembered how sleek and slender she had been singing "Down in the Depths On the 90th Floor." At the time, he was a janitor in a building on East 46th Street and the line about the janitor's wife having "a perfectly good love life" still resonated with Ralph.

"Right this way, Miss Merman. How are you today, Miss Martin?"

"Well, to tell the truth…"

"Come on, Mary!"

The bar at the Sherry-Netherland was sleek and luxurious and Mary, in her fur coat, fit right in. As it was still pre-cocktail hour, the two ladies were alone at their dark corner table.

"Where were we?" Ethel asked.

"So here I am," drawled Mary over a tall glass of Coke with a wedge of lemon, "a reluctant movie star approaching…" Mary could hardly get the number out.

"Approaching what?"

"Thirty! Oh, plop! I said it. Sorry to swear."

Ethel, who was on the other side of thirty and swore all the time, just smiled as Mary went on.

"I know I should be grateful. I mean, I got everything I ever wanted and dreamed of back in Weatherford. Well, be careful what you wish for, Ethel. You know what I learned in Hollywood? That movies are not the stage. I beat my brains out performing and nothing comes back. I like to hear the echo, do you know what I mean? All this radio work with Bing has proven to me that I need an audience."

"And I need another drink."

"I think you should have two."

"You're right. What'll *you* have?"

Mary slurped on her straw to get the dregs of her lemon Coke and began nibbling on the nuts from a bowl on the table. Ethel's two vodkas-on-the-rocks arrived at the table and Mary automatically reached for one.

"Slow down, girl!" Ethel chided.

"I have a wooden leg."

"You mean a hollow leg."

"Yes. And it's made of wood. Like that cute Walter Huston wore in *Knickerbocker Holiday* when he played Peter Lorre."

"That was Peter Stuyvesant."

Mary began to sing, "Oh, it's a long, long while from May to December…" Ethel joined her in a sweet, subdued voice. "But the days grow short when you reach September."

"Ethel, you're a tenor! Everyone thinks you're just this loud, vulgar belter, but you're a tenor!"

"What do you mean, loud and vulgar?"

Just at that moment, perhaps spurred on by the sound of two loud, but not vulgar voices harmonizing on the Kurt Weill-Maxwell Anderson song, three young, very well-dressed debutants came into the room. Their eyes lit up when they recognized Ethel and Mary.

"Are you Ethel Merman?"

"Oh, my gosh, Muffy, that's Mary Martin, the movie star!"

"Golly! Can we have your autographs?"

Ethel, actress *par excellence*, pretended to look puzzled and using her deepest, gruffest, and most masculine Brooklyn accent said, "Who da hell is Ethel Moiman?"

Mary giggled and went right along with the game using what she thought was a great New York accent, which coming from Mary came out as a cross between Butterfly McQueen and Wallace Beery.

"Josie, dees gals 'tink we're big stahs!"

"Don't pay attention to them, Bessie Mae!"

One of the debs admired Mary's fur. "What a beautiful coat. My mother has one just like it!"

Mary's mouth opened wide in despair. "Your mother!" Mary grabbed Ethel's other vodka and drank it. "Let's get out of here, Josie!"

"I'm right behind ya, Bessie Mae."

As Mikey watched *By Jupiter* unfold, he marveled at the star quality of Ray Bolger. Of course, Mikey and the rest of the world (even in 1942) knew Bolger as the Scarecrow in *The Wizard of Oz* movie. But here, live on the Shubert stage, in flesh and blood, playing the hilariously effeminate role of an Amazon warrior's "bride," was a whole other kettle of fish, as Rifka would have said.

What Mikey didn't expect was that he would see himself and Rifka on the stage singing and dancing to a song called "Life With Father." Of course, the rest of the audience saw Ray Bolger and Bertha Bellmore up there, but Mikey thought the resemblance between the strong pushy mother and the soft, childish son singing and dancing about the man in their lives hit very close to home. Morris Minkus was the only subject lately that united Mikey with Rifka. Everything else was a battle that was never won by either side.

But as much as he was enjoying the show, Mikey felt a little embarrassed every time the audience laughed at the jokes about Bolger (he was called Sapiens in the show) and his girly ways. Although Mikey joined in the laughter, he cringed inside.

Mikey realized how lucky he was. He had never been one of those social outcasts. He was not that little boy in school who got laughed at. Mikey was smart enough to hide any of his "unnatural" inclinations behind a veneer of boyishness. To be "girly" even for a moment would be a mistake, so he blended in and became part of the background, eliciting no jeers or snickers, as some of the other "different" kids might have experienced.

Away from school though, in his private world, Mikey and his best friend Ricky would play games that today might be called "roleplaying." In fact, they inhabited two female personalities: Suzie and Barbara. Suzie was a sweet and submissive girl in her twenties, while Barbara, her roommate, was bossy and domineering. They both lived in splendor in a mansion that looked exactly like the one inhabited by the TV clan on *The Beverly Hillbillies*. Their relationship was one of deep friendship, even if Suzie just sat around knitting and crocheting, while Barbara did… what? Bossy-boots stuff, Mikey remembered.

As Mikey remembered this secret and long-ago world of his childhood, he realized that he never had any real desire to be a girl. It was just that glamorous, rich women had so much more fun than the men he knew. Men just went to work and came home exhausted. Although, when Rifka was out, he liked to dance around in her ancient and scratchy crinolines, Mikey didn't really want to wear the dresses that might have pegged him as a drag queen or a transexual or whatever they called them. He just enjoyed fantasizing.

As the Intermission went on, Mikey's thoughts started to gel further. He started to realize that his idolization and love for Ethel Merman and Mary Martin might have sprung from those Suzie and Barbara days. Was Suzie, the sweet ingenue who knitted and crocheted using the strings from his winter parka, really a version of Mary Martin? And was the bossy and domineering Barbara really Merman? Suzie, Barbara, Mary, Ethel... He'd never thought of this before. Or had he?

Too deep, thought Mikey, as the lights dimmed for the second act. Mikey wondered if Rifka would show up again in Act Two.

On their way to the fabled Plaza Hotel, Ethel and Mary laughed and laughed; Mary, because she was pretty tipsy by now, and Ethel because her plan was working. Oil up Miss Martin and maybe the truth will slip out. The minute they got to the Palm Court, with the elegant little trio playing old show-tunes, Ethel turned left and pointed Mary toward the bar.

After ordering two champagne cocktails and Mary's non-alcoholic drink of choice, Ethel pounced.

"Now, before we're interrupted by fans, debutantes or Radie Harris and her wooden leg, spill the beans."

"What beans?"

"Why you really walked out of your Bel Air estate, got in a cab and had the driver take you to the airport without luggage to get on a highly dangerous flight to New York. Abandoning husband, baby and career."

"Oh, *those* beans."

The two champagne cocktails and Mary's obligatory lemon Coke arrived at their table. Mary pushed the Coke aside and started in on Ethel's champagne.

"Ethel, I don't know how you can still be sober with all those drinks you keep ordering. "

"Mary..."

"Ethel, I've spilled all the beans I am going to spill today. And besides, here come some of our brave boys in blue... or is it white? Anyway, the fleet's in."

Just as Ethel noticed the dozen sailors entering the bar, as if by magic, the piano came alive with a song that was very familiar to her.

"Ethel, he's playing your song." Mary began to croon, "Make it another old fashioned, please."

"Oh, shit! That means they all know who we are."

"Well, we are stars, darling," Mary said while downing Ethel's second champagne cocktail. "We're not exactly incognito. I didn't even wear my studio-issued sunglasses. Yoo-hoo! Sailor boy!"

"Come on, Mary! Like Horace Greeley said, 'Go west young girl.' In our case, that means the St. Moritz."

"Ethel, I am starving."

"Fine. Let's go up to the Sky Garden and get a bite before the dinner rush and then you can spill some more beans."

"Will you still be able to get a drink up there?"

"Don't worry about me, Mary."

They kept mum as the ladies ascended the elevator to the roof garden, as the elevator operator seemed to be all ears. When the doors opened, Ethel and Mary walked into what looked like a combination of boat deck and country club. Mary thought the place really was, as Richard might say, "the last word in swank." Mary had never been up there and delighted in the views north and west into the Park. The Maître d', still in his shirtsleeves but quickly pulling on his evening jacket, seemed unprepared to greet the public, let alone two stars, one from Broadway and the other from Hollywood.

"Miss Merman. Miss Martin. I am so sorry to tell you that we're not yet open for dinner. We start our seating at 6:00 PM, but I would be happy to fix you something myself if I may."

"You may," replied Ethel, as she and Mary sat at a table with a fabulous view of Central Park looking north. "How about two of your yummy seafood cocktails? And while you're at it, a couple of real cocktails. Let's see, we've had Scotch, vodka and Champagne… what's left?"

"May I suggest some very dry sherry?"

"Oh, Ethel," Mary cried, "he thinks we're little old ladies. I'm not even thirty!"

"Bring her a lemon Coke and bring me two double bourbons… neat."

"I'm so glad that you ordered them neat, Ethel. I hate messy bourbons."

Ethel ignored Mary and looked out the window. "You can see my building from up here."

"You can see my shame from down here."

"Mary," Ethel said with as much sympathy and warmth as she could muster, "what the fuck happened?"

Mikey joined in the huge ovation for *By Jupiter*. Now that the show was over, Mikey felt free to look around at the audience. First and foremost, he noticed that at this Wednesday matinee it was mostly a sea of ladies without escorts. Dotted among them were the men in uniform who, he had been told by the usherette, were given comps to see the show. Mikey suddenly remembered that this was World War II time. These were the boys who were shipping out any minute to fight and maybe die across the seas. Mikey found it odd that they would choose to see this musical as their last hoorah. He had always read about them going to see *Oklahoma!* before shipping out, but of course that would not debut until the next year, 1943. This was getting confusing.

Now, Mikey wondered about them, those service men, and wondered what people thought of him, at prime draft age, not going off to fight Hitler. He suddenly felt like all eyes were on him and felt the kind of shame that others like him must have felt at the time. Oddly, Mikey had two fears that accompanied him from his earliest childhood; fear of going to prison and fear of being in the army. Both felt like death to him.

Mikey turned to see a small pocket of men who were also not in uniform. Men like him, in civilian clothes. He noticed something different about them. A softness, an over-effusive quality as they applauded. Some of them even stood and cheered. He felt the blood rush to his face in embarrassment as he watched them, although he had no idea why that was.

Out the stars came. The bows and the applause continued. But before Ray Bolger could take the last of his ten curtain calls, the house manager of the Shubert tapped Mikey on the shoulder and beckoned him to his office once again. Mikey was not thrilled to miss one second of this fabulous show, even the exit music, but being the obedient child, he followed the manager up the aisle and to his office. Of course, the phone was off its cradle and waiting for him with a hyper Mr. Halliday at the other end. Mikey wondered if he had been drinking.

"How was the show? Was Bolger as good as his reviews? When do you meet up with Mary?"

Mikey was getting a little sick of being followed by phone but tried to be nice.

"The show was great. Ray Bolger was even better than in *The Wizard of Oz* and I will be seeing Miss Martin… I mean Mrs. Halliday in an hour or so."

Mikey heard Halliday gasping for breath on the other end, as if he was stifling tears. Mikey felt terrible for his pain, but after hearing what he had done and Mary Martin's reaction, Mikey's emotions were all over the place, mixed in a Mixmaster on high; sympathy, hatred, revulsion and even a little titillation. He found Halliday's actions repugnant, but also slightly arousing. He tried to stifle that last emotion. Why would he feel aroused? Before he could think any further, Halliday collected his own emotions and instead of issuing a command as Mikey had expected, his voice had a whining, pleading quality.

"Please… bring Mary back to me. Please."

Mikey replaced the telephone on its cradle and pondered the ridiculousness of marriage. The impossibilities of two people coupling and being together. How does it ever work? How did his parents Morris and Rifka make a go of it? At least they didn't have the added complications that Mary and Richard had. Two people who were thrown together by the studio "for show." Was Richard happy keeping his urges in check? Well, he didn't do a good job of that this time, Mikey thought. And what about Mary? She had to have known who she married, didn't she? Did she have secrets of her own? Mikey may have been 25 years old, but he felt all of twelve. He felt sure he didn't know one thing about the world, sitting in his basement under his mother's thumb. Even without any experience or knowledge, he knew how unhappy Mary was. Or else why would she run away? He decided to advise Mary not to go back to Richard.

Now all he had to do was find her.

The drinks arrived and, never one to break a habit, Mary automatically took one of the neat bourbons and neatly began drinking. This last drink finally pushed her over the edge and, as exhausted as she was, she imagined herself in a Paramount version of a movie of her own life, right here at the top of the St. Moritz in the Sky Garden.

FADE IN:

Traveling shot. The front of the St. Moritz traveling into the elevator and up to the roof.

New York theme music plays.

FADE IN:

INT. SKY GARDEN RESTAURANT

Closeup on MARY MARTIN finishing her drink.

> MARY (plunging in)
> I found him in our bed.

The music stops dead as the shot widens taking in ETHEL across the table, focusing all her energy on MARY.

> ETHEL
> Found who?
>
> MARY
> Richard. My husband. It happened last Thursday. The studio had me shooting holiday cheesecake. Mary Martin as a pilgrim showing her legs. Mary Martin as Santa in a very short skirt. Mary Martin as the Easter Bunny with great gams. Finally, just after lunch they ran out of holidays and sent me home early.

Mary's movie in her mind ended as the Maître d' and reality walked in with the seafood cocktails.

"Bon appetit."

"Yeah, yeah," Ethel dismissively said. "Thanks."

Ethel's stony stare made the Maître d' double his pace in leaving the room. The two ladies were alone. Mary could not retreat into a screenplay now. She had to tell the truth.

"So, you were sent home early from the studio…"

And Mary proceeded to tell the whole story, the same story she had told Mikey on the plane. She told Ethel about the dark bedroom and the two men she found in her bed, one of them her husband. She told about Richard scolding her, of her leaving and walking around Bel Air. Of her flight to New York. She had finally "spilled the beans."

There was a silence at the table now. Ethel felt embarrassed for Mary, who was openly crying. Ethel's empathy overflowed. She knew what betrayal felt like. The sting of her breakup with Sherman Billingsley still burned inside of her. Ethel had truly been in love. Now as she watched

Mary's tears fall, she remembered that final night at the Stork Club back in 1940. Could it have been only three years ago? Ethel wondered. Shit, she thought, I've been through two husbands since then. This one just had to last, or else why would she be having a baby? She recalled her red-hot anger at the ironically named Stork Club and burned all over again.

"What the fuck are you talking about, Sherm? Your goddamn wife is pregnant? You told me that you stopped sleeping with her. You told me I was the only goddamned woman in your bed. What a jackass I was to believe you."

"Now, Ethel," Billingsley said, trying to placate her.

"Don't 'now Ethel' me you motherfucker."

"There are sailors and truckers who want their mouth back, Ethel."

Ethel reached up and slapped the 6' 3" Sherman Billingsley right across the cheek. "Shut the fuck up. I loved you and you told me you were leaving your wife. All my friends said, 'Ethel, all married men say that.' But I told them this was real, that you loved me. What a sap I was."

Ethel's memory of that night merged into meeting Bill Smith and marrying him on the rebound. That sure didn't last, she thought as she looked at poor little Mary Martin, half in the bag and completely miserable. Men, thought Ethel, can't live with 'em and can't live without 'em. For all her empathy, Ethel didn't know how to comfort Mary, and before she could think of what to say, Mary spoke again.

"Richard has been my champion from the very start, and I guess I've always known this about him. I think Mr. Freeman at Paramount knew it too. But in his way, Richard always made me feel that this tomboy from Texas is… well, beautiful. Before Richard, I never felt that. Of course, we've never been wildly passionate. We both know that I save everything I've got for performing. Lust can just take away your talent. I guess I forgot that maybe he has needs too. Oh, Ethel, I just don't know what to do."

Ethel looked at her shrimp cocktail and didn't feel the least bit hungry now. She summoned the Maître d', got the check and paid it.

"Let's walk back to my apartment. I'm tired and you need a nap."

Mikey sat in the lobby of the Century Apartments trying to make himself as small and compact as possible. Not knowing where Ethel and Mary might be, Mikey had thought the safest plan was to find Ethel's apartment and wait. He found Merman's address on one of Mary's letters and walked all the way up Broadway from the Shubert Theatre on West 44th to Ethel's building on West 62nd Street and Central Park West. On the way, Mikey's eyes were filled with the marquees of all the great Broadway shows running in June of 1942. After scooting through Shubert Alley, Mikey took mental snapshots of the Booth Theatre where Noël Coward's great comedy *Blithe Spirit* was winding up its long run, of the Plymouth and Royale where *The Skin of Our Teeth* and *Counselor at Law* (he never heard of that one and vowed to look it up the minute he could hit a library) were playing, and finally of the Golden Theatre where *Angel Street* was still running after years and years. Mikey almost didn't want to leave that one street which also housed Gypsy Rose Lee in *Star and Garter* at the Music Box. And then to top it all off was his beloved Imperial Theatre, where he first met Mary Martin and saw her perform "My Heart Belongs to Daddy." Mikey wished he had a real camera to photograph it all. No wonder it took him an hour to walk uptown.

When he arrived and asked for Miss Merman, the haughty doorman told him that Miss Merman was not at home and pointed to the door, but Mikey insisted on waiting. As Mikey waited, the doorman never took his eyes off of him, making Mikey just a little bit nervous.

"I can walk, Ethel. Stop trying to hold me up. You're the one who's big as a house."

Mary Martin's slurred and twangy Texas voice, so familiar to radio audiences, rang through the lobby as both women practically flew into the plush lobby before the doorman could even reach the door.

"Fine," said Ethel placating Mary, "you can walk."

Mary turned her head and noticed Mikey sitting on a low divan.

"Michael! Ethel, look, it's Michael. Hello, Michael."

"Who?"

"My assistant. You remember, you met him the night that we first met, when I closed in *Leave It to Me*? How did you find us, Michael?"

"One of your letters to Miss Merman."

"That's good detective work... Isn't that good detective work, Ethel?"

"Yeah, yeah! Great work, kid. Now come on and help me pour Miss Martin into the elevator."

As Ethel, Mary, Mikey and the elevator man ascended to Ethel's apartment, Mikey spoke.

"I've spoken to Mr. Halliday several times today."

Mary looked at him and used her favorite expletive.

"Oh plop!"

Once the trio was safely deposited into Ethel's living room, and Ethel had gotten the first cup of black coffee into her, Mary spoke directly to Mikey.

"Next time you talk to my husband, you can tell him I am not going back."

Mikey surprised Mary by agreeing.

"You're right. I don't think you should go back either."

"Hold on! Hold on!" Ethel countered. "Let's think this through."

Ethel thought carefully for a moment. She was totally sober, and her mind was clear.

"Mary, I'm going to give you some advice."

"My mind is made up, Ethel."

"Your mind is made up of a lot of booze. Now drink that black coffee and listen to Auntie Merm."

Ethel took a dramatic pause and spoke straight from the shoulder. "Go back to Richard. Get on a plane and go right back to L.A. and your husband and baby."

"What?"

Mikey echoed Mary.

"Listen," continued Ethel in her calmest tones, "you told me you hate making movies, right?"

"Right…"

"What about Richard?"

"He loves it out there."

"Then you have a bargaining chip. It's always good to have a bargaining chip."

"What do you mean?"

"He wants to be Mr. Mary Martin, so let him prove it by moving to New York with you."

"But Richard works for Paramount."

"So do you. For now. Be your own agent. You make a deal. Mary, better marriages have been built on less. But here's what I got from your letters. This guy worships you. He sees you as a blank canvas he can fill with great art. It doesn't matter whether that translates to the bedroom. You, yourself, keep saying that you save all your lust for your performances, am I right?"

"Yes, but…"

"And Richard's whole world is Mary Martin. Your career can be his too. Isn't he happy to do all the things you never really want to do? Like pay the bills and decorate the house and…"

"Wash and color my hair."

"Yeah, that too. He really does that?"

Mary patted her perfectly coiffed blonde locks.

"Okay, we're neck and neck now as far as marriages go, you and me. We're both one-time losers, but here I am carrying Bob's kid and there you are with Richard's… it is Richard's, isn't it?"

"I think so."

"Good…" Just then Ethel did one of her famous double-takes and bellowed out the laugh line. "YOU THINK SO!"

Mary giggled one of her patented baritone giggles. "Oh, Ethel."

"Mary, you set me up and I'll take the punch lines. But kiddo, it's not fun being a bachelor girl and certainly not with two kids."

"My mother has Larry, which really is for the best. Larry's too much of a boy's boy for Richard and…" Mary suddenly realized that she might be going back. "Oh, Ethel, I've made such a mess of things. And the truth is, all I really want is to be… you!"

"Me?"

"Well, not you exactly. But to be back on the stage doing eight shows a week and sleeping till noon except on matinee days… how I hate getting up at 4:00 AM and having to go to the studio… I just want to sleep! And then the joy of not saying a word until curtain time. I want that applause at night, and I want to be able to just… smell that audience."

"Some of them stink, Mary."

"I don't care. I like 'em stinky!"

The ladies laughed and Ethel summed it up for Mary. "Well, Mary, you have a choice. You can leave Richard and start all over with a baby and no one to help you out… of course, you could always give Heller to your mother too…"

"No!"

"I didn't think so. Your other choice is to stick it out and make a marriage out of your career… or vice versa. Let Richard do all the dirty work… would he?"

"Would he ever! He loves being the bad cop and letting me be the pristine star."

Mikey interrupted. "I think he was crying the last time I spoke to him. He seemed so forlorn and sad."

Mary softened. "He did?"

"Well then, good," Ethel said, "I love a weak man. Listen kid, you let him be *Mr.* Martin and you can just be… Mary. And if you don't want that, maybe I'll marry Richard. I could use a fall guy too."

"What if he doesn't want me back?"

"I told you, he does." Now even Mikey was succumbing to the romance of it all.

"Mary… Mary. Without you he'd be just another four-hundred-dollar a week story editor at Paramount. But with you, he's the powerful husband/manager of a great star. Look at Kit Cornell and Guthrie."

"Kit and Guthrie are a great team and she's a huge theatre star and… oh…" Mary was a little slow on the uptake after all those drinks, but she was starting to get it.

"There's your future, kiddo." Ethel held out each hand weighing the couples. "Kit and Guthrie… Mary and Richard."

"But what about love?" Mikey's question hung in the air as Ethel and Mary looked at him.

"Oh, Michael," Mary said with a weariness that came both from life and the drinks she imbibed, "there are many versions of love, and it keeps evolving. Ethel, give me the phone. Oh, wait a minute, it's going to be really late in Los Angeles."

"No, it's three hours earlier," Mikey corrected. "I'm sure he's awaiting your call."

Ethel told Mikey and Mary that they could stay there tonight as they would both be flying back to L.A. tomorrow. Mary would use the guest room and Ethel showed Mikey to the library where there was a trundle bed. The library (or den, as Ethel called it) was wall-to-wall and floor-to-ceiling books. Mikey, the veteran library habitué, could not help but gawk at all the pristine looking books.

"My husband, Bob, is a journalist," Ethel said, as she put a pillow and blanket down on the leather couch. "He does all the reading for this family. These came with the marriage license. I think you'll be comfortable in here."

"Thank you."

Ethel closed the door from the other side and Mikey began to explore the shelves of great books.

Maybe it was something soothing and calming about being surrounded by all these books, the warmth and familiarity of it all, that made Mikey feel immediately at home and relaxed. He also felt a wave of fatigue taking over. Of course, he thought, you flew from L.A. for half a day and then went right to the theatre and then walked over a mile to get here. How could you not be tired? Mikey yawned and sat in a big leather armchair to skim through a picture book about London, but his eyes refused to stay open. Before he could even turn the page or pull out the trundle bed, Mikey had fallen into a deep dreamless slumber in the sleek armchair that seemed to embrace him in a way that he had never been embraced before.

After what seemed only a few minutes, Mikey's own snores woke him up and sent him into a coughing fit. He tried to go back to sleep but heard a strange noise that sounded like a vacuum cleaner.

"Didn't mean to disturb you, but Mrs. Leavitt told me to make sure it was tidy in here."

Mikey looked up from his chair, his eyes still crusty with sleep, to see a maid in a grey outfit pushing a heavy upright Hoover over the carpet.

"Mary?"

Mary2 smiled her secret smile and shut off the Hoover.

"I thought you'd never wake up. Come over here and take a good look at yourself, Mikey Marvin."

Mikey hated that she used his middle name, but he obeyed all the same as if he were in a dream. And wasn't he? He rose heavily from the chair and walked over to a full-length mirror, which he swore was not there when he first came into the room. But wait, was it on the back of a door and he just missed it? That has to be the answer.

"What do you see, Mikey Marvin?"

"I don't know," he answered with some annoyance in his voice.

"Neither do I. Mrs. Leavitt and Mrs. Halliday are schmoozin' in the parlor. Mr. Leavitt is out doing lord knows what. And what are you doin'? Sleepin'. This here mirror shows a short man. But you're what? Six feet tall?"

"Five eight."

"Can you imagine? A short, tall man like you and you almost made Mrs. Halliday obscure. If she didn't go back to her husband, who knows what might have happened? She might have stayed out in Hollywood and become... Mary Carlisle or Olga San Juan."

"Who?"

"Exactly."

Mikey was still staring at himself in the mirror and had an urge to reach in and touch his reflection.

"History is like a river, you know. It flows and seems to look the same, but it isn't. You almost touched history, Mikey Marvin, and shoved it the wrong way."

As his hand approached the solid glass, the mirror's surface melted and became like water, still reflective but soft and warm to the touch. Without any pause, Mikey's hand went right through the surface and touched its reflection, which was also soft and warm. Looking in the mirror, he could see Mary2 behind him opening Mary Martin's box of letters and starting to read one. Mikey flinched and cried out in pain as the mirror was once again just a mirror and cracked as his fist hit it. When Mikey saw the blood, he passed out. When he awoke again, he was back in the same dressing room at the Imperial where Sophie Tucker had held court in 1939. But now, in 1947, instead of plus-sized dresses, there were buckskins and moccasins, ceremonial Indian headdresses and cowboy hats.

"Michael! Hold your hand still while I bandage it," said a makeup-less and disheveled Mary Martin dressed in what seemed like a flour sack.

"What on earth were you thinking? You could have killed yourself!"

Chapter Five
White Kid Gloves
Imperial Theatre, NYC, September 1947

Mary Martin was dressed like a hillbilly and although Mikey had lost a lot of blood, he somehow realized that she was costumed for the first scene of *Annie Get Your Gun*. But Mikey knew he had to be confused because if this was the Imperial Theatre on Broadway, Ethel Merman was starring as Annie Oakley. So why was Mary in her costume? As she bandaged his hand, he noticed the letter that Mary2 had been reading lying on the makeup table before him. But that was back in Ethel's apartment and… now Mikey's head was beginning to ache. While Mary turned to get more tape for his hand, Mikey snatched the letter off the table and swiftly put it into his pants pocket.

"Does it hurt that bad? Oh, you poor baby. Maybe we should get the House Doctor in here."

"No. I'll be alright. And I have to get into the audience to see you."

"But you can't be bleeding all over Ethel. You will sit near her, won't you? Like we decided?"

"Sure," Mikey responded, remembering nothing about any decisions.

Mikey could feel that Mary was shaking like a leaf, and it was not like her to be nervous before a performance.

"I should not be nervous. I mean, I'm in my lucky theatre, aren't I? Of course, now Ethel owns the Imperial outright. I mean, did you see that marquee and her billing out there? It's big enough to scare Bernhardt, Duse, and Gertrude Niesen."

"Ten minutes, Miss Martin."

Mary quickly finished bandaging Mikey's hand and looked at her handiwork.

"How does it feel?"

"Numb."

"Will it stop you from clapping for me?"

"Nothing could stop that."

"Okay. You know your assignment. Get out there and enjoy the run-through and keep an eye on the Merm."

For some reason Mikey thought about Mary's son.

"How is Larry?"

"Who? Oh, Larry. I had a letter from him just yesterday. He's doing just fine. He's seventeen now, ya know, and going to Weatherford High. Just like I did. I just hope he's paying more attention than I did though. Lordy, when I was his age, I had just married his daddy. It seems a lifetime ago... now off with you unless you wanna see an old Texan cry."

Mikey began to leave but turned back to say "merde." Mary smiled as he exited through the same door he had used back in 1939 when he first introduced Ethel to Mary. This time Mary was the occupant. Mary, who had gone to Hollywood and returned to Broadway in triumph, taking up this dressing room when she played the title character in *One Touch of Venus*. But from all the photos of Ethel and her family and her personal items it was clear that Mary was only borrowing Ethel's room.

Mikey knew about Ethel's triumph in *Annie Get Your Gun*, and back in Brooklyn (after long playing records had been invented) he had played the Decca cast album until the grooves wore out. As he walked toward the stage door, he ran into Richard Halliday. Mikey automatically stiffened. His only memories of Halliday were of a man on the edge, a drunk who ordered him around in person and via long distance. But now Halliday seemed like a different man, someone more in charge of his emotions. A man who seemed to have finally found his place on Earth.

"What happened to your hand?"

Halliday seemed less concerned than annoyed. Annoyed that Mikey could have done something to take attention away from today's major event.

"I hit it on a mirror and it got cut."

"Well, don't bleed on Merman."

Mikey gave Halliday a mock salute as if he were in the military and waited in fear for Halliday's inevitable response. Shockingly, Halliday just smiled and patted Mikey on the back, streaming down through the hallway to his wife's dressing room, as if he were the Queen Mary on her way across the Atlantic.

Mikey watched as Halliday's sleek figure sailed down the grungy hallway and wondered if Halliday had changed. Had the deal that he and Mary struck to save their marriage and to propel her career mellowed Mr. Halliday? Had he, as Mary's husband and keeper, finally found his niche? He certainly seemed at home backstage, passing pleasantries to all the sundry show folk as he glided by. And surely his sexual life would have had to change as part of the deal. Or would it?

If Mikey could have looked into Halliday's heart, he would have found that he was half right. The "power behind the throne" job suited Halliday well and he reveled in it. That is, until it began to dawn on him that he, too, wanted... no, needed, recognition. During those sleepless nights when the booze would not kick in properly, Halliday found himself yearning to be more than Mary Martin's fall guy. More than the man whom Noël Coward blamed for the battle between the British genius and his miscast star. In fact, that bitter London winter and the even more bitter rift over the terrible flop of *Pacific 1860*, had put the Hallidays right where they were today, with Mary turning down another London production and deciding unilaterally that she would prefer touring the country in Ethel Merman's hand-me-downs. How well Halliday recalled that showdown on the Queen Mary returning home.

Halliday was still recovering from the Coward witticism circulating around the West End theatre scene: "Mary Martin is a talentless hillbilly, and her husband is her queeny mouthpiece. Why, one doesn't know where Mary leaves off and her Dick begins."

Mary, though, was oblivious as always and on the ship home she got more and more excited about touring. Richard was not convinced.

"But Mommy," Halliday chided, "taking Ethel's second-hand role to the hinterlands? What possible good will it do your career?"

"I just have a feeling about this, Richard. After London, I think for once you should trust me."

Outside the stage door of the Imperial, Mikey, as ever looking for answers, knew the information about what he had missed for the last five years might be contained in the box of letters. So, he opened the magic-Mary-missive box and lo and behold, found a letter that explained it all. It was written on Savoy stationery. Mikey plopped himself down on a bench near Eighth Avenue and read.

Mary Martin Halliday
THE SAVOY HOTEL
LONDON, SW1

April 1947

Dear Ethel,

I am so sorry that it has taken me so long to write to you from Jolly Old England. The reason for the silence is that England may be old, but it is far from jolly. I had no clue when I signed to do this show after the war that the war would still be going on over here. The rationing and the lack of heat and the dreariness of it all has affected my whole world. In fact, we have taken to calling Drury Lane DREARY Lane! Right from the start, I knew that this show was not going to go my way. Even Heller, who is only 5, had problems with Noël. Oh sure, he took her on his lap and read her a story… in French! At first it seemed that Heller understood it all, but after a few paragraphs, she looked up at Noël and said, "you look like a rat!" Well, Ethel, you never saw anyone drop a child faster. It was actually very funny. Imagine that clipped accent: "That Heller is going to give you trouble, Mary."

And imagine that I, from Weatherford, Texas, had to learn to clip all my consonants just like him! And of course, Noël wrote me a song that was obviously a showstopper, but also just plain dirty and Richard said that I should not sing it. It was all about the birds and the beasts of the field having at it with a girl named Alice. I think Noël thought that since I sang about my "daddy" and that made me famous, his song was tame. I have to admit I liked it a lot, but as Richard said, "Enough is enough. You're a married woman and mother of two." So, Noël reluctantly cut the song and grudgingly wrote me another number about doing a little dance, "There Is Nothing So Beguiling As a One Two Three… a One Two Three and a Hop." I started singing "one two three and a plop" on matinee days. I suspect I should have ignored Richard and kept my big Texas mouth shut and sung the other song.

Then there was the thing about the hat. Richard and I told Noël and his costume designer, Gladys Calthrop, before we ever came here that I did not look good in big hats. That I didn't have a hat face. So, there we were, trying on the costumes. All those hoopskirts! Oh plop! And what do they do but put me in the biggest picture hat you have ever seen. I sweetly told Noël that it wasn't right for me, and it would not do, but he pooh-poohed me and sent me out to rehearse some more. Well, I just had to tell Richard to take care of it, didn't I? That was the deal. Noël was livid. Well, you would have thought I started the next world war at the freezing Dreary Lane Theatre. In fact, the heated arguments were the only source of warmth for days. But we won. No picture hats for Mother. Of course, Noël stopped speaking to me, which was difficult because he was still my director.

Well, in any case, the show is a flop and we're about to close, which is more than fine with me. But this leads me to the cable I got from your producers, Rodgers and Hammerstein. They offered me a job! They knew I was over here and somehow… they must have moles at the Drury Lane box office… knew the show was on its last legs… so they offered me the London production of Annie. Well, I thought for two or three minutes and then sat down to write you first. After all, there would be no "Annie Get Your Gun" without Merman. How well I remember you telling me about Dorothy Fields coming to see you after you gave birth to Bobby and pitching you the show. You were in such pain from your C-section and you told her to... well, I could never say it. Wasn't Jerry Kern going to write the music, may he rest in peace? Oh, Ethel, great as Jerry was, could he have ever written all that hillbilly stuff that Berlin wrote for you? I doubt it.

But back to me doing the London production. I have four words to tell you my answer: I WANNA GO HOME!

Oh, Ethel, I cannot wait to get on that ship and sail back to civilization. To modern plumbing and overheated apartments. So, I had Richard cable back to Dick and Oscar and tell them to get another girl. And then I told them which girl to get. Do you remember when I was bored during "Venus" and took all those fresh young actresses and singers under my wing? Well, Richard put a stop to that double quick, but I put my foot down about one of the girls, a real talent, Dolores Gray.

Oh, Ethel honey, she's a cross between you and me, with a big brassy but silk and satin-y voice that could call hogs and then seduce them into marriage, all in the course of a song. Well, you know what I mean. You may have seen or heard tell of her in Cole's revue "The Seven Lively Arts" (Cole loved her!) and then last season in "Are You With It?" Well, if you haven't, you should. She is the real deal, Merman.

But what about me? Why am I giving up a good paying job? You know that when Richard saw you in your show, he teased me mercilessly because he knew I would have loved to be dancing in your size seven moccasins and shooting up the whole place. And he was right. Instead, I got to be a hoity-toity British opera diva in hoopskirts. Imagine that!

So, what would you think, old girl, if I took your show out on the road while you stayed the Queen of Broadway?

Richard thinks I am crazy, but the Lunts... you know Alfred and Lynn... well, they told me that going out on the road is the most fun ever. They said that if I went out on the road, the next time I was on Broadway, everyone from all over the country would come see me and think I was an old friend. It certainly has worked for Alfred and Lynn. So, Ethel darling, that's what I am thinking about. Of course, Dick and Oscar and Josh and Irving have to want me to go on the road and who knows what will happen. Still, I wanted you to be the first to know what was on my mind.

Hoping that Little Bit and Bobby are doing well and that your "love marriage" (isn't that what you called it?) is still going as strong as the grosses for "Annie."

Love from the frozen Tundra (aka the Dreary Lane)

Mary

Mikey digested the letter and wondered if he went to London with Mary. But how could he have gone with no passport? He always wanted to get one, but his mother Rifka didn't want him traveling too far from home, and now he had missed the opportunity of going to England and meeting Noël Coward and… this was ridiculous. Mikey laughed at his jumbled thoughts. Even if he did have a passport in 1983 it would never work for him in 1945. Back to the present, Mikey thought… or whatever this was.

So, reasoned Mikey, this must be Mary Martin's final dress rehearsal before she went out on the road with the show, what they called a gypsy run-through. And it was clear that Merman was here to judge Mary. No wonder Mary and Richard wanted Mikey to sit with her and report. He could almost sense a change in the Merman-Martin relationship since that night when Ethel advised Mary to go back to her husband and make a deal. It had been Ethel, after all, who encouraged Mary to return to New York and Broadway. That Mary Martin would take the town by storm in *One Touch of Venus* and grab the cover of *LIFE Magazine* for the second time had not been in Merman's plan. And now Mary was grabbing one of Ethel's greatest roles. Knowing Merman, this might not go down too well.

At 1:00 PM on that sunny September in 1947, the house was filling up with the casts of every show on Broadway. Row after row of the Imperial Theatre was stuffed with talent and ambition. Many of the actors, singers, dancers, and stagehands had already seen Merman as Annie Oakley and now they wanted to compare. All of them knew that Merman would be in the house, seeing her own show for the first time.

Mikey entered into this charged theatrical atmosphere, so different from the last time he watched a show in this theatre. Then it was a regular, if well-heeled, audience who paid dearly for their tickets and were out for a big night on the town. Now it was a house full of pros who paid nothing but knew how it felt to be up there on that stage. As a rule, this was a supportive, non-judgmental crowd.

On the other hand, Mikey imagined what it would be like to be Ethel Merman seeing a show she had never seen and watching someone else possibly triumph in a role that she created and played for over a year. He supposed it might be like looking into a funhouse mirror and finding a completely different version of what she thought was reality. With the way his life was going, he felt qualified to imagine just such a funhouse scene.

To many in the rapidly filling rows, this was not *Annie Get Your Gun* that they were about to see, but an alternate show, Merman vs. Martin, the Battle of the Annies! The air-conditioned air was thick with theatrical anticipation. Mikey recognized figures that, before today, were just black-and-white pictures in history books – Rodgers and Hammerstein and Josh Logan and Irving Berlin – and in color! Mikey peaked around and saw Herbert and Dorothy Fields sitting together, fountain pens poised over yellow pads, while several orchestra rows were filled with people Mikey did not recognize, people he assumed were somehow related to the show, the Merman cast, the costume and set designers, the orchestrators and various wives and significant others of the creators. The balcony was stuffed with the singers and dancers working on Broadway. The "gypsies."

Mikey, along with what seemed like the entire theatre community, held its collective breath when Ethel Merman entered from the lobby. Exquisitely dressed in a flamboyant red suit with her long pompadour hair pulled back in a neat ponytail off her heavily made-up face, Ethel seemed to have arrived with a private follow spot of her own. True to form, Merman was wearing enough baubles, bangles and beads to start a small jewelry store in the diamond district. Mikey remembered the Dorothy Fields quote: "whatever Mermsie couldn't wear, she would carry in her purse."

Ethel confidently strode down the aisle waving and greeting Dick and Oscar and Irving and Josh and took her seat, one off the aisle in Row D, close enough to the stage for Mary to see her, and back far enough for Ethel to get a full view of the show. Mikey saw his cue and sat down next to Merman.

"I'm saving this seat," said Merman without turning to see who was sitting next to her.

"I can sit on the other side," Mikey said, forcing Ethel to look up at him.

"I need that chair for my pocketbook."

Ethel was being imperious and treating Mikey like the enemy. Maybe he was. Mikey wondered if he still worked for the Hallidays.

Ethel finally looked up at him and noticed the bandaged hand. Her face softened.

"Fine, Michael, you can hold my purse while the show is on. And if I don't look like I'm having a good time, you can nudge me to smile. After all, I am paying you, right? Might as well get my money's worth."

Mikey smiled and shuffled past Ethel and sat on her right, holding her huge pocketbook.

I guess I work for Merman, Mikey thought, as they waited for the lights to dim and Ethel impatiently looked up the aisle for her husband.

Mary Martin's husband sat outside her dressing room door waiting to escort his wife to the wings. Mary sat on the other side of the door. Thinking. Mary did not like to think before a show. She liked to commune with her mirror and try to become her character before going out there to dazzle. But today, Michael had put ideas into her head. Ideas that would do her no good at all as the illiterate backwoods sharpshooter she was about to play.

As Mary looked at her hillbilly made-up face, she was thinking about her son. She had fibbed about getting a letter from him "just yesterday." Larry hadn't written her in weeks, and even when he did it seemed to be an obligation. Sure, he was now living with his father back in Weatherford, but Mary had a feeling that her almost grown son was going to be an eternally angry young man. Not that he didn't have just cause. Oh, he did, thought Mary. It was enough that she plopped him down with her parents, but then one by one, they had to die on him. The worst time of all was after Juanita died and Larry came to live with Mary and Richard. That didn't work out at all, mused Mary. Not one bit. Richard and Larry were like oil and water, constantly at each other. And then there was that time that Larry pointed one of his Texas shooters out the window at Richard down on the street and… well, that might not have ended well at all, so when Ben Hagman said he would take his son, Mary was so relieved that she kissed him for the first time in fifteen years. Richard had just smiled. He had won the battle.

Mary left her dressing room and, although the curtain was still down, found that small well-worn peephole she remembered spying through during *Leave It to Me* and *One Touch of Venus*. Back in 1938, Sophie Tucker had pointed the peephole out to her and said, "Mary, darling, always count the house before the show begins. Those gonif producers will gyp you every time." Closing one eye and peeping through, Mary saw the assembled bigwigs out there, ready to pass judgment. They didn't make her nervous in the least.

It was Merman. Merman in the red suit, bejeweled from head to toe. Merman with her lips scarlet and teeth all sharpened. Merman one seat in off the aisle, like the *New York Times* critic. For all she knew Merman had one of her Annie shotguns ready to blast her off the stage.

Although she knew that Mikey was working for Ethel, she also knew that he pledged allegiance to the flag of Mary Martin long before meeting the Merm. She was glad to see him sitting next to her. But what was he holding in his lap? Could it be Ethel's pocketbook?

"Oh, plop," Mary said loud enough for the cast to hear. Mary was so glad that when the lights hit her onstage, due to her slight nearsightedness, she became what she called "show blind." At least she wouldn't be able to see Ethel's reactions until the end of the show.

Mikey held tight to Merman's purse as he waited for the Overture to begin. He could feel Ethel shifting in her seat as she resigned herself to her husband Bob being a no-show. This did not improve her mood. Ethel sat impassively staring at the stage, remembering to don her Mona Lisa smile since all eyes were on her. She knew that just behind that curtain was something she never thought she would have to face in all her seventeen years as a Broadway star. Competition. Oh sure, Ethel thought, she had been the one to coax Mary Martin back to Broadway and Mary had been quite a hit, but now Mary was stepping into Merman-land and Ethel was not sure how she felt about it.

Suddenly the Overture, played not by the orchestra Merman heard nightly, but on two pianos, began with a fanfare. "Got no diamonds, got no pearls," mouthed Merman, and then when the Overture segued into "There's No Business Like Show Business," Ethel started to squirm a bit in her seat as adrenaline flooded her system, as if she were about to make her entrance onstage instead of sitting out here in the audience. She was like Pavlov's Dog – fourteen notes of Irving Berlin and she was off to the races.

Mikey dug his freshly bitten fingernails into Ethel's purse while, next to him, Ethel had to calm herself and not jump out of her seat and up on the stage when, after the first two songs, a shot rang out and her cue came. Instead, she held herself in check and watched wide-eyed as Mary Martin entered and got a huge hand from the invited audience. But it wasn't Mary Martin at all. It was Annie Oakley. How did she transform herself? thought Ethel, as she joined in the applause. And when Mary's – no, Annie's – first laugh line came a few seconds later, she found herself involuntarily laughing louder than anyone else. Was she actually enjoying Mary?

"Fuck," she thought, "I never expected to LIKE her!"

Mikey didn't just like her, he was enthralled beyond belief. He had seen Mary on this very stage knocking them dead singing "My Heart Belongs to Daddy," but this was someone else. He watched as Mary floated through the show. Scene after scene and song after song went by and the show was playing like a dream. Mary was rough and tumble and girlish and funny and warm and vulnerable and strong. Mikey had not seen Merman in the role, but he could imagine it clearly. She was surely dynamite, but Mary was dynamite as well. Mikey thought that there could never be such a role that used all the basic elements of Mary's personality. He knew from all his books that Irving Berlin had written the songs for Merman's voice, but Mary was making them her own.

Backstage watching from the wings, Richard Halliday was kvelling. Mary's gamble was paying off and he had to hand it to her. She had been right to go after this role. Of course, it was he who first saw the show and teased her.

"Slash your wrists, Mommy," Halliday remembered saying. "This is the role of a lifetime for you, and Merman got there first."

Mary had still been starring in *Lute Song*, applying Chinese makeup and wearing a long, black wig, and she was not amused. But once the *Annie* offer came and she decided to go on the road, despite his protests, she became Annie Oakley. And today, everyone in the theatre was feeling it. Gone was the prim soprano of *Pacific 1860*, gone was the smoky sex goddess of *One Touch of Venus*, and (thank God) gone was the Chinese bride of *Lute Song*. In their place was a real character in real situations, with a brother and sisters and a love story that was both believable and inspiring. And showstoppers. One after another.

The creators and producers exhaled after Mary's first number, and the audience, while still watching Merman's reactions, hoping she would grimace or frown, took Mary to their hearts. From the stage Mary felt that the audience was not only with her every step of the way, but enthusiastic to a degree she had never quite felt before. And despite her "show blindness," Mary saw a pair of magic white birds flutter in the air in Row D every time she finished a song. This had to be a sign. What were those birds? Whatever they were, they sparkled and glittered and shined.

During interviews Ethel was fond of telling the press that "Irving Berlin made a lady out of me." What she meant was that for the first time in a musical she had a softness about her. Oh, there had always been that vulnerability just below her hard crusty surface, but now she sang a lullaby to her brother and sisters and sincere love songs, as well as the boisterous comedy and swing numbers. Ethel was thrilled that Irving had written her a ballad that showed her soft and gooey center, "I Got Lost in His Arms." And Ethel rose to the task of being "a lady." It took some work, but she did it and she was proud. The ballad became her favorite moment in the show. But Mary started out a lady and her innate femininity, mixed with her penchant for being a tomboy, made her just right for the role, without even trying. Damn her, Ethel thought as the curtain for Act One fell to tumultuous applause.

During intermission, Mary sat silently in Merman's dressing room, looking at her reflection and redoing her makeup. She thought about how well Act One went, and thought about those magical, glittering white birds. Act Two contained several more songs for her including her favorite ballad, "I Got Lost in His Arms." Mary was aware that she was competing with the living ghost of Merman. Even now as she sat in her chair and looked into her mirror, Merman's ghostly presence was prodding her and pushing her forward, making her better and different than she had ever been. Mary, who always ran her own race, thought that this new sense of competition was good for her. It was making her strive to greater heights. Suddenly, Mary's reverie was interrupted as her six-year-old daughter slammed open the door and ran crying to her mummy.

"Heller! What is the matter?"

"I don't know, Mummy."

"I know. But you can't cry in your costume and makeup. You have to be a professional now."

Mary wondered if she had done the right thing, putting her small daughter in the show, as one of her sisters.

"But... I'm tired."

"You still have Act II to do. What did Mummy tell you? When we're in the theatre, we're not related, we're colleagues."

"What's that?"

"People who work together and respect each other and do their jobs without crying. Now, come give Mummy a kiss on the cheek and go and have them fix your makeup for the next scene."

Mary dried Heller's tears with a tissue from Merman's makeup table.

"Yes, Mummy. Is Daddy watching us?"

"Yes, he is. If you look you can see him offstage right. So, you better be good. And Mummy better be good, too." Mary softened and hugged her little girl. "Now run along, Minnie," Mary drawled in her best Annie Oakley voice, "I'll see ya on the cattle boat."

As Mary's impossibly small daughter ran off to be with the other children, the memory of that night several months earlier slid into Mary's head.

She remembered watching her husband smoking a cigarette as he stood outside his daughter's bedroom door. From the darkness of the room the glow of the cigarette mesmerized the child in her bed. Mr. Halliday thought his six-year-old daughter was asleep but, in fact, she was so used to waiting up for her mommy to come home and kiss her on the head after a show that she always woke up at about 11:30 and pretended she was still sleeping. After a moment, Mrs. Halliday joined her husband and looked in on their daughter. Mary whispered.

"I think she should be in the show with me."

"She's far too young to travel all over the country for a year," Richard said after taking a long drag off his Chesterfield.

"Richard," Mary said with clarity, authority and with the determination that got her out of Texas and on to Broadway, "I am not going to leave her with your mother or a nanny. I made that mistake once and I won't repeat it. I want her with me. She could play my youngest sister Minnie."

"What about the little girl who's been cast already?"

"I'm sure if you went to Dick and Oscar and Josh and firmly explained our needs, they would understand and replace the child."

"She'll be heartbroken, Mommy."

"She's a little girl. She'll get a new doll and forget all about the show in a day."

Richard sighed. "And what about your son? Is he to travel with us as well?"

"I wanted him to be in the show, too. I asked him, but he turned me down flat. He wants to go live with his father in Weatherford and be a cowboy."

Richard was relieved. He had no love for Larry and Larry felt the same about Richard. After all, hadn't Larry once thought about shooting Richard as he exited the apartment building?

"The boy is finally making some sense."

In bed, Mary and Richard's little girl was getting scared as she heard and understood snippets of what was being discussed.

"Alright, Mommy" said Richard, "I'll go in tomorrow and demand that she be in the show. They'll agree if it is something to make you happy and keep you on the road and make them money."

"Good! It'll keep the family together. It's the way it should be. And who knows? This could be the start of a great career for our baby girl. Heller Halliday… the HH will look marvelous on a marquee."

Mary walked off and back to her bedroom as Richard took the last puff off his Chesterfield and softly closed the bedroom door from the outside. He needed a drink badly. On the other side of the door, in her small bedroom, the six-year-old, without really knowing why, silently wept.

Mary's memory of Heller morphed to the memory of when she realized she was first pregnant. The mixed emotions embarrassed her and made her feel guilty. It was because of that surprise pregnancy that Mary lost her first Irving Berlin role, the leading role opposite Bing Crosby in a little film called *Holiday Inn*. There were times when the baby cried that Mary muttered under her breath, "Shhh, it's because of you that I didn't get to introduce 'White Christmas.'"

But that was water under the bridge and who knows, if Mary had made *Holiday Inn* and not had a baby, she might still be out in Hollywood. This was all for the best, Mary thought, as she put on her second act makeup, which was slightly more sophisticated and less backwoods-ish. This was about keeping the family together. Today, in 1947, Richard and Heller were on the board of directors of Mary Martin, Inc. But deep down, Mary knew that she was the creator, the president, and the product, rolled into one.

As Mary scooted her daughter out of her dressing room, Mikey stood in the corner of the lobby of the Imperial Theatre watching Joshua Logan chat with a very well-dressed man, whom Mikey would soon learn was the Hollywood agent, Leland Hayward.

"It's going well, Josh," Mikey overheard.

Never one for understatements, Logan said, "Well, she's brilliant. This tour is going to go on for years and make us all very rich."

Mikey's eyes bugged out when Irving Berlin came over to Logan and Hayward and spoke in his trademarked quiet rasp ("You know Irving; you have to hug him to hear him.") "What do you think, Josh?"

"I think we've got a second Annie. What do you think, Irving?"

"I think Merman hits the second balcony, but Mary hits my heart. Good to see you, Leland. I've got to talk to Dick and Oscar." And he was gone.

"Leland," Josh whispered, "do you know what rich is? When Irving buys a new pair of shoes, he has a private secretary wear them around the office and break them in. That's rich."

Hayward, who had left his Hollywood gig to become a producer, struck gold his first time out with a hit Broadway play. Now Hayward, knowing where the big money was, wanted to try his hand at musicals. That's why he was here today. His friend Josh had directed a bunch of hits and knew his way around a stage, but he too wanted to have more control, a bigger piece of the pie. And Josh had read a book. He had it in his bag, the bag that usually contained his scripts and scores. He pulled it out furtively and handed it to Hayward.

"Take it, Leland. Take it and read it and then we have to snap up the rights."

Hayward looked at the cover that read *Tales of the South Pacific* by James Michener. He had heard of it and the great reviews it had garnered.

Mikey could not help himself and interrupted. "That would be a show for Rodgers and Hammerstein!"

The two men swung their heads around in unison, almost spitting fire, as if they were a theatrical two-headed dragon.

"What show?" Leland Hayward demanded of Mikey. "And who are you?"

Logan knew Mikey. "This is Michael Minkus, Merman's personal press rep. He used to work for Mary out on the coast."

Mikey's eyes widened. He was a press agent. Wow! He had no idea what a press agent did, but wow!

Leland Hayward was nothing, if not polite. He put his hand out and shook Mikey's. "Pleased to meet you, Minkus. But... remember you heard nothing of this conversation, and you will not say a word to Dick or Oscar... or the press! Is that clear?"

Josh interrupted. "But the boy is right, Leland. In fact, he's a genius. Dick and Oscar would be perfect for this material."

Hayward looked closely at Mikey and smiled. It was as if he put this moment, like a card, into his pocket to save it for some future time when he would need it. Then Hayward spun around and wagged his finger at his old friend, Josh.

"Do not say a word to them! Not until we have all these rights sewn up. If they get wind of it, they'll want complete control. You know Dick better than anyone, Josh."

"We're old friends, Leland. Dick has been wonderful to me."

"Not a word!"

Mikey's head almost spun off of his neck in pleasure. He was there when *South Pacific* was being conceived! He might have even helped decide its fate by suggesting Dick and Oscar as the authors. Oh, how he hoped he would be around for the birth, too. He wanted to run backstage to Mary and tell her what her next Broadway show was going to be. He wanted to let her know she would be on the same stage as Ezio Pinza. He wanted to dance her around Ethel's dressing room and…

Suddenly there was Ethel Merman.

"Do you intend to hold my purse forever?"

Mikey had totally forgotten he was carrying it. Oh no! What did Logan and Hayward think of him? A grown man with a purse! He quickly relinquished the pocketbook to Merman and apologized. She had not said a word during the whole first act and just sat there with that Mona Ethel smile pasted on her face as the lights came up. He was dying to know what she thought. Before he could ask, she was making a beeline for the Ladies' Room, waving at everyone who smiled at her, her friends, her colleagues, the gypsies out for blood who were thrilled that Mary was good and hoped that Ethel would want to kill her. Ethel smiled and waved and kept the party line.

"She's great, right?" "Who knew the show was this good?" "I'm having a blast!" "Blah, blah, blah, blah!" "Yeah, yeah!"

Mikey would have to wait for the real Merman verdict until much later.

The audience walked back to their seats for the second act, but Mikey floated back to his. He was living more than a dream. He was helping to create theatrical history. And he was a press agent… for Ethel Merman! He hardly missed 1939 or 1943, not to mention 1983, where he was just an unemployed nothing. Maybe, Mikey thought, he could actually get somewhere. Wouldn't Rifka be surprised?

The second act was a blur to Mikey as he plotted and planned his future in 1947. Maybe Mary and Richard would take him on the road and he could do advance publicity in Dallas and Houston and Chicago and…

Before he knew it, the show had veered towards the Finale, when the entire company sang "There's No Business Like Show Business" segueing into "They Say It's Wonderful." When the curtain call began, Mikey saw Ethel getting up out of her seat. He was afraid she would just storm up the aisle and he would have to follow, pocketbook in hand. But no, Ethel was on her feet applauding.

From the stage, Mary – her "show blindness" gone – saw Ethel clearly for the first time. She was standing in her red suit and sparkly jewels applauding Mary with vigor and true joy, but no sound was coming from the hands that were clapping. Even as the rest of the audience's applause dimmed a bit, Ethel continued soundlessly clapping. It was then that Mary noticed that the fluttering white birds that were so enthusiastic during the show were the white gloves on Ethel's hands. No wonder there was no sound! And now Mary could see that the light had caught Ethel's jewelry and made the fluttering "birds" glitter. Mary started to giggle from way down deep in her soul and then she pointed at and applauded Ethel who was applauding her.

As the houselights came up, the audience of gypsies exited through the lobby and onto West 45th Street in rapture, while the inner circle – the creative team and staff – all stormed the stage and smothered it and everyone on it with love and congratulations. Hugs abounded, with none more fervently warm than the ones given to Mary Martin, still in her final curtain call costume. Rodgers got to Mary first and with a Cheshire cat grin said, "You were perfectly adequate." Mary took a dramatic pause and broke up laughing.

"You sure know how to flatter a girl!"

Rodgers' date, his 15-year-old daughter Mary, praised the older Mary to the sky.

"Oh, Miss Martin, you were wonderful," Mary Rodgers gushed. "I have seen the show five times with Miss Merman, but the one thing I noticed today was that Frank Butler is really singing 'my defenses are down.' All the other times I thought he was singing 'mighty fences are down.'"

Rodgers looked crossly at his daughter as he led her away. "Do not say that in front of Mr. Berlin!"

Oscar Hammerstein approached with a wagging finger. "Weren't you the girl who auditioned for me in Hollywood singing 'when I'm calling you double-o, double-o?' Despite that, I had a feeling you would go far."

Costume designer, Lucinda Ballard, rushed over to Mary with her arms outstretched, as if to embrace her, but instead fixed the small cowboy hat that sat on the back of her head.

"If you tilt this a little bit to the left, it will read better in the balcony."

And with that she departed, only to be replaced by Irving Berlin.

"Well, Mary," said Berlin with a kiss on the cheek, "here's to the new Queen!"

"We'll see what the old Queen says about that," Mary replied with good humor.

"Noël Coward isn't here, so he can't say a thing," quipped Richard Halliday, who was standing next to his triumphant wife. Mary raised her eyebrows at this. Did she smell liquor on Richard's breath?

"Did you tell Heller how wonderful she was?"

"Not yet, Mother. But I shall go backstage and bow down to our progeny now."

"Don't kiss her. She has to stay healthy!"

As Halliday departed, Josh Logan, Mary's intrepid director, approached her with love in his eyes. He was followed by Leland Hayward, who congratulated Mary.

"You were simply magnificent."

Josh topped him. "I bow to the champion!"

And with those words Logan did a deep Southern curtsy to his leading lady.

"Oh, Josh! Was I alright?" Mary demurely asked.

"Let's just put it this way," whispered Logan. "I saw steam coming out of Merman's ears."

"You mean she didn't have little white gloves in them? Where is that Merman anyway?"

And like the star whose instincts kicked in when a good cue came her way, Merman climbed up on the stage, followed by Mikey, still carrying the purse.

"This drop needs some touching up!"

"Ethel!"

"You know what, Mary? If you tilt that hat a little to the right, it'll read better in the balcony."

Mikey watched as the two Annies embraced. By this time, Mary's husband Richard had rejoined the group with little Heller in tow. Mary spoke in a small voice to Ethel.

"Well, Mighty Merm... was I okay?"

"Okay? Okay?" boomed Merman, "You killed 'em, Mary. And then you laid 'em in the aisles. You're a champ."

"Is that good?"

"Didn't you hear that applause? Especially from me?"

"Well, as a matter of fact, I saw your hands, but I heard nothin'."

Mary held up Ethel's gloved hands. Ethel began to laugh.

"Shit! You mean I was wearing the gloves the whole time?"

Ethel slowly and with mock innocence peeled off each white kid glove as if she were Gypsy Rose Lee in her prime. When they were off, she summoned Mikey over and put them in her purse, snapped it shut and proclaimed, "There," and gave Mary a new round of audible applause.

"Now get your ass to Dallas and sell some tickets."

Ethel, knowing just the right time to make an exit, took her own ass off into the wings and straight out the stage door onto 46th Street. Mikey did not follow. He wanted to give Mary his own congratulations.

After Josh and Dick and Oscar and Leland and all the rest did their final congratulations and left, Mary and Dick, Heller and Mikey went back to her dressing room so that Mary could change into civilian clothes. Tomorrow the Hallidays would all fly to Dallas for the big opening.

"Well," mused Halliday as Mary changed behind a screen, "it's not every day you see the visualization of a metaphor."

"What do you mean, Richard?"

"Didn't you notice? She took off the gloves."

"Oh?" It took a moment, but the lights went on for Mary who now emerged in street clothes. "Oooh!"

"Yes, Mother, the gloves are off. And may the best star win."

As the Hallidays exited the stage door on to West 46th Street and into a waiting limo, Mikey, who had held back all the knowledge he had about their futures, suddenly had a brilliant idea.

An idea only a press agent could concoct.

Maybe Richard was right, maybe the gloves were off. Now, what if they pushed the competitive envelope with the public? What if Ethel and Mary, the perfect blendship, exploited their rivalry? What if they became "frenemies?" Two Queens of Broadway vying for the ultimate crown. Mikey knew that Mary's next show, *South Pacific* would take the town by storm in a way that very few other musicals had ever done. And Mikey also knew that Ethel would run and run and run as Annie Oakley and then triumph in *Call Me Madam*. And with one lady being the Queen of Broadway and the other the First Lady of Musical Comedy, who would know which was which? And what if Ethel said, "Mary Martin's alright… if you like talent?" Oh, this was getting good. Mikey knew that this public rivalry would make columnists happy for years.

Now, all he had to do was sell Ethel and Mary on the idea.

Mikey felt empowered and decided to go out through the house and leave the theatre through the main entrance on West 45th Street. He crossed the street and walked east, past the Golden, Royale and Plymouth Theatres, just so he could take a good look up at the wonderful marquee again from a distance. Ethel Merman's name was bigger than the title of the show. Bigger than the name of the theatre, but he knew that if he could convince the two stars to become public rivals and remain private friends, both their names would blaze even brighter.

As he stood in front of the Plymouth looking across the street at the Imperial, he felt a tap on his shoulder. He spun around to come face to face with Mary2.

"Mikey Marvin! As I live and breathe. Fancy finding you on 45th Street."

Mary2 didn't seem at all surprised to see Mikey. It was as if she were lying in wait. Without letting Mikey interject, Mary2 took the conversation ball and dribbled it as fast as she could.

"Were you at Miss Martin's run-through, too? Wasn't she just grand? Grand I tell ya. Miss Merman must be blowin' smoke from her ears. I predict a big-time rivalry, don't you, Mikey Marvin? Something like a grand, grand feud. Kinda like Tallulah Bankhead and Helen Hayes… you know them both, right? Well, Miss Bankhead and Miss Hayes were both playin' on the street, around the corner from each other and they naturally wanted to kill each other. Of course, it didn't hurt that I was dressin' both of them and puttin' ideas in their heads, but never mind."

"You dressed them both? At the same time? How did you do that?"

"The tunnel, honey."

"What tunnel?"

Mary2 beamed and took Mikey by the arm.

"You just come with me and I'll show you."

Before Mikey could object, Mary2 took Mikey into the stage door of the Plymouth Theatre, into the house, across the orchestra seats and down the stairs to the lounge. As they walked, she explained with a manic kind of glee.

"Now… here's your history lesson, little boy. When the Plymouth and the Broadhurst theatre were built, back in 1917, the guy who designed them thought of them as twins. One is on 44th Street and the other right behind it on 45th. This guy had a funny sense of humor and wanted them to be connected, so he built a secret tunnel underground to keep them together, like Siamese Theatres."

"That's fascinating, but why are you telling me this?"

"I am telling you this, Mikey Marvin, because after Miss Bankhead's show closed… prematurely she said… I say it was mature enough… well, Miss B was furious that Miss Hayes was still running in her show. So, instead of going home to lick her wounds, Miss Bankhead just refused to leave the theatre. She decided that the show may be gone, but she was not goin' nowhere."

"That's crazy."

Mary2 laughed and agreed. "That's Miss Bankhead. So, another show opened and she had to get out of her dressing room, meaning I was off salary. Thank the Lord I still had Miss Hayes. But she … I mean Miss B… would not leave the premises while Miss Hayes still had a show running across the tunnel. So, she just moved in."

"Moved in? Where?"

"Into the tunnel. Lock, stock and Southern Comfort. Come on, I want you to meet her. The entrance is in here."

"The Men's Room?"

"You got it! I told you this architect had a funny bone."

She then opened the door and went in.

Mikey was aghast! "Mary! You can't go into the Men's Room!"

"Why not? You were in the Ladies Lounge at the Rainbow Room."

Mikey did a double take on that, remembering that was back in 1939 and his head began to ache a bit. By now, Mary2 was gone, and Mikey had no choice but to follow her. When he got in, passed the dirty urinals and grimy sinks, he saw Mary2 opening a small door, crouching and stepping into what looked like a dark tunnel.

Mikey summoned his courage and followed her into the dark abyss.

"Mary?"

Once he was in the tunnel, Mikey heard another voice. A familiar, low, raspy baritone voice. The unmistakable foghorn that was Tallulah Bankhead.

"Darling! Welcome to the tunnel of love."

Mikey, who remembered Tallulah Bankhead from the TV show *Batman*, was fascinated and walked toward the voice.

"Keep on, darling. You're almost there. Mary, help the poor boy to find me."

Mikey, who was oddly not as scared of small places as he had been, kept walking and walking, touching the walls with his arms outstretched, realizing this tunnel was not very wide. He wondered how Tallulah Bankhead could live in here. In the dark. And why?

"Darling," she called. "Keep walking. Keep walking… don't mind the dead body, just kick Helen aside. Ha Ha Ha!"

Mikey continued walking through the darkness and never found Miss Bankhead or Mary2. He was confused and even though his eyes were adjusting to the dark, he saw nothing. He put his arms in front of him and walked like a proverbial sleepwalker until he reached the end of the tunnel, where a similar small door awaited him. He pushed it open and shielded his eyes from the blinding light of the Men's Room of yet another theatre. This one was grand, with twelve matching sinks of shiny green, and tiled floors and walls that looked like Radio City Music Hall. Some papers sat on a long makeshift table over by the door, and Mikey picked one up and read:

Rehearsal Schedule: Ford 50th Anniversary Show
Starring Mary Martin & Ethel Merman
Hosted by Oscar Hammerstein & Edward R. Murrow
Center Theatre, Rockefeller Center
Producer: Leland Hayward
Sponsored by Ford Motor Company
Live on June 15, 1953
On CBS, NBC, ABC & DUMONT NETWORK
Director & Choreographer: Jerome Robbins
Mr. Hayward's Press Rep: Mike Minkus
May 1, 1953

Chapter Six

Some "I" Songs

Center Theatre, Rockefeller Center
New York City, May 1, 1953

The Men's Room door violently swung open and Ethel Merman stormed in.

"Because I need to know how you're going to stage it before I can learn it, that's why."

Ethel was not screaming, but her natural volume was a notch up from normal, and it was clear she was questioning authority. It was also clear that her emphatic statement was masking some kind of insecurity.

Following behind her was Mary Martin, holding two binders. Mikey took note that both Mary and Ethel had aged in the six years since he had last seen them. Instead of aging ingénues, each looked, well… middle aged. Of course, it didn't help that both ladies were wearing the glasses they never dared wear in public but needed for taking notes on their staging. The last through the swinging door was the short, compact, muscular dancer's body of director-choreographer Jerome Robbins. They all treated Mikey as if he were a ghost, which in a sense, he was.

"Now, Ethel," Mary said in her most soothing and placating voice, which had a touch of the Texas schoolmarm in it, "give Jerry a chance to explain what he actually wants us to do."

"He actually wants us to sing the medley over and over and memorize it before he stages it. I heard him. And don't play Miss Goody-Two-Shoes. You don't want to do it that way either."

Mary was silent. She always preferred not to be confrontational in public. She left that to her husband, Richard.

Robbins just wanted to pull out what was left of his thinning black hair, but instead, he took a deep breath and smiled at Ethel. He knew her well. He knew her ever since he was a chorus boy back in 1939; he staged her numbers in *Call Me Madam*. He understood her, he thought.

"Can we please go back into the rehearsal room, Ethel? Mary? Nothing will be solved in the Men's Room. I promise to make you both look fabulous," Robbins cooed, knowing he had no idea how he would stage the twelve-minute medley.

Mikey was impressed as he watched Robbins cajole Ethel and Mary. He had always read about what a tyrant he could be. Mikey remembered hearing about how when Robbins was yelling at a stage full of dancers, he kept walking backwards and as he perilously reached the orchestra pit, not one of the dancers warned him not to take that one more step back and... boom! That was how much he was loved in the theatre. But now, with Merman and Martin, Broadway's biggest stars, Robbins was a pussycat. Mikey had an unexplained urge. He wanted to get to know this contradictory man better. Before Merman could yell at Robbins again, the Men's Room door swung open and in came the impeccably dressed Leland Hayward, the gentleman who was with Josh Logan at Mary's *Annie Get Your Gun* run-through.

"Ethel! Mary!" Hayward exclaimed, as he hugged his two stars.

Hayward then turned to Robbins and addressed him by his pet name. "Gypsy, why don't you give the girls a break and you and Mike and I can have a little chat. It won't take long. Is that alright with you girls?"

Ethel surveyed the situation and spoke. "We 'girls' will be in the rehearsal room waiting for our director to come up with a decent idea. Come on, Mary."

Mary, playing the role of gentleman, held the door and let Ethel exit first, shooting an eye-rolling glance back at the men before leaving herself.

As the door swung closed, Hayward asked the two men to sit down.

"How is it going, Gypsy?"

"I may have made a mistake starting with the duet medley," explained Robbins. "The ladies are scared to sing together, Leland. Ethel wants me to show her where she is going to be dancing and where the lights will be, and of course Mary has intimated that she might want to wash her hair or something."

Hayward impatiently laughed but decided to dismiss this and get to the subject at hand.

"Yes. I am sure you can handle it and give us the eleven o'clock showstopper we need at that point. Look what you did with Gertie Lawrence and that bald guy in *The King and I*. And you and Ethel got along famously in *Madam*, didn't you?"

"Mostly..." replied Robbins wearily. Hayward may have produced *Call Me Madam*, but he was never in the trenches with the star.

"Good," Hayward said, dismissively. "Now, I asked Mike to be with us today because this meeting is really about... public relations and Mike has become my right hand man when it comes to the press."

Mikey stood outside of himself and smiled. He was impressed with what "Mike" had accomplished. The last time he had met Leland Hayward, he was a personal press agent working for Merman, and now, it seemed, he was in charge of a whole TV special with a lot more responsibility. The fact that he had no idea how to do a job he had never really done was now beside the point. Hayward believed in him.

"Mike has brilliantly engineered the 'fabulous feud' between our stars," continued Hayward. "When did you first come up with the notion, Mike?"

Mikey looked around the room to see if there might be someone else there named Mike, but he quickly concluded that *he* was Mike.

"Six years ago," Mikey responded in a deeper voice than he had ever used before. "Right after Mary did the run-through of *Annie Get Your Gun* in front of Merman. I saw the seeds of a rivalry and it just took some stoking and planted items in the press to make the public believe they were in constant competition."

"Well, it was brilliant," complimented Hayward. "Two friends doing a TV Spectacular is one thing, but two friends who are competing for the title of First Lady of the American Musical Theatre... *that* brings conflict to the whole enterprise. Something worth watching on all four networks."

"And that," Robbins explained, "is exactly what I am trying to inject into the finale medley. That sense of competition, but of course, keeping the joy and fun."

"Well," Hayward said, "you're the best, Gypsy. And that leads me to why I wanted to talk to you." Hayward took a dramatic pause and blurted out a name: "Ed Sullivan."

Robbins stiffened up and froze in his seat. "What about him?"

Robbins stared at Hayward as the silence in the room grew. As always, Hayward was impeccably dressed by Brooks Brothers. Robbins always felt a bit inferior around Hayward, with his tall patrician and frankly *"goyisha"* looks. Leland. Even the name was perfumed. And the perfume was decidedly non-Jewish. Hayward was the epitome of a Midwestern WASP who would date Katharine Hepburn, marry and divorce Margaret Sullavan, and wind up with Slim Hawks. In fact, Hayward had done all of those things.

"Leland, please get to the point. I have to deal with Merman."

"I envy you. This morning I was dealing with Henry Ford the Third."

"Oh?"

"Yes… And Mr. Ford had been talking to Ed Sullivan."

Jerry looked ashen.

Mikey looked down at the paper in front of him. This was the *Ford 50th Anniversary Show*. Henry Ford was their boss.

"You know," Hayward calmly continued as Mikey looked at the floor and Robbins began to sweat, "Ford is the leading sponsor for Ed's show."

"I know that," Robbins whispered.

Mikey grew up with *The Ed Sullivan Show*. Every week he would pray for an excerpt from a Broadway show and throughout the 1960s and into the early '70s, he was seldom disappointed. And Ethel Merman was a frequent guest. He can still remember his mother shouting, "Your girlfriend is on, Mikey!"

"I haven't seen Ed Sullivan since 1951," Robbins continued in a soft voice, "and I would be happy never to see the right wing bastard ever again."

"I'm sure," said Hayward. "Didn't he rescind his invite for you to be on his show?"

"The son of a bitch had me investigated. He found out I had been a member of the Party. But that was during the War years when Russia was on our side."

"Funny how that works," Hayward mused with quiet irony, "they're not on our side anymore."

Mikey was starting to put two and two together. They were in 1953, smack dab in the middle of what was to become known as the McCarthy era, even though Senator McCarthy had nothing to do with the House Un-American Activities Committee's infamous interrogation of people they suspected of having Communist ties. HUAC would force them to name names and, in a few cases, send those who refused to jail. Did Ed Sullivan tell Mr. Ford about Jerry? Was Robbins really a commie?

Hayward continued. "Not appearing on Ed's show has not done you a lick of harm. Look at you! He may be the Toast of the Town, but you're the toast of Broadway. You know how proud Slim and I are of you."

Robbins could take no more of this beating around the bush. If Hayward was going to take this long to get to the point, Robbins would get there for him. He took a deep breath and spoke.

"Leland, I've been subpoenaed. They want me to testify on May the fifth. Which is exactly what I intend to take—the Fifth."

Mikey tried to look nonchalant, but his mouth nearly hit the floor. This was serious. Today was the first of May, May Day in Russia, a point not brought up but one that sat heavily in the air. Hayward was relieved to have Robbins speak first and to have it all out on the table. He took the friendly, nonchalant tack.

"Mr. Ford tends to have other ideas about taking the Fifth Amendment and I was hoping you would see it his way. And of course, the Committee is making it especially easy for you by holding special hearings here in New York at the Federal Court House. You can take the whole day off and be back in rehearsal the next day. I mean it's perfect timing. And if you just give them what they want, everything will be fine here in Ford-land. If you persist in your idea of the Fifth Amendment then, of course, you can have *many* days off. But listen, Mike here can be of great help to you now… and after. Feeding the press what *we* want them to know, right, Mike?"

Mikey was taken aback, but he knew the power of cooperation, something Robbins would have to learn in four days.

"Right, Leland."

Robbins said nothing. Right, Leland indeed, he thought. Right as they come. "Oh, Leland, what did Ed Sullivan actually say to Mr. Ford?"

Hayward had been ready to leave the room. He turned back and smiled ruefully.

"He said that should you not cooperate with HUAC, he would expose you on his program as a homosexual."

A sense of *déjà vu* permeated Mikey's being. He knew he had been here before, but also knew that he had not. He sort of recognized the curved walls paneled in mahogany, but that was because this theatre was the plainer sister to Radio City Music Hall, even down to (up to?) the three-tiered chandelier weighing six tons! This he had read in a brochure in the lobby.

The brochure suddenly reminded him of the stack of *Playbills* and souvenir programs that his mother kept locked away after his dad had died. Mikey had sniffed them out and when Rifka was out at a hot Mahjong game or at the beauty parlor, he pried open her hidden strong box and found the treasured booklets. Among them, he remembered, were several from The Center Theatre, all ice shows starring Sonja Henie. Mikey loved looking at those *Playbills* because the ice-skating star had once made a movie with Ethel Merman, one that they never showed on TV. So, this is where Rifka and Morris saw all those extravaganzas before he was even born.

Mikey was jolted from his reverie by Hayward's sudden presence in the lobby.

"Leland! I had a great idea for a publicity piece about the theatre and its history."

"Not interested in the theatre. We're doing a TV show and no one will even know where it's coming from. Just live from New York. That's all they need. I need you, on the other hand, to get a puff piece into Earl Wilson's column about Jerry. Earl hates Sullivan and he already told me he will do an item for us. I want everyone to be reminded what a great talent Jerry is and, not incidentally, a great American. He did the dances for *Miss Liberty*, didn't he? Yes. You look it up. If Rodgers and Hammerstein love him, and they do, well, he can't be anything less than apple pie goodness. Hey, that's good, you can use it. Hit your Corona, kid. We're gonna paint him red, white, and blue. Of course, if Jerry doesn't cooperate, all bets are off."

Hayward started up the grand staircase to the mezzanine. Halfway up, he dramatically turned back to Mikey.

"Let me see the copy before you send it to Earl."

Ethel and Mary sat on opposite ends of the rehearsal room, each on her own high stool, waiting for Jerome Robbins to return. Jay Blackton sat on his bench in front of the Steinway upright, waiting as well. Jay, who had conducted on Broadway since *Oklahoma!* had arranged this grand finale. This medley of medleys that would top off over two hours of live TV. But so far, the ladies had only rehearsed separately with Jay. They had not yet put their distinctive voices together in song, and Jay was getting a little worried.

"Ethel," Mary said from her perch across the room, "what do you think about Jerry?"

As if on cue, Robbins entered the rehearsal room. He knew they would have been talking about him. He looked over at Ethel and knew that for all her bluster and resistance, she would do what he asked of her. He understood that she was putting on a little show for Mary. A power play – or a test.

First rehearsals were always like a test. Would the director or the star be in control, or would the director figure out the best way to let the star *think* she was in control? That was always tricky and now, with two stars of equal stature, it seemed trickier than ever to Jerry.

"I always stand stage right," Merman told Robbins.

Ah, the test begins, thought Jerry.

Robbins looked over at Mary Martin who was smiling her Cheshire Cat smile and cooed, "Whatever Ethel wants."

Later, Mary took Jerry aside and said, "I know how important it is to Ethel to be stage right and I'm fine about it… but don't think that I don't know that's the star side. I just don't have anything to prove."

Mary had enough confidence in her own star power and magnetic charm to not worry about what side of the stage she was on. She knew that, as opposed to movies where the editor does all the work for the audience, telling them where to look and how closely (and wasn't that one of the reasons Mary hated doing movies?), in the theatre, the audience chooses where to place its focus. The audience was its own editor and Mary knew that ever since that fateful night on the trunk at the Imperial Theatre, when she had turned those eyes just where she wanted them to be.

Jerry was impressed with Mary's composure, and it was Mary Martin, with whom he had never worked, he wanted to impress. He knew that Mary and her husband Richard were shopping around for a director for a project he coveted. Not only because of the story, but because it would give him a chance to be in full control of a new musical instead of just staging the musical numbers.

Control. Something Jerome Robbins needed desperately. Especially now.

He wondered how much the two ladies had discussed. Did their rehearsal books contain lists? Lists about Robbins?

Jerry wondered if Mary had heard the latest list of "Robbins Rumors:"

- That he was mean ("depends on who you are")
- That he tortured dancers ("they loved it")
- That he was jealous of anyone who was a star ("not so, since *I'm* a star")
- That he was a self-loathing Jew ("who isn't?")
- That he hated his father ("hmmm")
- That he loathed his mother ("not so")
- That he demanded complete control ("that one was true!")
- That he was a communist
- That he was homosexual
- That he refused to name names
- That he *might* name names.

Jerry was still shaken from his encounter with Leland and didn't know what to do about his testimony, but he *did* know what to do with his two stars.

"Well," began Jerry, "shall we get off the stools and gather around the piano? It's time for you both to sing together. Then, when I know how you sound and you have all the words and countermelodies, I will stage the number."

"You want us to sing?" Ethel asked.

"At the same time?" Mary countered.

Jerry nodded and Jay Blackton played the introduction. After a moment of hesitation, like Pavlov's dogs, both Ethel and Mary were at the piano and singing. As they sang together for the first time, they breathed a sigh and looked at each other in wonder. Maybe this could work out. They also wondered how the other one got here.

Ethel had been out in Hollywood just a few months earlier in her dressing room on the 20th Century Fox lot where she was shooting the final scenes of the film version of *Call Me Madam*. It was then that she got the call from Leland Hayward.

"Ethel, how's it going out there at Fox? Are you protecting my investment?" Hayward (who had produced *Madam* on the stage) asked over the phone.

"Leland! You sound worried. Listen, kid, the movie's gonna be a smash. I just shot "You're Just in Love" with Donald O'Connor and it's gonna stop the film the way it stopped the show. We're even doing the encore."

"Wonderful, Ethel. Wonderful." To Ethel's astute ear, Hayward sounded a bit nervous over long distance. "Listen," he continued, "I just got the most fabulous idea and had to run it by you. You know I was asked by the Ford Company to do a TV spectacular celebrating their fiftieth anniversary, right? I'm sure you read about it in *Variety*. Well, we're booking time on all four networks, including Dumont, so that everyone in the country will be watching." Hayward took a dramatic pause. "And I want you to be my top star on the show."

"That sounds swell!"

Hayward sounded relieved. "You'll get top billing and do several huge numbers throughout the evening. I've signed Oscar Hammerstein and Ed

Murrow to host, so it's going to be very classy. And Jerry Robbins is going to stage it all."

Ethel didn't hesitate for a second. This all fit into her newly minted plan. Ethel had a new man in her life, and she intended to retire gracefully from Broadway and become a Denver housewife with movie and TV gigs filling the time between PTA meetings.

"Well, I'm in. Talk to my agent and make the deal."

"Oh, I am happy to hear that, Ethel. And darling, Slim had this crazy idea for the big 11 o'clock number."

Slim was Hayward's wife, at least for the time being.

"What if... now, think this over carefully... what if we got Mary Martin to join you in a duet? She told me she was dying to sing with you, even if it was only for one minute. Wouldn't that be a lark? Of course, she would be a guest and you would be the star."

Although neither Ethel nor Mary quite knew why, their friendship had cooled a bit since Mary had triumphed in Ethel's role in *Annie Get Your Gun*, so she was a bit surprised to hear that Mary was "dying to sing with her." Still, Ethel took it at face value and, as she was called to the set to shoot a scene, ended the phone call on a high.

Mary's call came to her house in Connecticut. Richard Halliday answered and after some business talk about *South Pacific* (Richard was a co-producer), he passed the phone over to his wife.

It was as if Hayward had hired an expert scriptwriter and director, for he repeated the exact Merman conversation with Mary, changing it to "Ethel is dying to sing with you, but you will be the top billed star."

Leland Hayward had produced *South Pacific* for Mary and *Call Me Madam* for Ethel, so he knew how to handle each star. He had also poached Mike Minkus from Merman. Mike Minkus, who had, over the course of a few short years, convinced the press that the two beacons of Broadway were arch-rivals. Now Hayward had convinced them to perform together for the very first time... on live TV.

Saturday May 2, 1953

Mikey sat in the makeshift office that Hayward had pointed him to and, nursing his second cup of coffee, heavy on the milk, looked at the typewriter in front of him. He was glad that Mrs. Barbarash slapped his wrists with that ruler to make him learn how to type on a manual. His fingers were still nice and strong, and he could certainly pound those keys. This morning though, he had no urge to pound them. This morning, he could only think about Jerome Robbins and his dilemma. Against his will, he worried. He worried about the "what ifs."

What if Robbins did not cooperate? What if Ed Sullivan exposed him to the public as a homosexual? And what would that mean to him or his career? Mikey, a visitor from three decades hence where this "what if" did not come with so many consequences, had to wonder about this. Why was it so bad to be homosexual? What was Robbins afraid of? What if he just, as they would say in the future, "came out?"

Mikey had no answers, but he knew the whole thing made him very uncomfortable and scared, rather like when his mother would tell him about the Jews being persecuted by the Nazis and how half their family had been exterminated during the War. Mikey felt a kinship with those Jews and now felt the same kind of kinship to Jerry Robbins.

But this morning, Mikey had to turn back into Mike and type a red, white, and blue press release for Earl Wilson that would run in his Sunday column. This, too, made Mikey nervous.

That morning's rehearsal concentrated on a duet that Merman and Martin would not sing, but instead lip-synch. A vintage 78 rpm record would be played so that the two ladies, in male drag, could recreate an old vaudeville number originated by the Happiness Boys. Robbins still had not dug into the big finale medley. He felt blocked and was happy to have something else on which to focus his efforts. He was relieved when lunch rolled around, and the trio could shuck the rehearsal formalities for some gossip.

"Tricked?" asked Jerry, during lunch.

"Well, not exactly," said Mary, daintily eating one of Richard's cucumber sandwiches with the crusts cut off.

"Exactly!" replied Merman emphatically, as she chomped on her tuna-heavy-on-the-mayo ("and don't forget the kosher pickle") sandwich.

Ethel and Mary recounted their identical stories to Robbins, who laughed out loud for the first time in weeks.

"Does your contract stipulate top billing?" Ethel asked Mary.

"Of course, it does," Mary replied. "Do you think Richard would let that part slip?"

"The son of a …"

"Don't say it!"

"Mary! Don't tell me you're turning into Loretta Young with her 'Swear Box.'"

Mary bristled a bit and put on her most uppity, least Texan voice. "Whatever do you mean?"

"Don't tell me you didn't hear the story about when Tallulah went on Loretta's TV show?"

"Well, I might have."

Jerry chimed in quickly. "Well, I haven't! Spill it, Merman."

"Well," Ethel began with more relish than was in her tuna salad. "Loretta hates swearing…" And now she looked pointedly at Mary. "Like some people I know. But Loretta makes it a thing… a big thing. You see, she has this box – she calls it her 'Swear Box' – and if you say 'shit' or something like that, she makes you put in a dollar. Well, Tallulah is rehearsing and forgets her lines and says, 'Shit, darling.' So, Loretta says, 'That'll be a dollar.' Then Tallulah says shit again and Loretta collects another dollar. After a third slip, Tallulah shouts 'son-of-a-bitch,' but before Loretta can ask for the two bucks, Tallulah pulls out a twenty and says, 'Here's twenty bucks, Loretta. Go fuck yourself!'"

Jerry and Ethel looked over at Mary, who looked shocked for a moment and then burst into laughter, freeing the other two to do the same.

"Oh, Ethel! So, what do we do about Leland?"

"Why not kill him?" Jerry said.

Ethel jumped on the joke. "Or tell everyone he's a commie and get him blacklisted!"

There was an awkward silence as Jerry's spirit totally left the room. D-Day was only two days away.

That afternoon, Jerry left the rehearsal early, leaving the ladies to go over their medley with Jay Blackton. He could not face them. Or himself.

In the glare of late afternoon outside the Center Theatre on the corner of Sixth Avenue and 47th Street, Mikey saw Jerome Robbins trying to hail a taxi.

"Mr. Robbins! Mr. Robbins!" called Mikey.

But Robbins either didn't hear or ignored Mikey as he continued waving frantically and even whistling for that ever elusive Yellow Cab going uptown. Finally, Mikey ran up and tapped Robbins on the shoulder, making the nervous choreographer almost jump out of his skin.

"What the hell?" Robbins shouted.

"I'm sorry," Mikey apologized, quickly adding, "I thought we might share a cab."

Robbins seemed annoyed at first, but then stopped and took stock of this Mike Minkus. He had never really looked at him, this sort of cute guy of about twenty-five. Robbins smiled to think that the kid looked like someone who rarely got out in the sun, but stayed holed up behind a typewriter or a book. Not quite Jerry's type. Jerry favored other dancers or athletes, but this shy-looking Mike was not bad. Not bad at all.

Finally, a Checker Cab with extra room and two jump seats came by.

"So, hop in," Robbins ordered, as if Mikey were a dancer in his corps.

Safe inside the cab, Mikey sat on one of the jump seats, giving the whole rear bench to Robbins, who spread out, as if reclining on a divan.

"Where can I drop you?" Robbins asked after telling the cabbie an address on the Upper West Side. Mikey shrugged. He didn't really have any place to go. He had already messengered his press release over to Earl Wilson's office at the *Post* after having had it approved by Leland Hayward. He was free as a bird but had an urge to connect with Robbins.

"So," said Jerry, "you have nowhere to go… but up."

Mikey shyly smiled. "That's from *Knickerbocker Holiday*," Mikey nervously uttered.

"What is?" Robbins asked.

"That's the name of a song from the show."

"Oh… yeah, I remember. With Walter Huston, right? I think that played a couple of blocks away from my first show as a chorus boy."

"*Great Lady*?"

Robbins was duly impressed and sat up straight for the first time since entering the cab, which was now inching along through the traffic up Sixth Avenue, past Radio City, and toward Central Park.

"How did you know that?"

Mikey shrugged again. He was almost embarrassed by his encyclopedic knowledge when it came to musicals. Jerry reached over and petted Mikey's hand, as if he were a good puppy.

"Now," Jerry said while still holding Mikey's hand, "you must want to go somewhere."

"Where are you going? I mean, isn't it early to leave rehearsal?"

Jerry dropped Mikey's hand abruptly.

"I was not inspired," Robbins said coolly. "My mind is… elsewhere."

"Are you worried about your testimony?"

Robbins was aghast. "Wouldn't you be? I know what Leland and Ford want of me. But I have something called a conscience and becoming a stool pigeon does not appeal to me."

"But what about Ed Sullivan? Aren't you scared?"

Robbins looked at Mikey and Mikey looked back. Mikey thought that Jerry looked about ten years old. A balding little boy scared of his father's wrath.

"Terrified," he said as softly as he could, hoping it might not be true.

Mikey moved off the jump seat and sat next to Robbins as the wide Checker Cab rocked like a boat, rounding Central Park West and heading uptown toward Robbins's apartment.

"Richard," Mary began over dinner at seven. "I know I'm right about him. He's the man to make me fly."

Richard Halliday was flying himself, having started his cocktail hour at five, before his wife had even arrived home from rehearsal. But tight as he was, he still held strong opinions.

"Mother, I know you know best about your career, but… Mr. Robbins was, and might very well still be, a commie."

Mary sipped her iced tea and looked across the table at her husband with his glass of Scotch.

"Oh, pish-posh! He's going to testify in two days," Mary said in a modulated matter-of-fact voice, "and after that, he will be an American hero. You'll see, Richard. The press will all eat it up. And then he can direct me as Peter Pan."

"Mother decrees?"

"Mother decrees."

Both Richard and Mary smiled at their *bon mots,* and each went back to their own mental domain, Mary to her food and Richard to his Scotch.

As they ate the rest of their meal in silence, Mary thought back to that day ten years earlier when she had run away from home and Richard, and come to New York seeking Merman's advice. She thought back to Ethel telling her to go back to Richard and make it work. But make it work to *her* advantage. And she had. As her Broadway career blossomed though, her friendship with Ethel had withered on the vine. The publicity machine had turned them into rivals, and although Mary had at first taken it in her stride, it seemed to have caused a real rift that was hard to mend.

Mary was happy to defer to Ethel about where she wanted to stand, but then why did Ethel never look at her when they sang together? Mary was worried enough about her profile and how the TV cameras would accentuate the negative, meaning her nose, which on stage just added to the bigger than life quality she projected. On camera however, without Paramount's brilliant cinematographers and makeup artists, Mary was afraid her nose might make her come off as Durante's mother.

But despite those misgivings about her profile, she still turned to look lovingly at Ethel whenever they sang together and especially when Merman was singing alone. But Merman, it seemed, just intended to play straight out to the camera and never make eye contact at all.

Despite her reputation on stage, on this Saturday night Ethel Merman was making eye contact as she looked deeply into Bob's eyes. Not the Robert to whom she had been married for a decade, but a new one. He was Bob number two, but Six was his name. Tonight, with the kids asleep downstairs in Ethel's parents' apartment, she contacted his pupils in an attempt to look into his soul. Her eyes practically devoured Six's tough, ugly mug as she crooned in her sweetest most dulcet tones, her voice almost cracking.

"It's the wrong Bob at the wrong time… though your face is lovely… it's the wrong… I don't have a rhyme…"

Bob smiled and Ethel laughed. "Well, it's clear why Cole Porter gets the big bucks for writing 'em and I only get to sing 'em."

"I like how you sing 'em," Bob drawled.

Six and Merman had been married for three months, but due to Six's peripatetic work schedule, they had not actually cohabitated. They had met two years prior in 1951 at the Onyx Club on Fifty-Second Street. Ethel enjoyed reminding Six by singing a song she introduced called "When Love Beckoned (in Fifty-Second Street)."

Ethel's "love marriage" to the other Bob, now known as Mr. Leavitt or the kids' dad, had been on the rocks. And the rocks were usually in Leavitt's glass. His mood swings and heavy drinking affected everything and finally Ethel had had it. So, when Mr. Six walked into the Onyx, dressed in his usual blue suit and broad smile, Ethel had no trouble letting him buy her a drink.

Six, who recognized Merman from seeing her onstage, boldly and egotistically introduced himself as the president and owner of Continental Airlines. Usually, Merman was not impressed with such ego, but something about Six attracted her. It took Ethel only one moment to figure it out. That rough and tumble mug bragging about his company reminded her of another long ago mug, the man who got away – Sherman Billingsley.

Tonight, in the same apartment she had shared with the other Bob, and as Six waited for the morning flight back to Denver where Continental had its hub, Ethel popped the question.

"When are we going to actually live together? In our own home?"

"When are you going to become the official spokeswoman for my airline?" Six unromantically responded.

If Ethel could only look into the future, she would have run for the hills. But possessing no talent of prescience, Ethel just pulled Bob Six in for a deep kiss.

Sunday, May 3, 1953

Of all days, Sunday in New York City meant different things to everyone. Monday was always the same, that day of the week when work began again. Friday or Saturday meant the finish of labors, but Sunday was special and unique.

If Leland Hayward had his druthers, Sunday would be taken off the calendar, and with it the required day off from rehearsal. Not to mention that Tuesday, that not quite good news day, was fast approaching. As Hayward and his wife Slim silently sipped their black coffee, Hayward pondered the future. He loved Jerry Robbins and was of two minds about all this blacklisting mumbo jumbo. He wished it would just go away, but since he was now in TV and dealing with the most conservative sponsor in America, he had to hope that Jerry would do "the right thing." Meanwhile it was a gorgeous June day, and he was going to take his mind off Robbins with a walk in Central Park with his wife.

On opposite sides of Manhattan, both Ethel Merman and Mary Martin lolled around alone, each in her own big, lonely bed.

Bob Six had woken at the crack of dawn to make the first flight back to Colorado but had promised his new wife that he would start house-hunting in Denver. Ethel promised to fly back with him after her big TV show was over and check out the lay of the land. And she promised to bring the kids.

Richard Halliday was still asleep in his own bedroom and would be for some time. Mary contemplated her day off. With nothing to do (oh, what a joy and curse *that* could be, thought Mary), she picked up the needle-point bag beside the bed and went to work stitching the rug she was working on. She was basing it on a pastoral painting that hung over the mantel and, stitch by stitch, like Mary's life, it was starting to turn into a genuine, synthetic work of art.

Michael Marvin Minkus noticed that Sunday in New York in 1953 was nothing like it was thirty years later. As he walked the avenues and streets, he was shocked that Grand Central Station was totally deserted and, in the morning, with Manhattan's denizens either in Church or sleeping in, and with the bars not open until noon, the streets themselves had a canyon-like emptiness that he had never experienced. He was sure that if he sang or shouted, the echo would come rolling back at him with a Rikfa-like intensity. It was as if a bomb went off and everyone was vaporized, like in a B-movie.

Sunday in New York. The warm emptiness of June rather suited Mikey, he thought, as he tried to sort out his feelings about what had happened the night before.

The world had changed, that's for sure. His world, at least. And yet, the cracked and uneven sidewalks were still beneath his feet and the cloudless sky was still hanging over Mikey's head. It had not fallen and suffocated him as he feared it might. In fact, his fears of being imprisoned or drafted or pinned down amounted to nothing this morning.

Was it just last night that he followed Jerome Robbins...*the* Jerome Robbins out of that Checker Taxi and into his Upper West Side building? Did the doorman smirk or knowingly smile or turn away in boredom? Mikey could not recall. He was just following Jerry, following his fate into an elevator where a smiling, smirking or bored (but magnificently uniformed) elevator boy said, "Good evening, Mr. R," and pulled the old-fashioned lever chugging them to the eighteenth floor. Eighteen, Jerry later told him, was the Hebrew symbol for life and that was the reason he took this apartment. Did Mikey blurt out he was Jewish too and pull out his bar mitzvah pictures? No, he was sure he didn't do that. He was mostly silent, mostly mature, mostly terrified.

Jerry knew. But how? Was Mikey's twenty-five-year-old face such an open book? No. Yes. In any case, Jerry knew that this was Mikey's first time. Mikey didn't have to say a word. It was there on his person, like a label that had not been torn off yet. Mikey was fresh from the factory.

Do not tear this label off under penalty of law. Mikey always wondered about that tag on all the pillows on the couch at his mother's house. If he tore a label off one of those filthy pillows would the police show up at the door? Mikey's tag needed to be torn off, this much he knew. And if the police showed up and arrested him, well, so be it. He was no longer afraid of going to jail. Not if it meant finally being touched, and that was what Jerry did. He touched Mikey's arm and a shiver of electricity went through him. This same arm that had been touched countless times before. But never with intent. Intent, as any actor will tell you, is everything.

Jerry was a dancer. Jerry was a choreographer. Jerry was used to teaching his steps and combinations by using his own body as a guide or example. Jerry, who could be a martinet with dancers, was as gentle as a meal of tea and toast with Mikey. Never at his best with verbal directives, Jerry used his own expressive body and silent mouth to teach Mikey, to show him new ways to see himself. To mirror. To be a variation on a theme. And Mikey responded. He was a quick learner.

After the yapping dogs were locked away in the den, and even before any clothes were off, Jerry, unhurried, made Mikey feel that the student and not the teacher, was doing the teaching. Jerry was surprised by Mikey's own youthful moves and thought of the line from *The King and I*, "by your pupils you'll be taught." Even the shedding of Mikey's shirt and pants seemed simple and clear and uncalculated. Something Mikey had never experienced before.

Much later, walking through the Saturday night streets of Times Square, Mikey would realize that it had all been a dance. Impromptu, yes, but a dance that stretched back through the ages and then again into the infinite and unforeseeable future. A dance that Mikey would repeat in the ensuing years, but a dance that would never again be totally original and new, no matter how Mikey longed for it to be. Figuring out that this night was unrepeatable would take many years.

Lying together afterwards, Jerry had spoken for the first time since the elevator ride. He spoke softly but was as emphatic as a Dutch uncle.

"This is not an easy life, this choice you just made," Robbins said.

Mikey knew, but did not say, that it was not a choice.

"Homosexuals can be very cruel and there's a hierarchy of beauty that can drive you mad or leave you left in the dust. It can be very lonely."

Mikey listened as Robbins gently warned Mike about how homosexual men judged each other by looks and bodies and penis sizes. How youth was a drawing card ("Lucky you… at least for now") that eventually faded and that, perhaps, this was not the life for everyone.

"I almost got married. I wanted to. I still might," Robbins averred. "I like women, too. Not as much as this, but… if I had gotten married, all of this might not be happening."

"All of this?" Mikey asked, thinking that Jerry was referring to the two of them.

"This Ed Sullivan red, homo-baiting crap."

Mikey looked sadly disappointed, and Jerry sensed it, pulling the boy in for a kiss.

"You need to think all this through, Mike. Decide on your path. On your life. Figure out what's important to you and what you can leave behind or shove into the closet."

Mikey had the feeling that Jerry was really talking to himself, but he listened closely. He was just glad that the label was torn off and he suddenly realized that it was almost 10:00 PM and that he was starving.

Jerry let the grateful dogs out of the den and whipped up some scrambled eggs on the tiny stove in the even tinier Manhattan kitchen, and the two ate silently, with six beseeching eyes watching them. After they were sated and Mikey was dressed, Jerry took Mikey's hand and steered him to the door. At first Mikey was disappointed. He thought he would get to sleep in the big bed in the other room and cuddle. But Jerry explained that his boyfriend Buzz was due home after his show.

"Buzz? Show?"

"Didn't I tell you? Buzz is… well, we live together. He just opened in the new Rodgers and Hammerstein show and the reviews were not good. He needs attending. In any case…"

Mikey thought, "No, you didn't tell me," but he said, "Oh, okay" and put his face up to be kissed again.

"This is not an easy life, this choice you just made." Jerry's words reverberated in his memory now as he stood on the other side of the door waiting for the elevator to the lobby.

Monday, May 4, 1953

"You'll have all day off tomorrow, so get a nice dinner and a good night's sleep so you'll be fresh for tomorrow's… activities."

Robbins just looked at Hayward across the makeshift table in the Men's Room of the Center Theatre as he made this pronouncement. Could this be Slim's husband? Could this be the man who lovingly called him Gypsy?

Mikey sat as far away from Jerry at the table as possible. He was present at Leland Hayward's behest. He had not seen Robbins since Jerry had kissed him goodnight and locked the door. Jerry did not look Mikey in the eyes.

"Tomorrow's activities, Leland?" Robbins replied with some irony in his voice. "You make it sound as if I am going on a weekend cruise to Havana and there will be shuffleboard and a swim meet. The activities will include a light lunch of Robbins on a spit over an open fire. Lightly roasted or completely obliterated."

"Now, Gypsy, it doesn't have to go that way and you know it," Hayward said as he got up from the table and put both of his hands on Robbins's shoulders. "A car will pick you up in the morning and take you to the Federal Courthouse downtown. It'll be over before you know it."

Hayward strode out of the room leaving Mikey and Jerry alone.

Mikey spoke first.

"I'm going with you."

"No, you're not. I don't need a keeper, if that's what Leland thinks he is doing here."

"Leland has not asked me to go. I want to go."

Jerry Robbins was taken aback and the angry fire in his eyes softened as he looked at Mikey.

"Why?" Jerry asked.

Mikey shrugged and responded, "Moral support?"

Before Jerry could say a word, the swinging door swung open and Ethel Merman, in a rehearsal outfit consisting of flat shoes, toreador pants, and a man's shirt tied around her midriff, with her glasses propped on top of her generously curled coiffure, stormed in.

"Are we ever going to stage the finale, Jerry?"

Jerry's eyes were ablaze.

"No!" he responded emphatically. "At least not today. And certainly not tomorrow. I've asked my new assistant, Mike here, to put you through your paces for the next two days. I want the medley totally off book and second nature. You will see me on the other side of the moon."

Jerry stormed through the same swinging door that had propelled the now speechless Merm into the Men's Room. Mikey didn't understand how he went from press agent to assistant director, but he did understand that, without a word, his offer of company was somehow rejected. As his father Morris used to say, "Silence speaks volumes," and as his mother Rifka liked to say, "Which part of no didn't you understand?"

One hour later, Jerome Robbins was lying flat on his stomach with only a towel covering his still muscular dancer's bottom. This was not his first massage or even his twentieth, but for some reason he was nervous. Perhaps it was the new young masseur (Bob? Bill? Frank?) who was about to lay hands on the man who had not yet decided whether or not to name names.

"Stop it, Robbins," thought Jerry, "If you have a career, you do what you have to do. You do what is right. The chips will fall no matter what."

His father Harry Rabinowitz's Russian-Yiddish-accented voice came into his head. "Sure! You kip telling you'self deht."

By this time the massage, which he was lucky enough to book with such short notice, had begun. Jerry was beginning to feel both tense and relaxed, but best of all he started to drift into that twilight world between sleep and vague awareness. This was Jerry's favorite part of a massage.

As the over-muscled masseur worked on his back, reaching all the way down to his buttocks, Jerry's mind became a sea with tiny ships afloat searching for a harbor. One little ship led him to think about Ethel and Mary and the damned medley.

When should they get up? How should Mary look at Ethel? How to get Ethel to actually look at *Mary* and not just at the audience. Should he shoot the number from above to make sure the now middle-aged ladies didn't show any double chins?

As Paul… Bob… (names, Jerry thought, were not his strong suit) the new masseur, in any case, dug in with his thick forearms and sharp elbow, the little ship floated into a stormy sea and Jerry suddenly heard the voice of his lawyer, the lawyer Hayward and Ford had hired.

"Tell them what they want to know, Jerry. Then the networks will clear you and that fucking Ed Sullivan will get off your back. What did you ever do to him anyway?"

Jerry knew what he did to Ed Sullivan. He offended his "family first" Republican little heart by liking boys. Ed let Jerry know through the grapevine and eventually through Hayward that if he didn't testify and name names, Ed would expose him in his nationally syndicated column as a pansy. All of this Jerry knew in his waking state but now he was drifting again and envisioned himself the next day wearing a suit in front of the House Un-American Activities Committee. Except instead of the Congressmen who would be asking him questions, there were Ethel and Mary, dressed in their male drag for the Happiness Boys number, sitting in judgment.

"Hi, Ethel!"

"Hiya, Mary!"

"Let's sing some old songs."

"I think that'd be fun."

Jerry smiled as the massage reached his right leg.

The Congressman resembling Merman spoke. "Are you now or have you ever been a chorus boy in *Stars in Your Eyes*?"

"I refuse to answer the question on the grounds that it might incriminate me… that show was not a hit."

As the masseur returned to Jerry's back, he heard a gavel.

"Every *Merman* show is a hit!"

The Congressman resembling Mary Martin in a mustache was speaking now. "Ethel has never been in a flop."

"What about *Sadie Thompson*?"

"I quit in rehearsals," snorted Merman in drag.

"Did you know," the mustachioed Mary countered, "that they offered that show to me? But I couldn't play a prostitute. That's Merman's game."

Jerry's drifting dream-like state was interrupted by the masseur (Cal! Yes, that was his name) gently shaking his shoulder and telling him to scootch down and roll over.

Jerry did as he was told and, as he turned his body over, exposed his erection. Cal put the towel over it, but the towel tented. Jerry looked embarrassed, but Cal just smiled as he proceeded to pour some more massage oil on Jerry's chest and stomach area. Relaxed once more, Jerry drifted as his upper front torso got the treatment it deserved. This time, Ethel and Mary reappeared on stools. Stools so high they were touching the roof of the courtroom where Jerry's hearing was taking place.

"Mary, let's sing some 'I' songs."

"Like... 'I Was a Communist But I Repent and I Promise to Name Names?'"

"That's right!"

From their tall stools, Ethel and Mary told Jerry to sing.

And sing he did... naming every name he could think of. He sang so loud and long that he didn't even notice Cal giving him a "happy ending."

Wednesday, May 6, 1953

"I am not singing this goddamned medley one more time," Ethel proclaimed as she got down off her stool on the bare stage of the Center Theatre.

Jay Blackton at the piano rolled his eyes, hoping that Mike or Mary or anyone would catch a glimpse of his despair.

"Neither am I," agreed Mary, daintily stepping off her stool and closing her rehearsal book.

"Mr. Robbins will be here soon and he wants you totally off book," Mikey said with as much authority as he could muster. "And I have to say every time you do it, it gets better and it's one of my favorite things in the world."

Ethel looked at him like she wanted to spit.

"Now we're being policed by a press agent who loves medleys. What next? If you love this medley so much, why don't you just do it?"

Both Ethel and Mary looked at Mikey and sat down on chairs near the lip of the stage with "show me" in their eyes.

"Today, let us be the audience," Mary said with a giggle.

Even Jay Blackton got into the act, handing Mikey the music, but Mikey refused the pages.

"I know it by heart," Mikey bragged, recalling the dozens of times he had listened to it on his beloved ten-inch record where Mary got first billing on one side of the sleeve and Ethel got first billing on the other.

Mockingly, Blackton crossed himself and pounded out the introduction to the medley that he had devised. Both ladies crossed their arms in anticipation of Mike chickening out. They were flabbergasted as Mikey jumped up on a stool and launched into the medley beginning with "let's sing some old songs." Continuing on past the old songs and the "I" songs, he simultaneously yodeled the strains of "Indian Love Call" while munching on the foxtrot of "Tea for Two," just like he did in his basement room in Brooklyn.

"Picture you upon my… when I'm calling you-oo-oo-oo… will you answer… two for tea alone!"

Just as Mikey got to the finale of the medley and was belting out the last eight bars of "There's No Business Like Show Business," his eye caught Robbins, mercifully free of his "inquisition suit," standing in the aisle of the cavernous Center Theatre.

Robbins applauded and leapt onto the stage, carrying a rolled-up copy of *The New York Times* with his picture on the front page. He tossed the paper in a trash can and announced, "And that is how we are going to do it. On stools."

"Stools?" challenged Merman.

"Yes, stools," Jerry calmly said. "Every choreographer of every TV spectacular and variety show over-stages musical numbers with dancers leaping through the air and sets flying in and out. But television is not the theatre where our eyes are the camera, and we can look at anything we like. Television is also not film, with its ever-shifting camera angles, zooming in and out of the action, enfolding you in the color and music. Television is black and white on a tiny screen in someone's living room. And that, ladies, is the key. We are entering someone's home. We are intimate friends with them and each other, communicating through song the joys of life. We are at a private party in everyone's living room. And we don't have to dazzle them with staging pyrotechnics. Not at all. You are the two greatest stars of musical comedy, with personalities that can warm the coldest hearts. But you are both, if you'll pardon me for saying it, very different types. So, I am going to put cameras on your faces and show you reacting to each other and having a wonderful time performing for each other. The audience just happens to get to watch, like flies on the wall. Ladies, we are going to make entertainment history."

Ethel and Mary sat rapt in the spell of Robbins's soft voice. Mary knew at that very moment that she had to have this genius staging her dream show. She knew that only he could make her fly as Peter Pan. Ethel, the former stenographer that she was and would always be, took notes in shorthand of everything he said.

"Now," Robbins said as he placed the two stools exactly where he wanted them to be, "Shall we begin?"

Center Theatre, Rockefeller Center, NYC
June 15, 1953

"Camera Two on Hammerstein, go in a little tighter, please. Camera one, two shot on Ethel and Mary… Now go in tight on Mary's face…"

Hayward sat close to Jerry as Jerry barked out his orders to Clark Jones, the camera director, marveling at how well it was all going. Henry Ford III looked worried. Were the car commercials going over? Was it a good idea to have puppets, even if they were Kukla and Ollie, selling driving machines they could never actually buy?

Mikey sat in the house, smack in the middle of the audience of the cavernous Center Theatre, a few seats away from a sober Richard Halliday, minus twelve-year-old Heller, who had seen the dress rehearsal and was home with her nanny. Mikey noted that Halliday was chewing on his fingernail. He had no control over this show and that made him nervous. Mikey knew that Richard loved controlling Mary's career.

Bob Six, Ethel's new husband of only three months, also sat in the special cordoned-off section, in the same row as Halliday and Mikey. His new stepchildren – Ethel's kids, Little Bit and Bobby – sat a few rows away from him, wondering how they would take to living out in Denver with him and their mom. Also in the house was writer Pete Martin, there to soak up atmosphere and take notes for the memoir he was ghost-writing for Merman. Pete Martin (no relation to Mary) had an idea that history was being made tonight.

In the final weeks leading up to the broadcast, as Jerry Robbins worked on every aspect of the gargantuan show, all the while avoiding him, Mikey kept busy learning on the job and becoming a credible press agent. He got to know everyone associated with the production from Edward R. Murrow to Kukla and Ollie (well, Burr Tillstrom, anyway). He almost fainted when Oscar Hammerstein told him to call him Ockie. Ockie? This was the man who wrote *Show Boat* and *Oklahoma!* and *South Pacific* and would someday write *The Sound of Music*, for heaven's sake! He just couldn't do it and Mr. Hammerstein remained Mr. Hammerstein. Mikey observed this gentle giant of a man when he was not looking. He noticed the pockmarked face and thought of his own pimply teen years and how he thought they would scar him forever as a loser and a geek. But if Mr. H. could command the highest respect of the theatre community and ultimately the world with that pockmarked face, well, it proved that anything was possible. And here was Mike Minkus, press agent for the biggest TV spectacular in the history of this admittedly young medium, television, succeeding beyond his wildest dreams.

After his "performance" of their duet medley, Mike became a kind of mascot to both Mary and Ethel, even as he conscientiously stoked the publicity fires about their friendly rivalry. Part of him worried that they would grow further apart and follow the public's perception of them, but the other part just did its job. Occasionally, Mike even got to eat his lunch with them when he needed one or the other for some publicity. And sometimes they would even gossip, right in front of him.

"What do you think about Jerry?" Ethel asked Mary over her usual tuna fish sandwich.

"I think he's a genius and I want him to direct all my shows from now on."

"But what do you think about what he did?"

"What do you mean, Ethel?"

"Cut the coy act, Mary. You know he was a commie."

"Oh that. Ethel, he repented. He went before the Committee and told them he was sorry and then he gave them what they wanted."

Mikey chimed in. "You mean he named names."

Mikey didn't know to this day how he felt about it and, of course, Jerry had not spoken to anyone about it.

"To Richard and me, he's an American hero," Mary proclaimed.

"Some people think otherwise. Lots of people think he's a stool pigeon and did it for his career. Me, I don't like to think about it at all."

"I understand, Ethel. You New Yorkers are so liberal."

"Hey! You live here too."

"Honey, I was born a Texan and I will die a Texan."

"And I'm a Republican."

Mary was gob smacked. "You, Ethel? But…"

"But what? My Mom and Pop have always been that way."

"I thought you were Jewish. You know, Zimmermann."

"You thought wrong. Listen, I have nothing against being Jewish – my kids are half-Jewish – but I'm German on my father's side and Scotch on my Mom's. We're Episcopalian."

"Well… I'll be a monkey's uncle! But Jerry Robbins is Jewish, right?"

"Of course. And a fag."

Mikey blushed and hoped the ladies didn't notice.

"Is he?" Mary asked without any emotion, as if she would be as happy as Mikey to change the subject.

"Mary, he's a dancer."

Mary sloughed it off with a toss of her hand. "Well, it just doesn't matter to me," she said and then turned to Mikey. "Does it matter to you, Mike?"

Was Mary establishing some kind of kinship or bond with Mikey? He was speechless, but as usual, Ethel was not.

"Matter? Are you kidding? Every other man in show biz is a fag. The other night I went out to dinner with ten chorus boys and my friend Benay. When we got to the restaurant I said, 'Okay, we're gonna sit boy-girl, boy-girl.'"

Not for the first time, Ethel had defused the possible bomb with her ribald humor, but nevertheless Mikey was relieved when the lunch/gossip hour was over. It upset him to hear Jerry referred to as "a fag." For obvious reasons it upset him a lot. Jerry had warned him that this could be a tough life. Mikey had to remind himself that it was still 1953 and that times and attitudes would change. Or not.

In 1983, Mikey bought a bootleg VHS of this very show he was now watching from the audience. A grainy, blurry, and ghostlike black-and-white remnant of a dead era in television. Now, here he was seeing it all in living color, live on a stage that would be demolished within five years. Robbins's choreographic genius was evident in every musical and dance number, and when Mr. Hammerstein and Mary Martin did a scene from *Our Town*, the eyes of the most hardened grip and cameraman were moist.

Then at precisely 10:40 PM Eastern Standard Time, Mikey left his seat and went backstage to stand in the wings and watch the climactic eleven o'clock medley. There across the vast stage were Ethel and Mary seated on their stools and waiting for their cues.

With the cameras elsewhere on the stage, and the bright lights not yet shining in their eyes, Ethel and Mary could still see each other. Not as colleagues, although they were that. Not as rivals, although Mike and the press certainly proclaimed them that… but as fragile friends. Two powerhouses who saw the soft centers of one another. This moment would only last until the lights hit and the camera cues were given. Then Ethel Agnes and Mary Virginia would magically turn into Merman and Martin.

Mikey simultaneously watched both the color reality on the stage and the black-and-white illusion on a TV monitor at which a movie camera was pointed. A camera that would preserve what was on the TV screen and produce a film known as a kinescope, the only visible souvenir that live TV could produce at this time. But it was magic, because one day a boy in Brooklyn would shove a VHS video tape into a bulky video machine and watch this show over and over. Magic. And it was about to happen for real now.

Just off to Mary and Ethel's right, famed newsman and the voice of America during World War Two, Edward R. Morrow, looked directly into the camera and, after seriously warning the world of impending doom, turned it around to introduce Ethel and Mary and their medley. That famous deep radio voice emerged.

"But in good times or bad… in war or in peace… this is a singing country. And those of us who can't sing like to be sung to."

"Camera one to Merman," Robbins instructed.

Camera one caught Merman in a dress that made her look like a tank, Mikey thought, in front of a three-sheet poster of *Call Me Madam* (leave it to Hayward to plug his own shows) as she sang a rousing chorus of "There's No Business Like Show Business." Camera two showed Mary for just a second, watching and listening rapturously. When Ethel finished the chorus of her song, the orchestra waited for no applause (although there was some) and the camera swung around to find Mary Martin in front of the three-sheet poster of *South Pacific* singing about being in love with "A Wonderful Guy." And then they sat down on their stools.

Stools thought Mikey. Stools and stoolies thought Jerry Robbins in the booth. Ethel spoke first.

"Hiya, Mary."

"Hi, Ethel."

"Let's sing some old songs."

"I think that would be fun."

Mikey watched as the medley killed. He looked from the stage to the screen and back again and almost swooned with joy. It was then that a third camera began to dolly closer and closer to Mikey's face for a shot of his rhapsodic reaction. As the huge TV camera moved in on him like a predator, Mikey noticed that the man behind the predatory lens looked like a cross-dressing Mary2 wearing a man's shirt and pants with her hair slicked back, tight to her head. As the camera came almost to his face, Mikey backed up and tripped over a cable and fell and fell, as if into an endless void.

"Minkus! Minkus! Are you okay?"

The voice seemed distant and echoey as Mikey stood up.

"I'm f-f-fine," he stuttered.

"Well then, get off the stage and back to wherever you're supposed to be, please," the disembodied voice said. "Half hour, everyone…"

Another announcement came over the loudspeaker from beyond where Mikey was.

"Ladies and Gentlemen, as you finish your desserts, please remember that in thirty minutes, Live from the Astor Hotel, you will be the stars of the *1960 Tony Awards*."

Chapter Seven

Bucking a Nun

Astor Hotel, New York City
Sunday, April 24, 1960

Mikey dusted off his tuxedo and regained his equilibrium, picking up the spiral-bound script he had dropped when he tripped over the thick camera cable. The cover of the script read "1960 Tony Awards Presentation. Written by Michael Minkus."

As he flipped through the pages, Mikey saw speeches meant to be given by the likes of Eddie Albert, Celeste Holm, Helen Hayes, and Ray Bolger. Speeches he must have written. Mikey didn't remember becoming a writer, but then he had no idea how he had become a press agent either. Mikey was most impressed that he had written for Bolger, who had delighted him in *By Jupiter* way back in 1942, which in Mikey's crazy, time-warped mind seemed like a few weeks ago. His revery was interrupted by a young woman tapping him on the shoulder.

"Would you like me to show you to the booth in the back, Mr. Minkus?"

Mikey turned to see a pretty woman with long, blondish-reddish hair, not much younger than he was. Despite her age, she treated Mikey with a deferential respect to which he was totally unaccustomed.

"Thank you… uh… I'm sorry, I think I've forgotten your name," Mikey apologized.

"That's all right. It's Jane," the girl said with a wonderfully husky alto voice. "We met through Leland."

"Oh?"

"My father used to be married to his wife and… well, we met one night after my show."

"Are you an actress?" Mikey asked.

"Well, the Tony people think I am. They nominated me," replied Jane, with a laugh.

"Wow! Congratulations," Mikey said, still trying to figure out who this was.

"They put me up for Supporting Actress. I wanted to say, 'I'm not supporting. Do you think I'm a bra?' I won't win anyway. My show is closed."

Put two and two together quickly, thought Mikey. Her father was married to Leland Hayward's wife? And Hayward introduced them? So, is Hayward her producer? And is he the reason he got the job of writing the *Tony Awards*? The last he knew, he was Hayward's press agent. But that was seven years ago. What had he been doing for those seven years?

Mikey's mind drifted away from the guessing game of the actress before him. Wait a minute, he thought, if this is 1960, Mary Martin was starring in *The Sound of Music*. And Ethel? Mikey gasped without making a sound. Ethel was starring in *Gypsy*. Mikey almost geeked out in front of Jane. This was one of the best years for musicals ever!

Jane graciously led Mikey out through the door at the side of the stage into the huge and beautifully appointed Astor Ballroom. There before him were table upon table of stars, producers, writers, directors…

"Look at them," Jane proclaimed with a wave of her arm, "the freak show. Half of them are related to me."

As they squeezed by the front tables, Mikey saw Jackie Gleason, the "Great One" himself, scarfing down his second dessert. Mikey always loved Gleason on the reruns of *The Honeymooners*. Now here he was at the *Take Me Along* table. And there, at another table, was Dolores Gray sitting far away from her *Destry Rides Again* co-star Andy Griffith. Mikey always loved that record and had read that Gray and Griffith had a grand feud. Not a made-up feud like Ethel and Mary, but a real "knock-down-dragout-kick-'em-in-the-pants" kind of feud.

Mikey passed *The Sound of Music* table and wondered where Mary and Richard were. He took note of Howard Lindsey and Russell Crouse, the book writers, but also noticed that Rodgers and Hammerstein were absent. Sitting alone was an unassumingly shy-looking woman of middle years with a neat coif but lacking much glamour. He wondered who she was as he watched her sipping her coffee.

"I'm going to leave you here, but I think the booth is just at the back of the ballroom. Are you feeling good enough to find your way? I need to go talk to Josh Logan and… my father."

Mikey looked over where Jane was looking and saw the very familiar face with Josh Logan. His mouth fell open when he realized it was Henry

Fonda. That made this Jane, who was walking toward them and away from him, Jane Fonda! Of course.

Jane had dropped Mikey off right near the *Gypsy* table, which was totally deserted. Mikey nonchalantly went around the table looking over the place cards in front of the empty seats: Ethel Merman, Jack Klugman, Sandra Church, Jule Styne, Stephen Sondheim, Jerome Robbins, David Merrick…

Where was everyone? Mikey wondered.

Fifteen blocks uptown, Ethel Merman was at home in her furnished apartment at the Park Lane Hotel. She sat on her couch in a paisley house dress with her hair in curlers… alone in front of the TV. As the sun began to set, Ethel's large, overstuffed apartment felt empty. Her daughter, Ethel Jr. or "Little Bit," as her parents dubbed her when she was born, was 18 years old now and had just gotten married a couple of months earlier. Ethel was very uneasy about her little girl, still such a child, being a wife. But Ethel Jr. was as headstrong as Ethel Sr. and usually got what she wanted. The fact that her father was gone and Ethel was a single parent (by this point, the marriage to stepfather Bob Six was all but defunct as well), made it harder on Merman. Ethel's son Bobby was only 15 years old, and he had gone back a day early to the Hackley School in Tarrytown, New York, where he boarded five-days-a-week. Ethel was lonely and thought, "Maybe I should have gone."

No! No! No! Ethel practically screamed at her subconscious for even suggesting the thought. And yet… a deliciously evil smile came over that Merman face.

What if I just put on my best gown, Ethel thought. Mary's not the only one who has a Mainbocher original. What if I just marched into that ballroom just when the Best Actress in a Musical category was being announced. What if I did that?

At that very moment of speculation and folly, Ethel's phone rang. It was her doorman. She picked up the phone and whispered in a voice that could reach the lobby without a phone, "Yes. Send her up."

As Mikey neared the control booth in the back of the ballroom, he heard a familiar voice.

"Michael, as I live and breathe. I don't think I have ever seen you in a tux."

Mary Martin, resembling nothing so much as a Mainbocher Glinda, the good witch of Oz, practically floated over to Mikey. She was resplendent in her green-blue-colored Mainbocher ball gown, trimmed in scarlet satin, complete with hoopskirt and red bow in the front and long red bow in the back. She was certainly the best-dressed woman at the Astor. Mary greeted Mikey with a hug, but the hoops in her skirt rebelled and pushed him halfway across the room. Laughter bubbled up in both of them.

"That's why I never did *The King and I*."

"That dress is amazing," Mikey said.

"Try going to the Ladies' Room in it. But Richard insisted that I take it out of mothballs for tonight. I told him that everyone who saw me on TV with Noël Coward has already seen this dress. You know what he said?"

"What?"

"They haven't seen it in color, Mommy." Mary noticed the empty table for *Gypsy*. "Where is everyone?"

"I have no idea."

"Well, our table is a little sparse, as well. Dick and Oscar aren't here and Leland and my Richard aren't here. I might have to eat their desserts."

Mikey decided to take the plunge.

"Have you seen Ethel?"

"She's not here," Mary replied, matter-of-factly. "I mean," she continued, softening her tone, "I was told she wasn't feeling well and was staying home tonight. Between you and me, I'm a little worried about her. Of course, we haven't seen each other lately and… the newspapers make us out to be bitter enemies, which is absurd."

Mikey blushed to think that it was his idea to pit star against star. He remembered thinking it would be like Hope and Crosby or Fred Allen and Jack Benny, a friendly, but fake feud. But those were men who were very much in on the joke. Now, he had a feeling that the whole "feud" might have gone a bit too far, what with Ethel and Mary both starring in big shows the same season and being nominated opposite each other for Best Actress in a Musical. Maybe it was not such a joke anymore.

"Maybe it was all a bad idea," Mikey whispered.

"What? Just then another announcement came over the sound system.

"Ladies and gentlemen, we are at fifteen minutes. Would everyone in the ballroom please make their way to their seats. *The 1960 Tony Awards* will be live in fifteen minutes. Thank you."

"It's gonna take me fifteen minutes to maneuver this dress back to my seat. By the way, Richard and I are so proud of you, Michael," Mary warmly said while pointing to his name on the script.

"Thank you."

"Thank Richard. It was his idea and he pushed for you to get this job. Remember, you're riding with me and Janet after the show."

Mikey watched as Mary swept her hoop-skirted radiance past all the other stars, producers, directors, and writers scrambling to get back to their seats, until she was back at *The Sound of Music* table. She carefully sat down next to the unassuming middle-aged lady. Mikey watched.

"Janet," Mary whispered to her friend who had won the first Academy Award ever. "I sure do wish Richard were here tonight."

Of course, thought Mikey, the woman with Mary was Janet Gaynor!

As Mikey made his way to the control booth, he saw all the tables in the Astor Ballroom filling up. The *Gypsy* table, though, was still sparsely attended. Composer Jule Styne and Sandra Church (who played the title character) sat cozily next to each other. Mikey had heard they were an item. Sondheim and Merman's seats were conspicuously vacant, and Mikey saw that David Merrick was hanging out at the *Destry Rides Again* table, having produced that nominated musical as well as *Gypsy*. Another of the MIA was Jerome Robbins. Mikey nervously wondered if Robbins was still in the Men's Room. Mikey also wondered if he and Jerry had ever met again since that time back in 1953. But Jerry's seat remained empty as Mikey reached the booth and said hello to the director and his crew. The director seemed to know and respect Mikey, pointing to the stool emblazoned with the word "WRITER." Mikey kind of liked it. He had always wanted to write, but never got past just typing. Tonight's telecast would be shown live only on the local New York CBS station, but Mikey's pulse rushed as the lights dimmed. He opened his own script and read along with the show.

"The American Theatre Wing 1960 Tony Awards. Now, Miss Vivian Della Chiesa and our National Anthem."

"Stand up, kid," the director ordered. "It's magic time."

As Ethel waited for her first guest, she thought that despite having the triumph of her career as Rose in *Gypsy*, her real life as Ethel in *Merman* was going to shit. Like Mary at the Astor, tonight Ethel was minus one husband. Ethel's third marital experiment, Bob Six, had flown the coop after Ethel found out that he was "banging some broad in Honolulu." Add to this that her second husband, the first Bob, Bob Levitt, had killed himself in early 1958. Although their marriage had been kaput since the beginning of the 1950s, he was the father of her children and his sad demise filled Ethel with regret and some guilt to this day. Ethel sometimes wondered why she ever married at all when it always ended badly. Three strikes and I'm out, she thought, never guessing there would be one more in her future, one that would make the other three seem like gems.

"Look at you, Ethel! You look like fucking Marjorie Rambeau as Joan Crawford's mother in *Torch Song*!"

Benay Venuta came storming into Ethel's apartment like a brassy whirlwind. She was a raspy-voiced blonde version of Merman who usually got Ethel's sloppy seconds in the theatre. She sailed right through the living room into the kitchen shouting over her shoulder.

"Have you got any soda? I brought my own Campari."

Benay wore a stylish Chanel suit. It was a knockoff but fit her like a glove.

"Where are you going, all decked out like that?"

"I was coming to see my best pal, but you'll have to do. It's nice of you to dress for me."

Ethel patted her hair-curlers as she fiddled with the rabbit ears on her television set. "Only the best for my buddy, Benay. Help me with this antenna."

"You know, Ethel, you should get the Hotel to hook you up to their antenna on the roof. These rabbit ears are hell. By the time you get the station tuned in without any snow, your show is over."

"I don't watch that much TV, Benay, and I don't need to be hooked to the roof. You know me, the bare essentials."

"You mean like having them take your stove out of the wall? What if I wanted a cup of coffee or tea?"

"You always drink Campari and soda."

"Yeah, but what if I changed my mind tonight?"

"I have a portable plug-in immerser, like we use on the road."

"Like *we* use? You never go on the road."

"Yeah, well, I'm negotiating now to take *Gypsy* out when we close."

"Sure, you get the First National Tour stops and I get the Bus and Truck."

"Well, that's what the critics all call you, Benay, 'the bus-and-truck Merman.'"

"Fuck off, Ethel!"

As if on cue, Ethel's house phone rang again.

"Send them up!"

Benay took out the plastic bottle from her purse that contained her Campari and poured enough into the glass of soda to make it pink. Then she poured some more and made it red. She took a sip and smacked her lips. "Who else did you invite?"

"Dorothy Fields and that girl from the show I like, Maria Karnilova."

"What does she play?"

"Tessie Tura, one of the strippers."

"Oh, I like her. She's very Russian."

"Yeah, a Russki from Brooklyn, but her friends call her Maroush. I've known her twenty years… since *Stars in Your Eyes* when she was a prima ballerina in the chorus. Jerry Robbins was in that chorus, too, if you can believe it."

There was a knock on the door and then the bell rang.

"Hold your horses! Benay, you're closer, would you get the door?"

Benay rolled her eyes and unlocked the double deadbolt. The door swung open revealing Dorothy and Maroush, both dressed as if they were going out to El Morocco.

"Mermsie," cried Dorothy when she saw Ethel in the housedress, "so nice of you to dress for us."

The ladies all hugged and kissed.

"Get yourself drinks," ordered Ethel from her place in front of the TV, "and sit down. It's gonna start soon. I have some chips and popcorn in the cupboard. Maybe a few nuts, if you're lucky."

"Ever the gracious hostess," whispered Benay to Dorothy.

While the other two ladies foraged for drinks and snacks in Merman's stoveless kitchen, Maroush sat down beside Merman on the couch. She felt a warm sisterly affection for Ethel.

"How are you doing, darling?"

"As well as can be expected, Maroush."

"Well, for whatever it's worth, you made me cry again last night."

"Maroush, you would cry at a turnip."

"No, no, no! Standing in the wings and watching you sing 'Rose's Turn' makes me weep every time. It's brilliant. You're like Lady Macbeth out there. So, I cry. And then I have to go and reapply my makeup for the curtain call. I'm sending you a bill."

"I have to be great to top you broads bumping and grinding and stopping the show. You crack me up every time."

"Oh, Ethel, we just belong to a mutual admiration society."

"Hey! Don't remind me of *Happy Hunting* and that Lamas creep."

Dorothy and Benay came into the room carrying trays of refreshments.

"So, Ethel," Benay said, jumping right back into where they had left off, "why would you, who only know from Broadway and Hollywood, want to take the show out on tour? Do you even know where the Midwest is?"

Dorothy interrupted. "You're going on tour? But the show's doing great here on Broadway."

"Eventually, Dorothy, every show closes."

"You played *Annie Get Your Gun* for three and a half years."

"And I hope this one runs as long. But when it finally closes, I'm going to do the National Tour."

"But why?" asked Benay.

"Because eventually the show will play Los Angeles."

"Yes?" queried Maroush.

"And then everyone in the movie industry will come."

"And?" asked Dorothy.

"Once Jack Warner and his minions see me, the film version will be mine."

"Isn't being a Broadway star enough for you?" asked Benay.

"In a word? No! I want this show to be preserved and the only way it will ever be right is if I play Rose on the screen. I heard a goddamned rumor about Judy Garland. We all know how *Annie Get Your Gun* turned out for her."

"She never did it," recalled Dorothy, who wrote the original show.

"Exactly."

Benay gave Ethel a withering look. "You do know that I was in that picture."

"I never saw it."

"I know."

This subject was a bone of contention between the two friends.

"Benay, you know I love you, but I could not sit and watch that Hutton cunt ruin my show. Not after the things she said about me. She told all of Hollywood that I had her songs cut from *Panama Hattie* and that's why Buddy DeSylva felt sorry for her and brought her out to Paramount with him. Of course, she failed to mention that she was banging him backstage at the 46th Street, while I was singing 'Let's Be Buddies.'"

Benay didn't want to pursue this conversation which always led to the same place: Betty Hutton, whom Benay enjoyed working with, was a cunt. "Fine. Next subject. What did you do on your day off?"

"Stewed."

Dorothy, a musical comedy writer in her prime, asked: "Like a prune?"

"Save your jokes for your next show, Dottie."

Benay jumped in, "Ethel, if you're going to be so upset, you should have gone to the award show."

"I was not about to go to Elizabeth Arden to do my hair and makeup and get all dressed up to go and be humiliated."

"You don't know that's what would happen."

"Believe me, Benay, I know. Sit your asses down, girls, the humiliation's about to start."

When "The Star Spangled Banner" ended, the glittering crowd quickly took their seats and Mikey followed along in his script as the voice-over announcer intoned, "From the Grand Ballroom of the Hotel Astor in New York City, WCBS-TV brings you the 1960 Tony Awards presented by the American Theatre Wing."

The announcer then introduced actor Lee Tracy to talk about the history and significance of the Antoinette Perry Awards. Tracy was currently playing the President of the United States in Gore Vidal's play *The Best Man*, a role that would earn him an Oscar nomination for the film version five years later.

After more than four minutes of Tracy's dull, rambling commentary, Mikey muttered apologetically, "Gee, it probably sounded a lot more interesting when I wrote it."

"You're forgiven," the assistant director chortled.

Mikey was not at all surprised at how natural and charming Eddie Albert was when he came on next to host the rest of the program. Mikey knew Albert from his years on the ridiculous but funny rural comedy show, *Green Acres*. But Mikey's script took another hit when Albert began to stumble over his words.

"The writer's nightmare," Mikey said out loud.

"You watch," the director said. "He'll blame the cue cards."

"Well, I've already loused up the cards…" Albert said with a smile.

"See!"

The rest of Albert's introductions started to blur together as Mikey looked through the dirty glass of the booth to the monitors with all the different shots lined up.

Mikey's attention perked up when Christopher Plummer came on to present the award for the "Best Actress - Dramatic, Featured or Supporting," and Mikey rooted for his new friend Jane in *There Was a Little Girl*. But the winner was Anne Revere for *Toys in the Attic*.

"Camera three, closeup on Madam Horseface."

"She's an ugly old broad, but a good actress."

A freak show, Jane called it. Well, she seemed pretty confident that she was not going to win.

As the dispersing of awards moved on, Mikey realized that the Tonys were not like the Tonys he had watched religiously since he was a little boy. Something was missing. Of course, he thought, there were no musical numbers. Just talk, talk, talk. On came Carol Lawrence fresh from being in the flop musical *Saratoga*, but she didn't sing. Then came Robert Morse from *Take Me Along*, but he didn't sing either. Nor did Vivien Leigh, who in a few years would be starring in her own musical, *Tovarich*. Lauren Bacall didn't sing either and, of course, neither would Mary Martin or Celeste Holm later in the evening. What a wasted opportunity. With theatrical efficiency and calculated spontaneity, each celebrity awarded another winner who did not seem all that surprised to win. Mikey asked the director if it was normal for actors to look this calm when winning a prize.

"Well, of course they look calm. The winners were all informed yesterday."

"Rigged!" Ethel yelled at the TV set. "Can't they see it? Not one person is even trying to look surprised! Benay, you're missing this."

"Hold your horses! I'm getting more soda."

Dorothy Fields spoke up. "These awards are crazy. Tom Bosley plays the title role in *Fiorello!* and they give him Best *Supporting* Actor."

Ethel agreed. "I know! Isn't he the star of his show?"

Benay returned with a fresh drink. "I don't know, Ethel. Does that mean that Sandra Church who plays Gypsy in *Gypsy* is the star of *your* show?"

This stopped Ethel in her tracks. Ethel hated Sandra Church with a passion. She hated her for one reason and one reason alone. Sandra was dating composer Jule Styne, Ethel's latest crush.

"Do not mention that cunt in my house!"

"Next time I come over, would you send me a list of the cunts I am not allowed to mention? This way, we can spend a nice quiet evening without saying a word."

Dorothy had a great idea. "I think we should publish the Ethel Merman List of Cunts. It could be a bestseller. It'll certainly be a fat book."

"Jackie Susann!"

"What about her?" asked Maroush.

"Head of the list. Do you know what that... that... what she did? She stood outside my building pining away for me last week, while I was at the theatre. Told the doorman that she was my long lost sister from Lithuania. Then when I came home after an exhausting two show day, she started to cry and tell me how much she loved me. Then she tried to kiss me! Jesus! Do I need that? I have to admit, that broad kinda scares me."

"Look, Ethel," called Dorothy, "haughty old Celeste Holm is on your TV. Talk about indecent exposure. She's giving out the Best Musical Award. My show *Redhead* won last year."

The ladies noted that Miss Holm on the TV screen was beautifully composed and without the slightest twinge of surprise she informed the audience in the Astor Ballroom and the TV viewers that it was a tie between *Fiorello!* and *The Sound of Music*.

Maroush seemed crushed. "That means we didn't even come in second."

Ethel shrugged and gave her an "I told you so" look.

Mikey was half expecting Jerry Robbins to show up and sit down next to him in the booth, where he last saw him during the Ford Show of 1953.

But Robbins, who was nominated for Best Director, but not for Best Choreography, was nowhere to be seen.

Mikey looked from monitor to monitor, studying the reactions at different tables, reactions that would not be going out on live TV. He saw Mary Martin whispering to Janet Gaynor when the Best Musical medallions were handed out to *Fiorello!* and *The Sound of Music*. George Abbott accepted for *Fiorello!* He had a terrible time getting around all the tables and up to the podium. It seemed to take forever, but he made up for it with a witty speech. On another monitor, Mikey could see Jule Styne, sitting with the *Gypsy* contingency, angrily toss his napkin on the table. Sandra Church put her hand on his leg. Monitor number four had a closeup of Janet Gaynor patting Mary's hand under the table.

"I hear she's a dyke," the sound man muttered.

Mikey, who still worshipped Mary, did not want to hear that kind of salacious gossip, true or not, and blocked it out by listening closely to the acceptance speeches which were, naturally, not in his script.

Up bounded the book writers Howard Lindsey and Russell Crouse. Crouse was wryly amusing ("I'll do the speaking, but Lindsey probably wrote the speech.") when he announced that neither Rodgers nor Hammerstein would be there to accept the award. He explained that Hayward was in Nevada, Rodgers was in Italy, Hammerstein was in Bucks County and Richard Halliday was in Brazil, but "I've never known four nicer fugitives."

Mikey thought this was strange. What was Halliday doing in Brazil when the musical he produced was winning the Tony and his wife Mary was sitting at a table in a Mainbocher waiting for her category?

At her table, Mary felt nervous. How silly, she thought. I know the outcome and yet I'm as nervous as if I didn't. She shifted in her seat as Helen Hayes presented the Best Actress in a Play award to Anne Bancroft and the Best Actor in a Musical Award to Jackie Gleason. Mary was grateful that phony old Helen Hayes would not be the one to be in the photos with her when she won her award. What was it Tallulah Bankhead used to say about Helen? Oh yes: "Helen was always in shit!" Mary giggled to herself. When she put the water glass down her hand touched Janet Gaynor's by accident and Janet, sensing that her friend was nervous, held Mary's cold, quivering right hand and patted it with her left.

Janet had been in Mary's shoes. At twenty-four-years-old Janet had won the 1929 Academy Award as Best Actress, the first and only time a performer won the Oscar for multiple roles in multiple pictures. She did not remember being wildly nervous back then, but certainly recalled her jitters nine years later, when she was nominated for *A Star is Born* and did not win. Janet didn't know that Mary already knew she was going to get the Tony that night, so she felt sympathy for her friend. How nerve-wracking it all could be. Janet was happy that she was on the periphery of show business now. She had retired from films at thirty-three and had only recently come back to the stage in a disaster which made her grateful that she had had a busy and fruitful life with her costume designer husband, Adrian, and her close friendship with Mary. In fact, it was Janet and Adrian who introduced Mary and Richard to Brasilia and the joys of getting away from civilization. Noël Coward's song was always on their lips. Janet hummed it under her breath now to sooth her friend's nerves. Mary smiled at Janet as she hummed along.

"World weary, world weary... "

Mary smiled at Janet as she hummed along.

"I long to get right back to nature and relax."

Mary sipped some water as host Eddie Albert introduced the next presenter, Ray Bolger. Bolger, who would always be remembered as the Scarecrow in *The Wizard of Oz*, leapt onto the platform and joked about Mr. Abbott's inability to find his way to the stage.

"I don't see the trouble Mr. Abbott had getting up here. If I intended to be the recipient of one of these awards, I certainly would know the way. And especially if I were a director." This got a laugh from the audience who knew that Mr. Abbott had adapted and directed that very same *Where's Charley?* in which Bolger had triumphed. The one-hour show was running long, and Mary's corset was starting to pinch her, but Mary could not wait to get out of that chair.

"Mermsie! Get out of the can."

On the TV screen, Ray Bolger read off the nominees for Best Actress in a Musical.

"Oh plop! Janet," Mary whispered, "tell me when the camera pans over here."

"... and the nominees are Carol Burnett, *Once Upon a Mattress*... Dolores Gray, *Destry Rides Again*... Eileen Herlie, *Take Me Along*... Mary Martin, *The Sound of Music*... Ethel Merman, *Gypsy*..."

Maroush began to mutter under her breath, "Maybe this will be a tie too."

"And the winner is..."

There was a flush from Ethel's bathroom as Bolger gleefully announced, with barely a pause or even a reference to the script on his podium...

"Miss Mary Martin."

"Shit!"

"Camera three on Mary Martin. Closeup."

"Camera three is on you now, Mary," Janet said as she let go of Mary's hand and joined in the applause.

As the camera hit her, Mary looked at her friend and smiled radiantly, but her face was far from surprised.

The band played "I'm Sittin' On Top of the World."

Benay, with another Campari and soda in her hand said, "That song is not from *The Sound of Music*."

"Wideshot on Martin, follow her up to the podium. Do not lose her."

As the band played, Mary held on to her hoopskirt and with dancer-like precision neatly sidestepped her way through the jungle of tables, past Helen Hayes, past Anne Bancroft, past Vivien Leigh.

Mary seemed to be doing some magical choreography that had been rehearsed many times. In fact, she had come over between the matinee and evening performance the day before and scoped it all out.

Dorothy admired the way she moved. "I think Jerry Robbins staged her entrance."

In the booth at the Astor, Mikey thought that this entrance must have been Robbins's handiwork.

Ethel, watching the TV, added, "I'm surprised she didn't fly!"

Mary floated on the stage without being hooked to a wire, hugged and kissed Ray Bolger, and made sure to show off her Mainbocher. "George, I did it with a hoop," she announced joyfully to Mr. Abbott. The audience loved it. Richard had been right to take it out of mothballs.

"Didn't she wear that dress when she did the TV show with Coward?" asked Dorothy Fields.

"Shh. She's gonna talk now!" hissed Ethel.

"Camera one, two shot on Martin at the podium. Keep it steady."

Mary gracefully accepted her award from Bolger, who gracefully withdrew from the camera's view to let Mary speak.

"Here comes the sugar and Southern Comfort," Benay said.

"I am very happy to have this award," Mary drawled. "In fact, I'm very happy, period."

"That's it," exclaimed Dorothy Fields as she rose from her chair, "I'm going home now."

Mary's speech played on the TV as Maria Karnilova said, "Wanna share a cab, Dorothy?"

Mary began quoting lyrics of "Climb Every Mountain" as Dorothy, Maroush and Ethel hugged and kissed goodnight. Ethel looked into Dorothy's eyes, which began to brim over with tears.

"One minute, girls."

Ethel took Dorothy's arm, led her into her bedroom and shut the door.

"Here I am thinking only of myself, and never once did I ask how you're doing? How are you, Dottie?"

"What can I say? I'm glad March is over. It's been two years, but March for me is still the cruelest month."

"I know."

"Of course, you know. You lost your husband just about the same time."

Ethel was confused for a moment, then she remembered Bob Levitt's suicide. "Bob? We were long divorced when he... when he died."

"He was still your husband. The father of your kids."

Ethel thought about it for a minute. She never liked to think about it. The idea that someone could take their own life was unfathomable to her.

"Yeah, you're right, Dorothy."

"Life is funny for two tough dames with soft centers. I miss Herbie too."

"Good ol' Herbie," said Ethel remembering that Herbert Fields, Dorothy's brother and collaborator on so many shows, including *Annie Get Your Gun*, had died just before her husband... in March. "I always liked him. He never found anyone did he?" referring obliquely to Herbie's homosexuality.

"He had me, Mermsie. We were best friends."

Ethel held out her arms to Dorothy. "Come here, honey."

Dorothy Fields, urbane and tough as Merman, let herself be held by her friend.

"Wide longshot of the room and roll credits." At exactly 9:06 PM it was over. Mikey closed his script and shook the hands of the director, his assistant, the sound man, and one grip who had just entered the booth.

"That was a good script, Mikey Marvin."

Mikey had to look twice at the grip to see the face of Mary2 behind the male clothes and demeanor.

"Mary?"

"Shhh. It's Morris now. Women don't get into the union. We've both come a long way from backstage at the Imperial. Now, don't miss your buggy ride in a limo, little boy. It should be interesting."

Mikey looked at the deserted grand ballroom. Empty champagne bottles forlornly stood on tables like so many bowling pins waiting to be knocked down. Making his way out to the lobby where theatrical luminaries searched their pockets and purses for their coat checks, Mikey scoured the crowd hoping to see Jane Fonda again. He wanted to tell her what a big fan he would become when she started making movies.

As he got closer to the coat room, he spotted Mary and her son Larry Hagman in a muted argument. Earlier that evening, when Lindsey and Crouse had accepted their Tonys for Best Musical, Mary Rodgers and Jimmy Hammerstein had come forward to accept for their respective parents, Richard Rodgers and Oscar Hammerstein II. When it came to Richard Halliday's award, Larry had been chosen to accept for "his father."

Mary knew that that had been a mistake when it was first suggested. Now, with the ceremony over and the cameras dark, Larry, who loathed Halliday, tossed the box holding the medallion to his mother and stormed out of the hotel.

As Mikey waited for his coat to be retrieved, he began to ponder if there was a life for him in between these time-jumps. Did those seven years exist with a Mikey, Mike or Michael in them? Was it some kind of hypnotic amnesia that kept him from really knowing how he got here? Or was time a blank for him during those gaps in time? He was on some kind of journey, he knew, but what did it all mean?

When Mary's 1956 Rolls Royce Silver Cloud was finally brought around, Mary, Michael and Janet settled into the back seat for the ride home, Mary clutching two Tonys, hers and Richard's.

Mary spoke to the chauffeur through the glass partition. "Boris, do you mind if we take a little detour?"

"Anywhere in particular, Mrs. Halliday?"

Mikey thought that voice sounded exactly like Mary2 with a cold.

"Just go up the west side to Central Park West, Boris. I'll let you know when to stop."

As Janet dozed, Mary looked at her friend who had been through so much in the past year, having suddenly lost her husband, Adrian. It was common knowledge in the biz that costume designer Adrian (whose birth name had been Adrian Adolph Greenburg) and Richard Halliday were "brothers under the skin," and that was one of the reasons the couples felt so close to each other. For Mary, it was unfathomable to lose the person with whom you spend your love, whether it be a husband, lover or a best friend. Mary, wondering what Richard was doing at this very moment, turned to Mikey.

"Richard would have been so proud, Michael. But I'm sure he watched it tonight on the television."

"From Brazil?"

"Well..."

"And what about Leland?" Mikey asked. "Is he really in Nevada?"

"Reno."

"Reno?"

"He's divorcing Slim and marrying that horrible Pamela Churchill."

"What?"

"You didn't know? The former daughter-in-law of Sir Winston put her teeth into Leland while Slim was off somewhere looking the other way."

"Wow!"

Mikey noticed they were driving up the west side.

"Where are we going?"

Mary ignored Mikey's question and got to what was on her mind. Ethel.

"Sometimes I regret falling in line with this Mary and Ethel feud business."

"Sometimes I regret coming up with the idea," Mikey said as the car inched its way uptown to Central Park South.

"I don't think Ethel feels loved," Mary whispered, so as not to wake Janet.

"Loved?"

"By Broadway. Oh, I know on the surface she seems tough and difficult. I heard one chorus boy call her a monster. Noël Coward likes to call her '*un monstre sacre*,' if you'll pardon my French."

Mikey thought about it for a minute. He knew enough high school French to translate that into "sacred monster."

"Well," Mikey averred, "Ethel has to look out for herself. She has to fight her own battles."

"Meaning that I don't… but no, you're right. I have Richard to fight the dragons. And it was Ethel who told me to go back to him and make him my keeper. I crocheted my own velvet handcuffs."

"She gave you great advice. Now everyone loves you."

"Oh, Michael, I am not that naive. Everyone knows that Richard fires the gun, but that I load the bullets. But yes, I am loved, in the abstract. And I can't say I don't like it. But I can't help feeling that Ethel didn't show up tonight because…"

"Because she knew she wouldn't win?"

"Please stop the car on the next block, Boris."

"Is Boris a man or woman?"

"Michael Marvin Minkus! What kind of question is that? But speaking of questions… how have you never aged since 1939? For some bizarre reason I'm twenty years older but you look exactly the same."

From the front seat of the Silver Cloud came a loud guffaw and then the car abruptly stopped, waking Janet Gaynor.

"Are we home?"

"Not yet, sweetie. Mikey and I have something to do. We'll be right back. Just close your eyes, honeychile."

Ethel looked at the house phone as it rang. It was nearing 10:00 PM and she had no intention of answering the nervously jangling device. When the ringing stopped, Ethel pressed the privacy button that told the doorman she did not want to be disturbed. Ethel was sure that it could only be one person at this hour, and she had no intention of giving Jackie Susann an ounce of encouragement.

"I'm sorry, Miss Martin, she has her 'Do Not Disturb' button lit. Was she expecting you?"

"No, I don't think she was."

"Can I give her a message?"

Mikey stood silently as Mary thought long and hard about that question. She really didn't know why she felt compelled to come here tonight. For a few crazy moments, she thought she would make a grand gesture and give Ethel her Tony Award, but now that just seemed ridiculous. Ethel was not the type to take charity or accept a meaningless gesture.

"Tell her that her friend Mary dropped by. That's all."

Ethel Merman smiled as she climbed into her big, empty four-poster, remembering the good feeling of a couple of hours earlier, when Dorothy Fields and Maria Karnilova left her and Benay alone.

"Well, old pal," Benay said as she put on her jacket and put her empty Campari container in a shopping bag, "we waited one hour and seven minutes and you're not humiliated, right?"

"That's 'cause I have friends. Thanks for being here, Venuta."

"Any time, Merman."

The two old buddies embraced.

"So, what are you doing tomorrow, Ethel?"

"Going back to being the biggest fucking star on Broadway."

"That's my little stenographer from Astoria. You took it well."

"Well, Benay, I learned one thing tonight. You can't buck a nun."

The Silver Cloud sped north through Central Park as Mary looked out the window at the darkness of the park. Janet Gaynor was dozing. Mary knew her friend was still depressed over losing Adrian. Friendship.

"Remember that first night, Michael? The night you introduced me to Ethel, and we rode in Cole Porter's sleek limousine to the Rainbow Room?"

"I remember."

"It seems like a million years ago."

Mary told Boris that there would be one more stop before he could drop Michael and take her and Janet home to 233 East 49th Street in Turtle Bay. The car smoothly glided out of the park and stopped at 525 East 68th Street.

Janet woke up again.

"Are we ever getting home?"

"Soon, darling," replied Mary. "Come on, Michael. We have someone else to see."

Mary and Mikey got out of the car and entered the twelve-story graystone building that faced the East River. They were stopped at the reception desk by a night nurse who looked to Mikey like Nurse Ratchet from the not yet filmed *One Flew Over the Cuckoo's Nest*. "Ratchet" did not recognize Mary but gave her a look that let her know that she thought it odd to find a glamorous woman in a ballgown before her.

"I know it's late, but I wanted to leave something for a patient. My husband, Richard Halliday. And I know it's against the rules, but we need to see him."

Mikey was confused as to where they were, and "Ratchet" looked disinterested, but she flipped through some pages in a book and found the name.

"And you are Mrs. Halliday?" she said in her less than welcoming tone.

Mary smiled and nodded, thinking how useless her fame really was.

"And who is this?"

Mary answered for Mikey.

With a grunt and a groan and a look that could kill, "Ratchet" went back to consult a superior in the next room.

"Now *there's* a charm school graduate for you," Mary whispered as she sat down on a bench, her dress taking up the whole space. Mikey took the opportunity to look around at what seemed like the lobby of an upper-middle-class residence. There was a beautiful and ornately carved mantle over the fireplace and above that a plaque that read:

THE WISDOM AND GENEROSITY OF
PAYNE WITNEY
ESTABLISH THIS HOUSE FOR THE HEALING OF
THE SICK AND TROUBLED
1932

"The Sick and the Troubled," Mary mused as she too read the sign. "Well, that's a charming way of putting it."

"Mr. Halliday is here? Not in Brazil?"

Before Mary could answer, "Ratchet" returned.

"My supervisor was not pleased, but she said that since it was still before ten, it might be alright. But only one of you can see Mr. Halliday."

Mary got up off the bench.

"I took the liberty of telling Mr. Halliday you were both here and he said to only send up the boy."

"The boy?" Mary quickly asked.

"What boy?" Mikey also asked, for the first time thinking of himself as a man, not a boy.

"Mr. Minkus can come with me. You can wait."

Mary was taken aback for a moment and felt the kind of hurt that only Richard's rejection could impart. She quickly composed herself and handed Mikey the Tony Award in its velvet box.

"Tell Richard I'll come see him tomorrow during the regular visiting hours. And give him my love."

Before Mikey could follow, "Ratchet" held out her hand for the box containing the Tony Award medallion.

"I have to make sure that there is no contraband in the box."

"Contraband?" asked Mikey.

"Pills. Amphetamines."

"It's a Tony Award," Mary said, with a roll of her eyes.

"Rules are rules and Mr. Halliday has proven himself a consistently clever man."

"Ratchet" opened the box, took out the medallion, felt around the velvet case, shaking it a few times, and then returned the award to its soft nest, snapping the lid shut. She motioned to Mikey.

"This way."

Mikey looked back at a rather forlorn Mary, who managed to smile in any case, and followed "Ratchet" up the elevator. As the elevator ascended, he had a kind of *déjà vu* experience. Although he had no memory of ever being in this building, he knew deep in his bones that he had been on this elevator before. And the ride made him more than nervous. Mikey was scared.

The Seventh Floor of Payne Whitney had special significance. This was the maximum security floor. This was where the sickest and most troubled walked the floors and did the dance that the nurses called "the Thorazine shuffle," interminably dragging their bodies and souls back and forth in their paper slippers. Richard Halliday, Broadway producer and husband of a star, never thought this would be his home away from home.

When the doors opened, Mikey was sweating and had trouble breathing. He hesitated to exit the elevator. He had been here before.

When he looked back at "Ratchet" through blurry pupils, she had changed. She looked much more like Mary2. But wasn't Mary2 driving the limo? Wasn't she the driver Mary Martin called Boris? Whoever it was, she gave him a little shove and pushed him out of the elevator and onto the floor, where he started to hyperventilate. She had seen this behavior before many times and methodically walked to the nurses' station and grabbed a paper bag from under the desk where they were stacked. She handed it to Mikey, who was now sitting on the floor holding on to Halliday's Tony for dear life.

"Breathe into this. Come on. Just do it," she commanded.

Mikey breathed into the brown paper bag with his eyes closed and he started to calm down. When he opened his eyes, Richard Halliday was standing over him in a ratty bathrobe and paper slippers. Mikey's pulse started to quicken again.

"Well, if it isn't the prodigal son."

Chapter Eight
The Quiet Room
Two Months Earlier, February 1960

As Michael Minkus entered the building at 525 East 68th Street, he brushed by a curvy woman in large, dark glasses with her dyed-blonde hair covered in a kerchief. She was being led out to a taxi by a tall man who looked as familiar as she did.

"Isn't that…?" Mikey asked the receptionist.

"It is," the receptionist murmured conspiratorially.

Mikey gave the receptionist his name, just as Joe DiMaggio protectively put his arm around a shaky Marilyn Monroe and exited the building with her.

Mikey had never been to Payne Whitney before, so when Leland Hayward and Richard Rodgers summoned him to the Rodgers and Hammerstein office at 488 Madison Avenue and entreated him to "visit" Richard Halliday, he was overcome with trepidation to say the least.

"What should I expect when I see him?" Mikey cautiously asked Richard Rodgers a few days prior.

"Expect to see Dick," Rodgers impatiently replied. "The same pain-in-the-ass Mary's been yoked to for almost twenty years. But expect to see him in paper slippers."

"Michael," Hayward said with the kind of warmth reserved for an old friend, "you are our only hope now. Richard won't see either of us. He likes you."

"He does?"

"Leland brought you into this because he thinks that Dick Halliday sees a kindred spirit in you. And now that I have met you myself, I agree."

Mikey was not sure he liked Mr. Rodgers' tone. What was he implying anyway?

"Michael," Hayward interjected, "you will be doing us and the show a very big favor by getting Richard to sign these papers."

Mikey remembered Hayward's tone. It was the same tone he used to cajole his pal Jerry Robbins into naming names.

"But what are they?" Mikey asked. "What do they say?"

Rodgers, despite having had mouth cancer a few years back and losing half his jaw, flashed his warmest this-is-only-for-photographers smile.

"Michael, Dick Halliday's been ill for a while now," Rodgers said with the kind of simplicity and sincerity that made his melodies soar.

"I know that he drinks, but…"

"Oh," interrupted Rodgers, "it has gone way beyond booze. Dick has a problem with amphetamines… drugs, pills."

"And that's on top of the booze," added Hayward. "We just need to have things in place… just in case. The show must go on, but there is a business to run as well. *The Sound of Music* is a corporation, and it needs to be cared for. You understand?"

"Nope. Not a word," Mikey responded.

"You don't have to," Rodgers said.

Mikey knew that *The Sound of Music* had opened in November to less than enthusiastic reviews. But the public loved the show, and it was selling out, due to the reputations of Rodgers and Hammerstein and especially because of the star power of Mary Martin. Although Rodgers and Hammerstein had their names above the title, looming large on the posters were the other two producers, Leland Hayward and Richard Halliday. In fact, it was the team of Hayward and Halliday that did all the heavy lifting on the producing front.

"Does Mary know that you want her husband to sign away his rights to the show?"

Rodgers reacted quickly.

"We are not asking him to sign away any rights. He is an equal partner, making his wife an equal partner, but we need to know that we have the power to make decisions should his condition become… more debilitating."

Hayward put his arm around Mikey.

"We would never do anything to hurt Mary," Hayward reasoned. "Mary has one job and that is to go out on that stage eight times a week and captivate the audience as Maria von Trapp. Richard has always taken care of the rest. But now, Richard's only concern should be to get well. That's why we want to take the burden off of his shoulders and not worry Mary with petty details."

Yes, thought Mikey, this was the same Hayward who knew how to negotiate huge contracts with the Hollywood studios for stars like Katharine Hepburn, and the same Hayward who turned Robbins into a stool pigeon, one who would never really be forgiven by the Broadway community. Hayward's honeyed tongue was as forked as they came, Mikey reasoned. And now it was Richard Halliday who was to be… "forked."

"What we are really afraid of, Mike," Rodgers said with more familiarity than before, "is that we might have to close the show if something happens to Dick and that would be a catastrophe for all those actors and kids, not to mention our Mary."

Rodgers seemed to know how much Mikey loved Mary Martin and he used the threat of her unhappiness as leverage. On top of that, Mikey, who had witnessed Hayward's duplicitous friendship with Jerry Robbins, had quit in a huff back in 1953, burning his bridges, so he thought. And now, Hayward needed him. Hayward had three Broadway shows running at the same time and Mikey needed a job. Maybe this was a way back into the good graces of one of the biggest producers on Broadway.

And of course, if it was for the good of the show, it was good for Mary Martin. Wasn't it?

It was a snowy February afternoon when Michael Minkus got off the elevator on the Third Floor of Payne Whitney and entered through the large mahogany doors that separated the elevator bank from the ward. Upon entering, he was relieved to see that the third floor was furnished less like a hospital than a run-down seaside resort. The couches and chairs were worn but neat and clean and, despite the cloud of cigarette smoke in the air, or maybe because of it, the floor smelled less disinfected than other hospitals Mikey had visited. He took off his coat and hat and loosened his muffler as he awaited Richard Halliday in the anteroom. In his hand was a large bouquet of flowers with a card attached and, in his inside coat pocket, a manila envelope holding a set of papers for Halliday to sign.

Before he could inquire as to Mr. Halliday's whereabouts, a fit-looking Halliday walked in wearing well-pressed pin-striped pajamas covered by a silk, Noël Coward-like dressing gown. On his feet, as Richard Rodgers predicted, were paper slippers. Mikey must have stared at the slippers a bit too long.

"They are made of the best Parisienne papier, I assure you," Halliday said as he put his arms out to Mikey. "Come on, drinking is not contagious. Or is it?"

Mikey let Halliday embrace him. Maybe he does like me, thought Mikey. And maybe we have been in touch since 1953.

Mikey handed Halliday the huge bouquet. "These are for you. Mr. Rodgers sent them."

Halliday opened the note and made a "this pudding is disgusting" face.

"Rodgers, the prick!" Halliday said as he read the attached card. "'I hope you get out soon,' he writes. It's the exact greeting I sent him when *he* was in here a few years ago. He means it as much as I did. Is he the one who told you I would be wearing paper slippers? He should know," Halliday laughed. "He wore them longer than I did."

"Richard Rodgers was at Payne Whitney?"

"Oh yes. He'll tell you it was for depression, but he was only depressed when he ran out of vodka."

"I guess you don't like Mr. Rodgers."

"Richard Rodgers is the greatest genius of the musical theatre," responded Halliday with great sincerity. "There is no one better than Rodgers as melodist, dramatist and theatrical mind. And he's a prick. Now what other goodies did you bring me?"

Mikey held out the manila envelope.

"Mr. Hayward and Mr. Rodgers want you to look these over and sign them," Mikey sheepishly said, as if he had rehearsed the line all day, which he had.

"And Oscar? He demurred?"

"Mr. Hammerstein wasn't there."

"No. Poor dear Oscar is ill. More ill than anyone knows. In fact, he's dying. It was a very big deal to get him to write one more song for the show when we were out of town. But write it he did. 'Edelweiss.'"

"I love that song," Mikey quietly said, knowing it best from the movie that had yet to be made.

"His last song, I suspect. Did they get you to bring these papers by saying the show would close if something happened to me? Did they play the Mary Martin card?"

"Well…"

"If Mother knew what those scoundrels were up to…"

"Mother?"

"Yes. Mary. Miss Martin. The Texas Tornado in a habit. In any case, I am glad you are here. Today they are allowing me to leave the premises. But only with a chaperone. And voila! Like magic, you appeared. *Mon ami du jour.*"

"You get to go out?"

"Yes! Look, Ma, no straitjacket! We of the Third Floor go out all the time. We walk the manicured but deeply walled gardens. Back and forth. Forth and back. The smokers smoke and the others hold their breath. But today is different. After weeks of being here and shifting from the dreaded Seventh Floor to the Fourth to the luxury of *Chez Trois*, I am to be permitted to go out to lunch as long as I have a signatory. That would be you," Halliday pointed at Mikey, "as long as we stay within a ten-block radius and a two-hour time limit."

"But…"

"There's a charming tea shop just two blocks from here and it will be my treat. Think of the scones and tea with clotted cream."

Halliday dangled the culinary goodies before Mikey as Henry Higgins dangled sacks full of chocolate before Eliza Doolittle.

"Of course, I have no money," Halliday added, "so you will have to pay."

"Well, then how is it your treat?"

"You're a sharp young lad. I have to get dressed."

With his paper slippers and high spirits intact, Halliday practically slid across the heavily-waxed floor toward his room. Mikey, not knowing where else to go, sat down and waited. The manila envelope in his hand felt like a time bomb about to go off. Mikey tried to make sense of where he was.

There seemed to be gaps in Mikey's time travel memories. He wondered if he actually lived during those in-between years or if he just jumped ahead—and now back—in time? Because of this, Mikey had no idea how long it had been since he last saw Richard Halliday. He knew that he had first met him that day in Mary Martin's Bel Air bedroom. Back then, Halliday was a drunk screaming at Mikey and railing at the world. Check.

Then he met him again in 1953 when Mikey (as Mike) was the press agent for the *Ford Show*. Halliday was not as in control of Mary during that time, so he didn't see much of him. The few times he did see him, Mikey remembered a man stripped of his power, a power he would soon regain the following year when he produced *Peter Pan* in Los Angeles and on Broadway, followed by two live television broadcasts. Check.

Now, he was the producer of one of the biggest hits on Broadway, *The Sound of Music*. Check, check, check… But what the devil was he doing in this loony bin?

"Let's get out of this loony bin," Halliday declared as if reading Mikey's mind. "I cannot wait to feel some fresh air on my pale white face. How cold is it out?"

Halliday was dressed in a very nice suit and tie and no paper slippers. He began putting on his overcoat.

"It's snowing," Mikey said. "And pretty cold at that."

"Good. I am sick of overheated rooms and under-heated patients. Come with me to the desk and we'll sign me out. Oh, and ditch those papers. I'm not signing that shit."

Richard Halliday's face was flush with excitement and the sudden gust of January wind that whipped around from the East River.

"Which way is the tea shop?" Mikey asked.

"Taxi!" shouted Halliday.

Mikey thought Halliday was joking until a Yellow Cab pulled up to the curb.

"Get in," ordered Halliday.

Mikey didn't know what to do, but being his mother's son he followed Halliday's command.

"233 East 49th," Halliday told the driver.

"Where are we going?" asked Mikey as the taxi and panic meters both began to click.

"Home. I am going home."

Mary Martin was not used to being at home alone and in charge. She was not used to being that free. Ever since marrying Richard Halliday back in Hollywood in 1941, Mary had been under his spell at first and under his thumb after that. But Mary was under no illusions that she was not part of the deal. In fact, she had initiated that deal after leaving Halliday for the second time. It had been her friend Ethel Merman who advised her on how to forge the deal. The deal that would both free and imprison Mary. The deal that let Mary and Richard leave Hollywood and create Mary Martin, Inc., a Broadway factory that produced only one product, Mary Martin.

And it was all a success. But successful contracts can take their toll on the parties of the first and second part. Mary learned how to be the product—a star—by being the party of the first part, and (according to their unwritten agreement) by leaving all the other tasks to the party of the second part, who learned how to perform his two tasks masterfully—control the star… and drink. And when drinking didn't quite do the trick, amphetamines were employed. It was the combo plan of pills and booze that brought Richard Halliday, then at the peak of his control and success on Broadway, to Payne Whitney. And this act brought Mary back to where she had been for those few days back in 1942 in New York—to a place called freedom.

On that cold January morning in 1960, Mary, on her one day off from being Maria Von Trapp, was going shopping. On her own. With her own money! This was not as simple as it seemed. Mary had been sheltered for so long, simply hailing a cab or remembering an address was now a monumental task. The Silver Cloud and driver were always there when she needed them. Until, that is, last week when a blizzard hit the tri-state area.

The snowfall was so heavy that the city was totally blanketed, and the Halliday car and driver failed to show up. On a show night!

Mary waited and waited in her lobby as the doorman called and called to no avail. Finally, Mary told the doorman to hail her a cab and, by some miracle, he flagged one down. As Mary settled into the backseat, the driver spoke.

"Where to?"

At that very moment, Mary, who had played the Imperial, the Winter Garden, the Majestic and Lord knows what other theatres, realized that she had no idea in which theatre she was currently starring.

"Take me… take me…" Mary stammered, "take me to *The Sound of Music*."

Lucky for her, the cab driver was a Broadway enthusiast. He dropped her, safe and sound, at the Lunt-Fontanne Theatre's stage door.

On that night, Mary looked up at the marquee with her name blazing in lights over the title and vowed never again to not know where she was going.

Now, on this cold morning, as the snow fell again, Mary hailed her own cab and took great pride in knowing exactly where she was headed.

"Take me to Tiffany's on Fifth and 57th and don't spare the horses."

The elevator stopped at the designated floor and the uniformed operator opened the doors onto a small vestibule with a single door painted a super-glossy red. Redder than Dolly's dress, redder than David Merrick's Broadway posters.

"Here you go, Mr. Halliday," the operator said. "Mrs. Halliday went out a few hours ago and isn't expected back until teatime."

"Thank you, Jimmy," Halliday said with a smile, as he stepped out of the elevator. "It seems that I forgot my keys this morning. Would you mind opening up for me?"

"Of course, sir." Jimmy pulled out his key ring and found the appropriate key. "Here you go, Mr. Halliday," as the door swung open.

"Thank you."

As Halliday and Mikey stepped into the apartment, the bright January sun cloaked the lemon-yellow couches with a warmth broken up only by the dozens of needle-pointed pillows on every seating area. The immaculately buffed black Steinway piano was similarly covered with ornately framed photos of Richard and Mother posing alongside every celebrity and politician of their era.

The curved marble staircase that went up to the bedrooms looked perfect for star entrances and Mikey could just see Mary, who would one day come floating down the red staircase of the Harmonia Gardens in a Mainbocher gown in the not-yet-written *Hello, Dolly!* to music that only he could hear. As Mikey imagined that scene, Halliday looked longingly at the very same staircase. He then then turned and closed the front door. "So Mother is out for the afternoon. Good."

"But all the way over here, you said we were going to see Mother — I mean Mary — and have a nice long chat."

"Did I? Well, the fellow said she wouldn't be back till teatime, so why don't you just wait in the kitchen for me," Halliday said as he pushed Mikey toward a set of swinging doors. "I need to get some things I forgot from my upstairs closet. Do not move and, for heaven's sake, don't touch anything. I will be down in a jiffy, and we can go back before they even have missed me. Here's some reading material you can skim."

After plopping down a pile of newspapers, Halliday bolted through the swinging kitchen door.

Mikey flipped through the newspaper on the top of the pile and thought about how much he didn't want to sit in the kitchen and wait. He was in Mary Martin's house, for heaven's sake! He wanted to explore. To go through her closets and touch her Mainbocher originals and Tony Awards. But instead, he obeyed Halliday and skimmed through a copy of the *Herald*

Tribune, happening on a dreadful, dog-eared review of *The Sound of Music* by Walter Kerr, describing it as "not only too sweet for words but almost too sweet for music." He added, "the cascade of sugar is not confined to the youngsters. Miss Martin, too, must fall to her knees and fold her hands in prayer, while the breezes blow the kiddies through the window." The now highly regarded critic clearly had no idea how important this show was and would be to millions of people. Sheesh, thought Mikey, wait till this guy sees the movie, then he'll be sorry.

"Hello?"

Mikey almost fell out of his chair.

"What are you doing here?" demanded an ice-cold Mary Martin.

She must have snuck in through some back entrance, unseemly as it was, perhaps in the service elevator. Despite her icy tone, Mikey was happy to see her. This is why he came along with Halliday in the first place. To see Mary.

"Well, Michael?"

"I'm waiting for Richard," Mikey managed to mutter.

"Richard? My Richard? What is he doing here?" Mary asked.

"I don't know. He told me we were coming to see you and…"

Mikey's last words fell on deaf ears as Mary stormed past the kitchen table and pushed through the double doors. He could hear her high heels clattering up the curved staircase.

Mikey held open the swinging doors a bit to hear what was going on. He heard the muffled voices of Richard and Mary arguing. He heard isolated words like "trouble," "pills," "disappointed," and then some foot-stomping from the floor above. Through his slightly cracked doorway, he saw Halliday quickly descending the staircase with Mary following at a more leisurely clip. This was not the Mary Martin "Dolly" entrance Mikey had fantasized about.

"Come on! Let's go," Halliday barked at Mikey, as he retrieved his hat, put on his coat and opened the big, polished-red front door.

Mikey sprinted out of the kitchen past Mary and mumbled a quick goodbye. He was still holding the *Herald Tribune* with the terrible *Sound of Music* review. Mary did not respond beyond folding her arms and waiting for the two men to exit. Mikey's last impression of Mary Martin that day was one of anger and bitter resolve. She seemed a tower of strength as she closed the red door on them.

The taxi ride back to Payne Whitney was fraught with tension. Halliday's demeanor, both agitated and dour, forced Mikey into silence. When they arrived back at Payne Whitney, Mikey once again had to pay the cab driver for the ride, leaving him with little left in his pocket. They rode the elevator up to "Chez Trois" but before Halliday and Mikey could reach the big mahogany doors, their path was blocked by three enormous nurses, two male and one female.

"Look at him! He's flying!" proclaimed the meanest looking of the nurses, referring to Halliday.

"Ah, what a charming welcoming committee," Halliday jested with a bit too much energy and his eyes blazing. "Ladies and gentlemen, the Andrews Sisters! Getting a bit beefy there, Laverne."

Just then, "Laverne" grabbed Halliday by the scruff of his collar and "escorted" him back to the elevator.

"Where the hell are you taking him?" Mikey asked, but before he could get an answer he was held in a headlock by the largest of the nurses. A cacophony of voices rang in Mikey's ears as the pain increased.

"Never you mind!"

"Owww!"

"I think he needs to be quiet."

"The Quiet Room?"

"Exactly."

"But!" Mikey finally got out of the chokehold. "Wait! I'm not a patient here!"

Ignored by the nurses, Mikey was pushed down the hallway and through a doorway. He fell on his knees and caught a brief glimpse of the room. It was as far from Mary Martin's yellow living room as he could get. The Quiet Room indeed, he thought. It's a padded cell. The walls and floors were all covered with a colorless mattress-like foam, apparently to protect the patient locked inside from harming himself. Mikey noticed dried blood on the padding on one of the walls. Had former patients knocked their heads against them? What kind of force would it take to draw blood when the padding was so thick? Mikey wondered if this was the very same room where they had put Marilyn Monroe?

Before he could ask himself the next question, he heard the door of the Quiet Room slam behind him, followed by the sharp, cold metallic sound of a deadbolt locking the door.

The room was now pitch black. For the first time, Mikey was scared. If they could mistake him for a patient, might he be stuck in here forever? After all, no one even knew he was here at Payne Whitney. Mikey started to long for his mother, which made him wonder if he really was crazy. She didn't know the adult Mikey was even alive in 1960, because he was only two years old and still home in a crib in her bedroom.

Mikey's head ached and he tried to clear his mind. All this darkness and quiet made it difficult to gather his thoughts. This was certainly not part of the deal he made with Richard Rodgers and Leland Hayward. Wait! They knew he was here. But would they ever think this might happen? Would they even call to find out where he was? Maybe if they wanted those signed papers enough. But they would not miss him. Not for days.

"Hey, let me out," he shouted to no avail. "Can't I at least get a phone call, like a common criminal would? Somebody, call Mary Martin and she'll vouch for me..."

Mary Martin. She must have called ahead to alert the powers-that-be that Richard had gone AWOL and maybe she blamed Mikey and this was his punishment.

He banged on what he thought was the door, but there was no sound. Of course not, Mikey thought, padding covered every inch of the room. Mikey tried hard not to panic but he was sweaty from the tense cab ride and now his forehead was dripping as if he had just eaten a dish of jalapeno peppers.

Panic. Panic.

Mikey remembered the terror of being locked in that fun house as a kid, how he banged on the walls and stomped on the floor until the proprietor let him out. This time was different. He was older and wiser, and the intense blackness of the room told him that there was no way out. This was not a house, and it was certainly not fun. Mikey settled down and tried to relax. He had no choice but to wait until they let him out and he could clear up the whole big misunderstanding. To top it off, he was starving. He had not had one bite to eat all day and had been counting on Halliday taking him to lunch.

Now Halliday was god-knows-where, getting his own punishment. And Mikey was alone. Having all the time in the world, Mikey tried to put it all together about Halliday. He must have gone back home, knowing Mary was out, so he could get to his hidden stash of pills. And he must have taken some before Mary found him. That's why he was both agitated and dour on the ride back. And the nurses who were waiting for him? Mary had to have tipped them off and they could see Halliday's intoxication a mile away.

Mikey's stomach growled so loudly that he was sure Richard Halliday could hear him on whatever floor he was.

"He can't hear you where he is," an unseen voice said.

Mikey knew that voice. Or did he? Oh, sure, thought Mikey, now I'm going to hallucinate, and they'll really think I'm nuts and give me shock treatments. Is this how it's going to end? Is this really "the cuckoo's nest?" What was this time-travel journey all for anyway? To put him in the funny farm in 1960 before he could even have his bar mitzvah?

"That's a funny thought, Michael Marvin Minkus."

Now Mikey was sure he knew the voice. It was Mary2. Was she residing in his head now? If she appeared out of a padded wall carrying a lit candelabra, Mikey knew he would faint. Mikey waited but there was no recurrence of the voice. Having no idea how long he was going to be in the Quiet Room, Mikey decided to just curl up in a ball and see if he could sleep. The warmth, the dark, and the silence conspired to send him into a neat little oblivion which was almost immediately broken by a Brooklyn-accented voice he knew too well.

"Who's munching on a foxtrot now? Where are your girlfriends Ethel and Mary now that you need them?"

Mikey's mother Rifka sat on the other side of the Quiet Room being anything but.

For some reason, Mikey could see her in the dark as the glow from the toilet paper covering her newly washed-and-set hair illuminated the padded walls and bounced off of her bra and girdle combination.

"Ma! Put on some clothes. You can't sit around in your bra and girdle," Mikey whined, shielding his eyes as if the sight of his half-naked mother might burn his retinas.

"What? Who's gonna see? You might not have noticed, but we're in the loony bin, kiddo. I'm even wearing the latest in shoes – paper! I'm *toujours* stylish here. It's you who don't fit in. But that's nothing new."

"Ma… please!"

"Tell me, *Tatala*," Rifka asked, softening her tone, "what has this whole *fakocta* time-trip done for you? Have you had enough yet? Every minute you're in a different year. It makes me dizzy. And the basement is empty without you there. Come home already. I'll make you some nice *kishka*."

"You know I hate *kishka*."

"No, you don't. Your father, may he rest in peace, loved it."

"What are you talking?" another male voice responded.

The voice came from behind Mikey and when he turned to look, there was his father.

"I hated *kishka*," his father said. "Nobody likes *kishka*. It's... *kishka*. The word alone is disgusting."

"Dad?"

Mikey was visibly moved and tears came to his eyes. He had not seen his father since he was twelve years old. He didn't remember him looking this young.

"Shut up, Morris. You love my *kishka*," Rifka said flirtatiously.

"Mom!"

"Oh?" Mikey's father responded, flirting back, "I do, do I?"

Suddenly Morris and Rifka were reclining on one of the padded walls, defying all the laws of Newton. Then they were embracing on the ceiling. It was like a crazy version of the Fred Astaire number in the movie *Royal Wedding*, Mikey thought. They danced on the padded walls and padded ceiling (why in heaven's name was the ceiling padded, Mikey wondered?) and finally landed on the padded floor by Mikey's feet.

Mikey tried to get his father's attention but, as always, Morris only had eyes for his wife, whose toilet-papered head was now transformed and covered in a wimple and a veil, making her look like a Jewish version of Mary Martin as Maria von Trapp.

True to her new look, Rifka started to sing, "Let's start at the very beginning..."

As she sang, Mikey watched Rifka and Morris grow younger until they were the couple they were before Mikey had been a glimmer in Morris's eye. They sang, as Mary Martin and Theodore Bikel sang, "An Ordinary Couple." Even the room had been transformed in Mikey's dream. No longer colorless, the padding on the walls looked like Scottish tartan. This now, to go along with the kilt that his father Morris sported as he knelt down to ask Rifka to marry him.

Mikey was embarrassed watching his romantically young parents, and he squeezed his already closed eyes even tighter. When he opened them again, Rifka and Morris were gone, and he heard the sharp cold sound of the deadbolt opening.

The door opened, letting in the light and hurting Mikey's eyes. How long had he been locked up? How long was he dreaming?

"You Michael Minkus?"

"Yes..."

Silhouetted against the light, he could see that this was the large female nurse who threw him into this room. But now, still officious as she was, she also sounded a bit contrite in her brusque way.

"Come with me. There's a lady here to see you."

The nurse helped Mikey up off the floor and as he rose, he noticed he had wet himself. The nurse handed him a robe.

"You can put this on for now."

Mortified, Mikey wrapped the robe around himself and tied the tie, covering the wet spot on his crotch and pant leg, and followed the nurse out of the Quiet Room to the front entrance near the large mahogany doors where Mary Martin was waiting.

"Oh, baby boy! I am so sorry. When I called them about Richard, I was so angry. I told them to lock him up and throw away the key. But I never thought they would treat *you* this way. Are you alright?"

The nurse spoke for Mikey.

"He's fine. He just had a nice lie down and some quiet. We're sorry for the mix-up, but how could we know he wasn't a patient?"

Mary grew serious. "How? I'm sure he told you that before you locked him up. We could sue you, you know. This young man could sue you. He arrived as a visitor and is walking out of here as a victim. Shall we sue them, Michael?"

"I just want to go home."

Mikey stopped and listened to what he had said. Home? Where? When? Back to the basement with his mother above him in every sense of the word? Home had changed its meaning since he took that LL train from Brooklyn to the Upper East Side.

"Come along then," Mary said, holding out her arm to Mikey. "You people are very lucky this man is a forgiving soul."

In the elevator, Mikey asked about Richard.

"I saw him on the Seventh Floor just before they gave him a shot. Thorazine, they called it. He'll be out of it for a while, but the next time I see him, he'll be off the pills and alcohol. Oh, and Michael, he was very contrite about pulling you into this whole caper of his. But we're going to make this right for you. You're a very good writer, Michael… don't be modest. We happen to know that they're looking for someone to work on the Tony Awards. Richard told me to put in a good word for you with NBC. We have a contract with them, and they want me to do another *Peter Pan*, so a suggestion from Richard carries great weight. Believe me, Michael, when Richard gets behind someone… well, I am the living proof of his tenacity and devotion."

Now, two months later, it had all come true. Richard and Mary's influence had gotten Mikey the job and he had written the Tony Awards and met Jane Fonda. And now, tonight, he was back at Payne Whitney handing Halliday his Best Musical medallion.

"How long before you get to go home?"

Halliday's response was slow, deliberate and slightly incoherent. The Thorazine had done its job well.

"I am home. Thanks for the Award and thanks to all the lovely ladies here in the dark."

Halliday turned in his paper slippers and shuffled away on the arm of a male nurse. Mikey watched as his once tall, patrician form seemed smaller and smaller. As he reached the end of the hall, Halliday crumpled to the floor with the grace of a dancer taking a deep curtsy. The big, strong male nurse picked him up and carried him around the corner until Mikey could see them no longer.

"How was he?" Mary asked when Mikey returned to the lobby where she was still waiting in her ball gown.

"Fine," Mikey lied to the woman who knew the truth.

"Did you give him my love?"

"Of course. And he sent his back as he danced into the sunset."

"That's lovely," Mary said and believed it. "Shall we?"

"You go ahead. I feel like walking."

"At this hour? Can't we drop you at home?"

"Thanks, but my home is… a bit too far out of the way."

"But…"

"Congratulations on your Award."

As Mikey watched the be-gowned and bejeweled Broadway star leave the "loony bin" where her husband now resided, Mikey had an inexplicable urge to get back on the elevator, although he had no clue where he would be going. Certainly, he was not going back to the Third Floor where the Quiet Room was, nor was he going back up to the Seventh Floor where Halliday was perhaps still being carried around in the strong, loving arms of his male nurse. As the elevator signaled its arrival with an electronic ding, Mikey walked in, shut his eyes and let the doors close behind him. He decided to let fate and the Otis company take him either up or down.

Time stood still for a moment and the doors opened almost immediately. Mikey was sure he had gone nowhere, but when he exited, he was not in the mahogany-and-pine lobby of Payne Whitney, but in the ornately marbled rotunda of the Brooklyn Public Library in Grand Army Plaza, near Prospect Park.

And there, seated at a table all alone and surrounded by books, was his twelve-year-old self.

Chapter Nine
When I Went Home
New York City, September 1970

"…where dreams are born and time is never planned…"

When he was still a little boy, one of Mikey's favorite records was *Peter Pan*, and when he found that it was a TV special and was to be repeated as a special holiday event for Easter, his joy knew no bounds. What was it, he sometimes wondered, that attracted Mikey to buy that recording? It was kind of strange that a lady was playing a little boy, but her voice was so lustrous and un-ladylike that he actually believed that she was Peter, the ultimate lost boy. Or was part of it the fact that Mikey felt a kinship to a lost boy, a boy without parents, one who ran (or flew) away to a Neverland where he could play and play without any adult responsibilities? Or did he just love the songs? As Mikey researched *Peter Pan* at the library, he found out that there were other songs that were taken out of the show before it came to Broadway and then television.

One title that haunted him was a song called "When I Went Home." According to one of those magical library books, it was to be sung by Peter about what happened when he decided to go back to find his home and family after years of being "a lost boy." When he got home and looked in the window at the nursery where he used to sleep, he saw another child, a new baby. A replacement. He realized then that there was no place for him anymore, no home. He suddenly knew that there was no going back. He was erased, replaced, and forgotten. Mikey thought this song, which he had never heard, which Peter never sang on Broadway or on TV, had to be the saddest song in the world.

He recalled it now and made up the melody and lyrics in his head, as he looked over at the boy he used to be. The young Mikey, not yet fully formed, hidden behind the books that could kill or cure. Twenty-five-year-old Michael knew every emotion that the boy he watched was experiencing. He knew that he had schlepped on three buses to get to this magical library from their house in Brooklyn, New York. He knew that he sang to himself while waiting for the buses, not only because he enjoyed it, but also because it kept away the fear. The fear of being noticed and picked on and even beaten up and robbed. The song in his heart and on his lips was like the happy tune that Anna whistled at the beginning of *The King and I*. It let people know, or at least made them believe, that you were not afraid.

But now the grown-up Mikey was afraid. Afraid to approach the ghost of his younger self. So, for now, he just observed. As in *It's a Wonderful Life*, everything appeared to Mikey in sweet, warm sepia tones. As he took it all in he was visibly shaken to see the boy he was, sitting at the same table he remembered, pouring over stacks of *Theatre World* annuals from the 1950s. Mikey always thought he was a fat little kid with pimples, but this boy before him was of average size, maybe a little chubby, but very cute, with curly brown hair and an open face that wanted to trust the world. On that face, there was not a trace of acne.

Mikey watched his young doppelgänger and tried to remember what it was like on that day when he fled to the library, as he sometimes did nightly. What was he thinking? Was he happy? Was he escaping from Rifka's boiled chicken? He could not recall that very ordinary September afternoon. It was like so many when he was nine and ten and eleven. It was then that Mikey decided to literally confront his past.

Before he could approach the twelve-year-old boy, he stopped to wonder what he might even say. How could he be sure not to come off as a creep or pervert? Mikey remembered how he felt when adult males approached him, using their mutual love of musical theatre as a come on.

"Say," one such man of about thirty said to Mikey when he was about eleven, "have you ever heard *Anyone Can Whistle*? Nah, you're too young to really get that show."

Mikey remembered how embarrassed he felt. Not because he didn't know the show or own the record, but because of the good/bad feeling it gave him. The mixed emotions he didn't really understand. So, could he now approach his younger self and possibly give him the same bad feeling? Before he could decide, the younger Mikey closed the last of the *Theatre World*s and got up to leave.

Mikey knew the route and decided to follow himself home, keeping a respectable distance so as not to tip the kid off to his presence. He wondered if the boy would recognize his own future, and Mikey decided that no one could ever tell who or what they would be or look like thirteen years down the road. For young Mikey that would be double his age. No, the elder Mikey thought, he was safe.

After completing the three-bus journey, Mikey let his younger self run on ahead and took in his neighborhood as it used to be. That place before. The place and time where his father was still alive and his mother had not yet calcified into the wicked witch of Canarsie. A time before Mikey worshipped Ethel Merman and Mary Martin. It was beyond surreal, a scenario that even Thornton Wilder conjuring up the third act of *Our Town* hadn't fathomed.

They say that when you go home again everything seems smaller, but for Mikey the opposite was true. The street seemed immensely long, and the trees and front yards were ablaze with green. It was to be an Indian Summer for sure. The rose bushes that grew wild and untended still held red blooms that longed to be clipped for bouquets for Rifka.

And the house of his youth was almost forbiddingly large. Those years before moving down to the basement, literally burying himself alive under his mother Rifka's rule, meant everything was more open and larger and filled with possibilities. He could hardly remember it, but there it was right in front of him, the house with its cement stairs leading to a porch where his parents smoked nightly. And on the porch was his father. The Dad who called him "Poochie" and brought him a glass of water before kissing him on the forehead and bidding him goodnight. There he was, on that cement porch. Alive. Reading the newspaper, smoking a Winston and coughing.

"Hey Mister," his father called down to him, "tell me something. Why are you wearing a tuxedo in broad daylight?"

"Where is Marvin Minkus?"

Ethel Merman was sitting in the star dressing room at the St. James Theatre putting on her makeup for the Saturday matinee. Her dresser, Mary2, shrugged as she got her first costume ready for Ethel to step into.

"I told you, Miss M, I said 'that boy was gonna be a no show,'" Mary2 chided.

"You never told me anything of the sort," Ethel said dismissively with a wave of her hand. "All you did was praise him to the skies when he needed the job. Mary Martin flew the coop and went to live in Brazil, you said, and I should give the kid a chance, you said. He was a good writer, you said. I told you I didn't need a writer. He could take dictation, you said… but *I* take it faster. And I do Pittman!"

"I know," placated Mary2 in mocking tones. She had heard this all before. "You were the best private secretary and stenographer in Brooklyn. What's Pittman?"

"First of all, Astoria is not in Brooklyn," Ethel corrected. "It's in Queens. And Pittman is the most difficult kind of shorthand. Anyway, Mary, I entrusted him with my house seat book and now he disappears, just a few days before the record-breaking performance. I'm getting calls left and right for seats."

Mary2 rolled her eyes and mocked Ethel, who ignored her as usual. "Longest-running musical in the history of Broadway! Mmm-Mmm… and all because of you. You are making history and lining the pockets of David Merrick. I have heard it all before."

Ethel looked into the mirror and up at Mary. Her features softened a little and a twinkle appeared in her eye.

"Well, you know I turned down the role of Dolly, don't you? I always say 'I didn't open Dolly…'"

"But you closed her?"

"Not yet, Mary. For all I know they'll replace me with Rin Tin Tin or even Tiny Tim. But no matter what, I made her the longest-running musical in history."

"Carol Channing always loves it when you say that."

"Carol Channing can kiss my…"

Just then, the phone in Merman's dressing room rang. Merman ignored it at first, as if the ringing came from some other dressing room. Then she realized the ringing phone was her own.

"Who the hell is calling me right before a Saturday matinee? Please turn it off, Mary. I knew putting in this phone was a mistake, but Merrick insisted I have it, like this air conditioning that is drying out my throat. 'Ethel,' he said, 'you are a star, and a star deserves…'"

Finally, unable to take the ringing another second, Ethel screamed, "Mary, would you answer that fucking phone before I need a straitjacket."

Mary2 picked up the phone and announced in her most lady-in-waiting tones, "Miss Ethel Merman's Star Dressing Room. To what does this pertain, please?"

Ethel rolled her eyes at Mary2's fake pretension as Mary2's face lit up.

"It's Miss Martin," she shouted to Ethel. "All the way from the jungle… I mean Brazil." Mary2 yelled into the phone, "Miss Martin, are you wearing fruit on your head?"

"Give me that phone," Ethel ordered as she pulled the receiver away from Mary2.

"Hello, Mary? Do you know how much this is costing you? The payroll for *South Pacific* didn't cost this much. Oh, well, isn't that lovely of you!"

Ethel put her hand over the mouthpiece of the receiver and shouted at Mary2, "Mary Martin thought *today* was the day we beat *My Fair Lady* as the longest-running musical. I guess time is different down there."

Ethel uncovered the mouthpiece and listened.

"Oh, you could hear that? Well, whataya know! That's right. But it's not today, it's this coming Wednesday. Yes, at a matinee no less. You are a darling though to call. You have no idea how much fun it is to play Dolly to such an adoring crowd. Oh, you did? Where? What the hell were you doing in Vietnam?"

Mary2 hissed at Ethel in quiet, but admonishing, tones, "You know she did Dolly in Vietnam and in Japan and in London. I was there with her, in the foxholes!"

Ethel smiled and spoke into the receiver, "I was just kidding. "They called you Foxhole Mary, right?"

"They called us both that," Mary2 said with pride.

Ethel looked at Mary2 and rolled her eyes to heaven as if to say either Mary Martin is crazy or you are.

"So, how's Richard? Uh huh… uh huh… mmm… oh… uh huh… no… really? Even in Brazil?"

"What?" asked Mary2 in a stage whisper that rivaled Merman's. "What is she saying? How is he?"

Ethel ignored Mary2 and continued to sympathetically listen to Mary Martin on the phone, injecting the occasional "tsk tsk" and "oh my" and even the occasional "shit," followed by the obligatory "sorry, Mary."

Noticing that it was approaching half-hour, Ethel tried to get to the end of the Richard subject.

"Well, you were right to retire to Brazil. Now no one on Broadway will see him making a horse's ass of himself. But everyone is saying how much they miss you. So, listen, Mary, what did you do when that Marvin Minkus disappeared on you? I mean should I put out a missing person's report or just get someone else to do my house seat orders?"

On the other side of the world, Richard Halliday silently sat sipping his Scotch and watched his wife, Mary, rolling her eyes to heaven.

Twelve-year-old Mikey Minkus's summer was ending as it did every Labor Day weekend. For adults, Labor Day was a three-day holiday, but for kids still in school, it denoted the end of the summer. Mikey was not sorry to see summer go. He knew he could still ride his bike and daydream, and he also knew he would always have the library. He would not miss the other kids in the neighborhood and their daily stickball or handball or baseball or basketball. Mikey was not athletic, and that summer Mikey felt he was a target of ridicule and scorn as he rode his bike past the schoolyard where the boys would play their games.

In reality, none of those athletic boys paid the least bit of attention to the twelve-year-old riding his bike past them over and over. Mikey had to admit that he enjoyed watching them play handball or stickball, even if he had no urge to join in. His twelve-year-old libido had no clue why he was attracted to them, but he was.

Mikey was confused and lonely and something was going on with his Dad that no one wanted to talk about. Every time Mikey would come into the room, his parents would clam up or change whatever the subject was. This only made Mikey even more nervous. Riding his bike by himself and staring at the handball players seemed his only relief. And so, he rode. And stared.

The twenty-five-year-old Mikey stood before eighty-five-year-old Sergei Rostropovich, the ancient Russian owner of "the best thrift store in Brooklyn" (according to Morris Minkus), modeling his vintage tuxedo for him.

"Very nice material," Rostropovich said in his thick-as-borscht Russian accent as he touched the lapel. "Most people merely bring in the suit and ask me to buy it. Very classy of you to model it for me. Do you want to sell it on consignment?"

"No," replied Mikey, "I want to trade it for some regular clothes."

"Are the shiny sissy shoes included?"

"Everything but my underwear," Mikey replied.

"This is a very unusual business deal. I like it. This is a vintage tux, from the forties, I think."

"And only worn once. At the Astor."

"The hotel?" asked Rostropovich. "Didn't they just tear that down?"

Mikey was unsure but ventured a guess.

"I think so."

"Oy, this city of dreams," Rostropovich said with the kind of Russian melancholia born of centuries of darkness and cold. "So many beautiful buildings reduced to dust. Like we all will be soon. Alright," he decided, "I'll take the tuxedo. In this neighborhood it will probably never sell, but it will look good in the window, right? Of course right. Take it off and pick out whatever you like. Don't forget the shoes."

As Mikey took off the tux in the makeshift dressing room in the back of Rostropovich's store, he double-checked his pockets, finding some cash (useful), Mary Martin's address in Brazil (interesting), Jane Fonda's phone number(!), and Ethel Merman's *Hello, Dolly!* house seat book, with a backstage pass made out to Marvin Minkus. Somehow Mikey surmised, he must be working on the show and going by his middle name.

Was he a press agent again? He knew he didn't write the show; that was Jerry Herman and another Michael named Stewart. But was he working for David Merrick, the producer? Or did he work for Merman again as he did back in 1947? Like Scarlett O'Hara, Mikey would think about that tomorrow.

As Mikey emerged from the dressing room wearing the everyday clothes he was trading for his vintage tux, he noticed a box on the counter that seemed familiar.

"What's the box?"

"What box?" Rostropovich asked.

Mikey opened the box and saw that, like the box he had lost somewhere along the way, this one was also filled with letters, letters to and from Mary and Ethel.

"Is this for sale?"

"Didn't you bring them in yourself? Aren't they yours?"

Mikey looked deep into Rostropovich's eyes and thought he saw a reflection of Mary2 in there.

"Take them," Rostropovich commanded. "I have no customers for ephemera."

And so it was that Mikey got a box of letters to fill him in on the last ten years, plus several changes of clothes more suitable for the Brooklyn Indian Summer of 1970. As for Sergei Rostropovich, he got a vintage tuxedo that was worn by a dummy in the window of his store till the day he died.

Cancer.

A word to be said in the most whispered tones, if at all. A death sentence for a smoker who refused to quit smoking. Twelve-year-old Mikey had heard the word before, but never in relation to his father. He stood outside of his parents' bedroom as he heard only scattered phrases mixed with tears. "Morris, are you sure?" "Cancer, Rifka…" "No, no, no… It's not true." "Honey…" "We will never speak of it again!"

When the door to the bedroom opened, Morris and Rifka were all smiles, as if nothing bad was happening. Mikey looked at them both, waiting for a sign that they were going to tell him the bad news, but they swept right past him down the long hallway to the kitchen where Morris lit up, inhaled, and started to cough. Mikey silently went out and took his bike out of the garage and started to ride. He rode on East 100th Street and turned on Avenue K and took a left on Rockaway Parkway toward the bay and the pier. Mikey was angry. Mikey was sad. Mikey was more confused than he ever had been in his life. Mikey was lost.

"My name is Marvin," the elder Mikey told Morris as they sat on the stoop in front of the house on East 100th Street. Mikey had decided it would be too coincidental to have the same first name as his younger alter ego.

"My son Michael has that as his middle name. The letter M is big in this family. I'm Morris with no middle name. My parents were too poor to afford one," Morris quipped between coughing jags. Marvin tried not to take note of his father's hacking cough, but Morris was pragmatic about it.

"I'm dying. It's my own fault, but what can you do? Years ago, the doctors told me to quit smoking or they'd cut a hole in my throat and make me breathe out of a straw. I just laughed at him. And look! No hole and no straw. Just impending doom."

"I'm sorry," Marvin uttered with not much voice. His father was finally saying the words he never uttered when Mikey needed to hear them. Finally, he was hearing the truth. Just then, Marvin's twelve-year-old self rode by on his bike. Mikey looked quizzically at the stranger talking to his Dad but kept on riding. Morris noticed and pointed to his son whizzing by on two wheels.

"There's the only reason I'm sorry for smoking. I'll never see him grow up. And he's got a lot of growing up to do. You have any kids?"

"Me?" Marvin asked incredulously. "No, I don't have anything."

"I waited a long time to have this one. My wife and I were happy just being us. We were very selfish and thought we were fine all alone. Until twelve years ago, there was a blizzard and the heat went out. Well, you can imagine the rest. I couldn't get out to buy condoms and…" Morris raised his eyebrows in a salacious way that reminded Marvin of Groucho Marx.

Marvin/Mikey (for he felt both 25 and 12 at the same time now) blushed at the thought of his parents actually "doing it." Even now with his Dad gone, he found it hard to think of them together in that way. But as he looked at the forty-six-year-old Morris, he saw a real person, an actual sexual being, not just the memory of the Daddy who tucked him in. Morris was just another man talking to a man, never knowing he was looking into the future as the future looked back at the past.

"Have you told him?" Marvin asked, knowing that Morris never did or would.

"No. He's just a kid."

"Don't you think he'll be devastated when you're gone?"

"Kids get over these things. Why burden him now with something he can never really understand?"

"So, you're just going to go on as if nothing is happening?"

"I think that's the best course of action. You know, I don't know you at all but, somehow, I feel like I can tell you stuff. Is that crazy? You said you used to live here?"

"Yes," Marvin replied. "Now I'm in between residences."

"Hotels can be fun. Remember the Astor? My wife and I had lots of fun there. I would take her to a show or a nightclub like the Latin Quarter and sometimes we would take a room instead of lugging ourselves all the way back to Brooklyn. Fun times. What do you do?"

Unsure exactly what his job was, Marvin took the plunge. "I work for Ethel Merman. She's in *Hello, Dolly!* now."

Morris was impressed and it showed on his face. Mikey/Marvin, half boy and half man, but all son, was gratified to see the look of approval on his father's face.

"Ethel Merman! Now that's a Broadway star. My wife can't stand her. She calls her 'the loudmouth.' But I've always secretly loved her."

Marvin smiled. This made him happy. He never knew his father liked Ethel.

The bicycling Mikey rode by again and waved this time.

"I'm a little worried about him," Morris admitted. "I think he might be a *fagela*… you know what that is?"

Marvin blushed again, getting younger by the second.

"Yes," he admitted. He knew. But he never knew that his father knew or even suspected. What year was this? 1970. The year after Stonewall, Marvin thought. What did his parents think when they read the *New York Post* with the images of drag queens rioting in Greenwich Village? Did they look at their eleven-year-old son and wonder about him? Did they picture him in a dress and a wig with outrageous mascara and lipstick painted over his little boy features? Were they worried about his future? When Mikey/Marvin was only Mikey, he was oblivious to all this. But now he knew. Now he knew that his father was worried. And those images on the front pages were what he thought his little boy would turn out to be.

"The kid sits in the library every night after supper. That can't be healthy."

"Maybe it means he's smart."

"Of course, he's smart," Morris, now filled with pride instead of shame, said. "He's a good boy. Does well in school, but that doesn't mean I'm not worried. Not so much about what he'll do, but I'm a man of the world. I know about perverts who would take advantage of a boy. I work in Harlem and let me tell you the things I have seen. That's one reason I don't want to go."

"That's a good reason. But… and I know there's no reason for you to believe me… your kid is going to be okay. I mean, someone must be watching out for him. And that someone will be you."

Morris laughed.

"You believe in that bullshit? God? Heaven? The afterlife? Not me. Nope. It's bullshit."

"I remember," Marvin imprudently blurted out, recalling all of Morris's outcries of "bullshit."

"Remember what?"

Marvin caught himself. "My Dad used to always say, 'It's bullshit,' too."

"So, tell me about Merman," Morris said, changing the subject. "Does she really hate Mary Martin?"

Marvin smiled, happy to have something other than his future and Morris's impending death to discuss.

"Funny you should ask…"

Just a few hours earlier, exiting the thrift shop, Mikey wondered if the frost between Merman and Martin had melted over the ten years since Ethel lost the Tony to Mary. This new treasure trove of letters he got from Rostropovich began to tell the story.

Mary Martin
Dolly Company
Hanoi Hilton, Vietnam

April 7, 1965

Dear Ethel,

It has been forever since we spoke. I have no idea if it's my fault or yours, but I tried to get in touch with you when you were on the road with "Gypsy" back in 1961, but all my letters must have gotten to you too late or too early, as they all came back: UNKNOWN RECIPIENT.

Later, I invited you to my opening of "Jennie" at the Majestic. That was 1962. Not my favorite year. Ethel, you were smart not to come... don't ask... it was a disaster of the first degree. Richard and I tried to get Cheryl to close it out of town, but the boys (Arthur Schwartz and Howard Dietz) threatened to sue us if we didn't allow the show to come to Broadway. So, I had to endure playing a terrible book (some lovely songs I must admit) about Laurette Taylor and yet not be called Laurette Taylor. Insanity! So here we are and the years are passing.

I am writing this (actually dictating it) from a chopper. A chopper flying over Vietnam. Oh, Ethel, if you ever get to come here, do do do. It is incredible to be touring a big fat Broadway show in the middle of war-torn Vietnam. I never got to entertain overseas during World War II, did you? No, we were both too busy in hit shows (or flops if you count "Pacific 1860" and I do not).

You know what show I am doing? You must have read about it in Variety... "Hello, Dolly!" And I know that you were the first person offered it, way before Miss Channing. Why did you ever turn it down? It's such a fun role.

We actually tried out in Tokyo and how divine that was. The sights and the people... oh, Ethel, the Japanese people. So delicate, so lovely. I cannot believe we were ever at war with these people. Our friend Mary (I have decided to call her Mary Two so that we don't get mixed up; she is the one taking this down) is along with me as my dresser and general confidant and buffer, since Richard decided that it was much too dangerous for him. I think he was afraid to be away from America, or at least American liquor stores. Oh plop! Did I say that? Surprisingly, he's been a conservative drinker since getting out of that awful Payne Whitney.

Mary Two is the only colored person on this trip and she is attracting lots of attention from the soldiers, not to mention that I believe she had a fling with one of the Kabuki dancers in Japan. She sends her love.

Oh, Ethel, if I have done anything to damage our friendship, I want you to know I am miserably sorry. I mean it. That blasted Tony Award should never come between us. I blame all that ridiculous publicity. The machine that ground out the Ethel and Mary Competition Show. You and I have never been in a race. We are not competing. And I know you never said, "Mary Martin's okay...if you like talent." How did we ever start believing our own publicity?

Darling, we're about to land and I hear bombs going off. That can't be a good sign. When we first began this trip, I sat down and told the company that I would be there with them... in the foxholes. Now they call me Foxhole Mary. It would be rather sweet if I didn't think there was a dig in there somewhere.

Please write me back to let me know we are all copacetic. You can write me in care of Uncle Sam or David Merrick. They both hand deliver my mail.

Love, Dolly Levi.

Mikey noted that Merman never did write Mary back, or else the letter was lost, either on the way to Vietnam or London or to the ages. As he shuffled through the letters, he found letters from producers offering Mary new musicals: *Funny Girl, Walking Happy, Mame, Do I Hear a Waltz*... Each offer was paper clipped with a charming but firm rejection from the Hallidays. Then finally at the bottom of the box was a handwritten note on blue stationery from Merman, dated 1969.

Dear Mary,

I cannot thank you enough for your note of sympathy about Little Bit. I never thought I would live to see one of my children go before me. It is not in a mother's playbook. Ethel Jr. was a troubled girl. She never found her place. She wanted to be an actress but had a mother to compete with. She wanted to be a wife and mother and couldn't hack that either. But one thing I know. I am sure she did not take her own life, like her father did. How could she do that? Not with her own little babies right there sleeping. No God would let that happen. No. I am sure that it was an accident. A tragic accident.

Right now, I can only trust that my baby is out of her misery and in a better place. And yet, Mary, I am more miserable than I have ever been. And more alone. I know that we have not been the best of friends in recent years, but your reaching out now, all the way from Brazil, in my time of sadness… well, it means a lot. We are both mothers. And I know neither of us played by the rulebook, but we both love our kids. How could we not? Your boy Larry has done very well for himself. I watch his TV show every week and think, "Mary must be so proud." And we both have grandkids. Did you ever think that would happen?

Mary, I want you to know that whatever you decide to do, retire to your hacienda in the jungle and needlepoint your ass off or come back to take Broadway by storm again, I want us to be friends like we were. Back before. Before it all went to shit.

What say, let's be buddies?

Fondly,
Ethel

Mikey was touched and warmed by the feeling that the two ladies could maybe reconcile and undo the rift that he helped to create. He wondered if he screwed around with history by inserting himself into their lives or would this all have occurred in any case?

As he talked to the father who is no more, he hoped that this time his visit to the past could change history in a small but healing way. If not for himself, then for the Mikey he used to be.

As Marvin turned the corner to Avenue J, he ran smack into his twelve-year-old self standing by his bike.

"That's my Dad," said Mikey.

"I know."

"Do you have a Dad?"

"No. I mean I did. But he's gone."

"Oh."

The elder Mikey felt as if he were in a pint-sized Pinter play. The dialogue seemed to be innocuous, but the undercurrents, the subtexts, were being played between the lines.

"Did he tell you?" asked Mikey as he got off his bike.

"What?"

"Nothing."

"Okay."

"I know."

"What do you know?"

"Everything. Also… who you are."

Before Marvin could reply, Mikey hopped back on his bike with the banana seat and high handlebars and rode off.

"Well, look what the cat dragged in!" Merman sarcastically intoned as Marvin sheepishly entered her dressing room at 7:30 that evening. "I'll take that," Ethel said, as she forcibly grabbed her house seat book from his clutches.

"Have I been missing in action?" Marvin asked as Ethel disappeared behind a slammed bathroom door.

"Honey," replied Mary2, "Miss Merman was havin' conniption fits. You've been gone for days. Nice duds. Did you get them in Brooklyn?"

"How did you know I was in Brooklyn, Mary?"

Mary just looked at him with her sphinxlike kisser, but her eyes twinkled with knowledge.

"I know lots of stuff. And I think you'd better think more than twice about what you're thinking."

Marvin was astonished. Could Mary2 read his mind? He had sat for over an hour on that LL train from Brooklyn to Manhattan and had nothing but time to think. Between Rockaway Parkway and Lorimer Street in Brooklyn, Marvin decided to kidnap his younger alter ego and save him from the unhappiness ahead; the drawn out illness of his Morris and his ultimate death and the despair of Rifka which would eventually bury Mikey in that basement.

Yes, the elder Mikey would find that last portal back to 1983, wherever it was, and take his twelve-year-old alter ego with him. Yes, thought Mikey, as the dilapidated train chugged into the Livonia Avenue stop, why should the boy endure all the pain of the next thirteen years if I can help him? But as the train lurched and lumbered down the tracks through Brooklyn, Mikey reconsidered. He had no idea if the boy would simply disappear in that long portal back to Merman's closet. And wouldn't he be terrified to find himself in another time period?

By the time the LL train went through the long dark tunnel under the East River and emerged into Manhattan, Mikey had decided his idea was idiotic. After all, he had no clue if he could even get back to 1983. This was starting to weigh on his mind. Up until now he didn't even consider that he might have wanted to go back.

He seemed to be hurling himself through the seas of time without any harbor, like a musical comedy Flying Dutchman. This thought made Mikey laugh… a musical comedy Flying Dutchman made him think of those vaudevillian Dutch acts like Weber and Fields, who portrayed their comic characters with German accents. By the time Mikey got off the train at Eighth Avenue and 14th Street to switch to the Eighth Avenue uptown local, he put on his Marvin persona and forgot all about the silly scheme. He had to find some other way to help Mikey. And with Morris's impending decline, he had to do it fast.

As he looked at Mary2 in Merman's dressing room, she seemed to know his every thought. Mikey noticed that she never seemed to age and told her so.

"You should talk," Mary2 responded. "You were twenty-five in 1939 and now it's 1970, isn't it? And you are still prime draft age."

Mikey visibly blanched at the thought of Vietnam and being drafted. He had been thrilled to be only twelve when the older boys in the neighborhood started either getting their draft cards or disappearing to Canada.

Mary2 saw his fear, which gave her a slight jolt of joy, but she ignored it and continued. "Not a wrinkle on your kisser, even after trying on all those new personas like you tried on those used clothes you're wearing. But don't you worry, little Mikey Marvin, they never notice. These star ladies and theatre folk are too busy ignoring their own mirrors and imagining themselves as sweet, young things to notice whether you've aged or not. In fact, if you look young, they make *you* their mirror."

Mikey looked deep into Mary2's eyes and echoed the words that his younger self said to him just an hour earlier.

"I know."

"What do you know?" echoed Mary2

"Everything."

From the bathroom came the voice of the Merm.

"Thank God I have my house seat book back."

Marvin glided past the St. James Theatre house manager and ticket taker, both of whom smiled at him and nodded as if they knew him well. He seemed to command the kind of respect that he lacked back in Brooklyn. Was it all because he held Merman's house seat book? Or used to.

Mikey/Marvin (for he was beginning to morph back to his true self) was more excited than he ought to have been for someone who had supposedly seen the show dozens of times (at least according to Merman). In reality, this would be the first time he'd ever seen Merman live on stage in one of her signature roles. He wondered if the happily buzzing crowd filling the orchestra seats knew that this would be her last Broadway role.

Now back to being Mikey, he noticed that there were standees leaning on the low wall at the back of the orchestra seats. He climbed up a few steps of the staircase to the mezzanine and balcony and found a comfortable step on which to sit with a view of the whole stage. The lights dimmed and Mikey closed his eyes as if he were doing a private incantation for the magic he was about to experience. As he opened his eyes, a blast of music filled his ears, the curtain went up, and Mikey suddenly wished that his twelve-year-old self could be there beside him to experience the joy. Entranced by the show, Mikey found himself listening a bit more closely toward the end of Act One.

"Ephraim, it's time to rejoin the human race."

Suddenly, he knew what his plan should be.

Chapter Ten
World, Take Me Back
September 2 – September 9, 1970

During intermission, Mikey went backstage. Normally this would be a thrill for him, just sauntering into the star dressing room and saying hello and *merde* for the second act. But tonight, Mikey was nervous. His idea depended on Ethel Merman being kind and sympathetic, but her majesty the Queen of Broadway might not be feeling generous toward Marvin, the errant keeper of her house seats. Although he knew that deep beneath that tough exterior was another even tougher exterior, somewhere buried under those layers was a vulnerable, sweet woman. Mikey/Marvin just had to crack through a few layers to get there. When Mary2 answered his knock with a shake of her frowning head, Mikey/Marvin knew this was not the time to crack anything harder than an egg.

"Watch out! Mrs. Levi's on the warpath," Mary2 hissed under her breath. "Her red Dolly dress got shrunk at the dry cleaners." And did Mary2's eyes roll at that statement? Uh-huh. Mmmm. Mikey unsuccessfully tried to suppress a giggle. He failed and Merman heard.

"What the fuck is all that laughter out there. Did you find the seamstress, Mary? Is she on her way with her goddamned needle?"

"I'd like to give that woman a needle. With a sedative or ten."

"Mary," Mikey whispered as he looked right into Mary2's eyes, "where are we going?"

"I don't know about you, Mikey Marvin, but I am going straight to heaven. Or home to bed, whichever comes first."

Mikey was feeling a little homesick now. "I think maybe it's time for me to go home too."

"Not to that bedroom in the cellar though."

Mikey didn't even question how Mary2 knew about where he lived for the last thirteen years. He just took it for granted that she was some kind of sorceress or enabling force. Or was she a fellow traveler on this weird journey? Was Mary2 on her own track that just happened to crisscross with Mikey's?

She was clearly giving him hints to that effect but, as always, Mary2 was indecipherable to the nth degree. The proverbial riddle wrapped in an enigma.

"Do you think Ethel would mind if I used a couple of her house seats for a sick friend?" Mikey asked.

Mary2 didn't even have to think. "She would have a shit fit... pardon my French. So, just don't tell her."

"Don't tell me what?"

Ethel appeared in her tight Dolly dress looking like an overripe cherry pie dipped in bugle beads.

"Don't tell her that Marvin is gonna scream at the dry cleaners for you and not let you even raise your voice."

"You mean I don't get to yell at the son-of-a-bitch myself?"

"Nope," Mary2 calmly replied. "You are saving those brassy but golden tones for your audience. You got a big day coming next week. You and Dolly gotta pass that finish line and wipe out *My Fair Lady*'s long-run record. Mr. Merrick is counting on you bringing down the house. Now, let me take a look at that seam, Miss M."

With a sidelong glance and a flick of her brown eyes, Mary2 showed Mikey where the house seat book was. As Mary2 turned Ethel around to the wall, Mikey ripped off two of the house seat order forms and quickly put them in the breast pocket of his jacket.

"See you at the Harmonia Gardens," Mikey/Marvin said as he headed toward the door and back into the auditorium to see Act Two.

"Make sure I hear you cheering out there when I come down those stairs, Marvin," Ethel shouted. "Carol Channing and Mary Martin have husbands to cheer for them, but I only have you. And that's why I pay you the big bucks."

Later that night after the show, Mikey/Marvin rode the LL train back to Brooklyn. He felt that he had known Ethel Merman on and off for thirty years, which made him giggle to himself since he was still twenty-five. Nevertheless, there had been a change in her since those early days before she married those four husbands. A sadness (understandable considering what he had read about her daughter dying last year) that went along with her mood swings. He wanted to make sense of the middle-aged Ethel who yelled at him after the show when he was trying to tell her how brilliant she was as Dolly.

He dug into the letters for a clue to her behavior and found one from Merman to her friend Dorothy Fields.

EAM
Chateau Marmont
Sunset Blvd.
Hollywood, CA

August 2, 1964

Dear Dorothy,

Thank you so much for the lovely wedding present which, due to the abrupt demise of my marriage to a certain Mr. Borgnine, I am herewith returning to you. I hope that you can get a refund or credit, but if not, perhaps you can use it yourself.

Notice my new temporary address. I will be back in New York by September.

I know that all of Broadway and Hollywood are buzzing over my brief marital fling but if anyone asks, please tell them that it was the worst mistake of my life. They say if you marry in June, you'll be a bride all your life. Well, your Mermsie killed that adage dead in its tracks.

I know you are dying to know the dirt, but the truth is I can hardly type the words. Let's leave it with the fact that I'm a lover not a fighter and though I seem "a tough broad" to many, I am really made of flesh and blood and my flesh didn't like being hit so hard that my blood was on the wrong side of my skin.

Oh, Dorothy, what the fuck do I do now? How about we do Annie again? The twentieth anniversary of our triumph is coming up and to have you show me how to do "the goon look" again would be more than I could bear. I know that Irving is dying (almost literally… he is so old!) to revive the show. Maybe we can get Dick Rodgers to produce again. Wouldn't that be a blast? The whole original crew back together again, as if time had never passed. Oh, I know a few wrinkles have gone under the bridge (of my nose), but with enough makeup and a very tall leading man, I can look positively middle-aged. I truly feel like an old fool.

Yes, honey, I can hear you now. You can dig yourself out of this. I know I can. No more men! That's it. I am a four-time loser, and every guy was some kind of uglier substitute for Sherm (except for Mr. Leavitt, who was, it's starting to seem, the man that got away). But that's all over and it's time to just live for Ethel now. I have two healthy kids and two grandkids and as some smart songwriter wrote, who could ask for anything more? I know nothing is ever going to mar my happiness ever again. NO MORE MEN! Especially if they're in show biz!

By the way, who the hell buys a set of pots for a woman who doesn't cook? Dorothy Fields, that's who!

Love,
Mermsie

Mikey knew that Ethel Merman and Ernest Borgnine were married and that it ended quickly. Hell, didn't Ethel have a chapter in her not yet written memoir entitled "My Marriage to Ernest Borgnine" followed by a blank page? Critics found it all very amusing, but Mikey understood now that that blank page was filled with pain. This letter filled in the blanks a bit. Poor Ethel.

Sometimes Mikey wondered if anyone in 1983 missed him. Did Rifka go down to the basement wondering if he was out looking for a job or sleeping at a friend's house? Was she worried at all? How long was he really gone? Surely, she would miss him if he never returned. Facing facts, Mikey knew that not many others would miss him. This bothered him a bit. Who would mourn if he never returned?

And he also wondered where Mikey slept on those nights in those times when he had no basement home to go back to? Did he lay his head on the straw subway seats and ride the train from end to end? Were there times when he was so flush with money that he took a hotel room? That night in 1953 with Robbins, did Jerry take pity and let him stay in the den, while Jerry and his then-boyfriend cuddled in the bed next door?

Or did he sleep at all in these foreign lands called 1939 or 1942? He remembered sleeping on that flight from Los Angeles to New York City. He remembered sleeping in the Quiet Room at Payne Whitney. He remembered those sleeps because of the vivid dreams. But were those dreams dreams or real?

For that matter, was *he* real or something of his own imagination? Was he still asleep all this time in the back of Merman's closet in 1983? Mikey had no answers.

He only knew that now, in this less than foreign country called 1970, his own very kind father offered him the use of the basement to, as Morris said, "stay for a while." And despite Mary2's warning to him about not going back to that bedroom in the cellar, Mikey accepted the offer.

Since Mikey was due at the theatre every night that Merman was on in *Hello, Dolly!* (she never missed a performance!) and Morris Minkus went back to work and decided to ignore his illness and take no treatment, their time together was restricted to late-night talks after Mikey returned from the St. James on the subway. But those late nights down in the basement of the Minkus house were precious.

As with most precious memories, time seemed to speed up as he was living them and started to feel like a musical montage where one scene led to another at a furious pace, underscored by a dazzling tune as it rolled on.

In the twelve years he was Morris's son, he knew little about his dad except for his warmth, the warmth that counterbalanced Rifka's starchy coldness to her son. Now, though, dealing with his father on a man-to-man basis, adult to adult, Mikey was nervous.

"My wife has closed the door on my illness," Morris confided at 1:00 AM on Friday morning. "She won't discuss it."

"Why not?" Mary2 asked that night at the theatre.

"Morris says that she's just too scared to deal with the truth," Mikey responded.

He had taken to confiding in Mary2 in a way that he had seldom done with anyone. She didn't question why he was staying out in Brooklyn or why he was getting so close to the man he called Morris. She seemed to have a keen interest in their budding relationship and prodded him with more questions.

"So, he's just not going to seek treatment at all?"

"That's right," Mikey sadly replied.

"And what about the boy?" Mary2 asked.

"My son does not need to know everything," Morris responded when Mikey relayed that question in their next late-night talk. "He's just a kid. I don't know how… I mean, I don't know how he's going to wind up or even if he'll remember me."

"I hope you told him that was not true," Mary2 shouted at Mikey at the Saturday matinee while Merman (with no love for matinee audiences) walked through Act One.

"I did! I told him that I never forgot my father."

"And did you give him the gift?"

"Not yet."

Mary2 rolled her eyes and threw her arms in the air dramatically. "Time is fleeting, Mikey Marvin. Do you think either of us is gonna be here forever?"

Mikey looked at Mary2 as the applause thundered in by way of the dressing room squawk box. Act One must be over.

"Don't just look at me. I have less time than you do, little boy, and I have to sew Miss M into that red dress again. Lordy, it's like my Sophie Tucker days all over again."

That night after two shows of *Dolly*, Mikey and Morris settled in for their usual early morning talk.

"You don't smoke," Morris said as he hacked away in the basement room he was lending to Mikey. "Smart kid."

"So, Mikey starts school again on Tuesday, right?"

"The day after Labor Day. Every year like clockwork. So, how's it going over in Ethel Merman-land?" Morris said as he flicked his eyebrows in that salacious Groucho way he had.

"Well, I'm glad you brought that up. Wednesday is the big day. The day that *Hello, Dolly!* becomes the longest-running musical in history."

"Beating *My Fair Lady*. You know how I know that? The kid. Mikey. He is so excited about it. He read it in Earl Wilson's column."

"Really?" Mikey said, remembering how excited he was and then how disappointed he was to never see Merman as Dolly. Mikey took the plunge.

"I could get you both in to see the historic performance. I have one of Ethel Merman's precious house seat orders. It's a matinee, so you both would have to take off."

"What did he say?" Mary2 hungrily asked at her labor day lunch with Mikey in the Village.

"At first he balked," Mikey slowly said, drawing it out for effect, "but then…"

"What? What?"

"He said 'no.' There was no way to take Mikey out of school for a day when he was just starting the new semester."

"Say what?" Mary2 said.

"That's what he said," Mikey replied.

"Did you tell him that this would be a memory you would keep for the rest of your life, after he was dead?"

"*I* would keep?" Mikey asked.

Mary2 ignored Mikey. "What are you going to do, Mikey Marvin?"

"I already put the house seat order in, and the tickets will be at the box office in Morris's name, pre-paid."

"Maybe you need some help from a pro, little boy."

And the montage rolled on. Later that day at the annual Minkus Family Labor Day Barbecue, Mikey brought the subject up to Morris again.

"I cannot take such a gift," Morris declared as he crossed his arms over his chest defiantly. "Rifka, do not undercook my steak," he shouted across at his barbecuing wife.

Rifka turned over the huge slab of bloody beef. "I know, Morris. If it's not shoe leather, it's not done."

"What gift?" twelve-year-old Mikey asked.

Silence.

"What gift?" repeated young Mikey. When more silence ensued, little Mikey's eyes started to water and his fury mounted. "No one tells me anything!" he yelled as he ran from the yard back into the house. Passing him through the swinging screen door, wearing toreador pants and a sparkly-top cut down low to show her assets, was none other than Ethel Merman.

"Hey, kid! Watch where you're running!" she shouted. "You could kill a musical comedy star that way."

Ethel nonchalantly entered the Minkus backyard in her idea of Labor Day attire plus about six pounds of costume jewelry.

"Oh, my God! Rifka," Morris excitedly called. "Did you see who just walked into our backyard?"

Rifka almost dropped the burgers she was flipping. "It's the loudmouth!"

"Hey!" Ethel said in mock outrage.

Mikey/Marvin smiled and thought to himself, "The big guns are here."

Ethel and Morris went to the front of the house and out on the porch, as two Mikeys waited and Rifka burned.

"So, Morris… can I call you Morris? Good. That's settled," Ethel plowed ahead as Morris opened a pack of Marlboros, took out a cigarette, tapped it on the box, put it in his mouth, and lit it. He sighed with satisfaction as he took the first puff. Suddenly he remembered his manners and proffered the box to Ethel.

"No, thanks. I quit in 1957. Those things'll kill you."

"Now you tell me," quipped Morris.

"So, Marvin invited you to my big record breaker, I hear."

"He did."

"Have you seen me in the show yet?"

"Sadly, no."

"Well then, this is your great opportunity. And the kid likes musicals, I hear."

"Miss Merman…"

"Do you need a whole song and dance, Morris? Cause I am not supposed to be singing on my day off. But Marvin thinks this is important somehow."

"Marvin and I have become close during our short acquaintance. I think I've told him too much."

"Marvin has not mentioned one word to me. He likes to gab with my dresser Mary, and *she* tells me only what she feels is important."

Morris threw his cigarette onto the porch and stubbed it out with his foot. "Did she tell you I'm approaching the exit ramp?"

"Yes," Ethel answered quietly. "All the more reason to bond with the kid and leave him something to remember."

"You don't think he will remember this day? Ethel Merman at his Labor Day barbecue? I know I will… it's just that my memory is going to be a short one."

"I don't know if you know this, Morris, but I lost my daughter last year."

"I didn't know. I'm sorry."

"Yeah. Me too. I keep her ashes in my front closet so I can always say hello and goodbye when I go in or out. But be that as it may, I had no clue she was going to leave me, no warning, no nothing. And neither of us got to have that moment. You know… one sweet moment of sharing that I could cling to instead of the millions of little battles that never got won."

Morris was silent but put his hand on Ethel's as they sat down on the beach chairs that now filled the porch. They both looked out over the empty streets of Brooklyn, each in their own world of thought; Ethel contemplating the past, while Morris thought about the future. It seemed to them that all of humanity was in their backyards with their grills all aflame with Labor Day burgers and hot dogs.

In the Minkus backyard time was standing still, and the air was thick with anticipation from the Mikeys and from Rifka's seething jealousy. The older Mikey could see his mother as she was before; before his father died. What he saw were the hints of the metamorphosis that would happen in just a few short months. The lines of bitterness around her mouth were just beginning to sprout their own lines and now, finally, Mikey could see where her hate of all things Merman came from. It all began on this day that never happened.

But in opposition to Rifka's hate, what also began on this day that never happened was Mikey's intense love for Ethel. His idolization began on this Labor Day. This day in which history, perhaps only in a small personal way, was changed. The day that Merman stepped in and changed their lives.

As the senior Mikey contemplated all this stage worthy confusion of reality and fantasy surrounding him, Merman and Morris re-entered the backyard scene. Ethel sat down on a reclining lawn chair and put her feet up and took some sun. Behind her huge sunglasses, she closed her eyes and smiled her secret smile. Morris looked at Marvin and nodded, as he approached his son.

"So, Poochie, you wanna take off from school on Wednesday and see a show with the old man?"

Back up in her Harlem flat, Mary2 played an ancient game of solitaire and, as she flipped each card, laying down her suits, she laughed.

At 2:00 PM on Wednesday, September 9, 1970, Michael Marvin Minkus sat on the steps leading up to the mezzanine of the St. James Theatre and got the odd pleasure of watching both the historical show and his own past as happy as he would ever be. And when Merman sang "World Take Me Back," one of the two songs that were put into the show when she took over, Mikey knew in his heart that indeed, "the world is full of wonderful things to believe in." And that it was time for him, as Dolly says, to "rejoin the human race." To stop time-jumping and figure out how to live in the time in which he was born and get out of Rifka's basement. Not to rejoin the human race, but to finally join the freak show.

The only question now was how to get to 1983 without waiting thirteen years.

As Mikey pondered how to escape from his escape, his crystal ball of a mind flashed forward with his young alter ego. He looked in the glass and saw Morris taking the boy to other Broadway shows: *Promises, Promises*; *1776*; *Applause*; *Company*... One every week, until Morris's cough got too bad to suppress with cough drops and he had to leave in the middle of each act to hack it out in Shubert Alley. Then, finally, would come the day when Morris was too sick to take the boy to see a show. Then Morris went into the hospital and never came out. Mikey remembered and looked into the future to the horrible day when there were no more Broadway shows with his Dad, because his Dad was no more. To the time when he moved down to the basement to get away from his mother. Away from Rifka's grief and anger. Rifka, who never got over losing Morris. Rifka, who wrapped her head in toilet paper as if it were a widow's veil.

With all the sad knowledge of what awaited him back in 1983, Mikey still wanted to go home.

"Well, little Mikey Marvin," Mary2 whispered later at the party at Sardi's, as if she could read his mind, "how are you going to do it? I mean how did you get here in the first place?"

"Here or in the first place?"

"Have you been drinking, little boy?"

"My Dad and his son just left, and I have never seen them look happier."

"Then you deserve a drink. You did good. You'll remember this day forever."

Mikey knew there were many ways to the past but there was only one sure path to his future—the closet of the star dressing room at the Imperial Theatre. It was the first portal that brought him to 1939 and if he were to return to 1983 and bring all his newfound knowledge to his present, he had to go back the way he came. But Mikey knew from all those days in the library pouring over *Theatre Worlds* that right now the Imperial Theatre was between shows and dark. He knew that *Minnie's Boys* closed at the end of May and *Two By Two* wasn't due to open until November.

Mikey looked hard at Mary2 and asked the question on his mind.

"Do you know any way for me to get into the Imperial Theatre?"

Mary2 said she didn't and then went off to celebrate with the other backstage people.

Mikey, alone in the crowd of strangers, resolved to go home now. He knew how but needed access to the Shubert-owned Imperial Theatre. Suddenly, his mind flashed back to that afternoon in 1942 at the Shubert Theatre when the house manager had escorted Mikey to his office and to a long-distance call from Richard Halliday.

"How did you find me?" Mikey remembered asking.

"I have spies at the Shuberts," Halliday told him.

Now, standing in Sardi's across the street from the Shubert Theatre in 1970, Mikey had his answer.

Halliday. Of course.

Mary2 might have had no access to the Imperial, but she had the key to Ethel Merman's star dressing room and Mary Martin's phone number in Brazil. In these antique days of 1970, it took Ma Bell and her fleet of operators some time to finally get through, but when Mikey heard the cheerfully chirpy voice of Mary Martin, he knew it was worth the wait. It was 8:00 PM in New York and 9:00 PM in Brasilia where Mary and Richard had their ranch.

"Hello?"

"Spirit who haunts this dark forest tonight, dost hear me?" Mikey began playing the game of being Captain Hook. From the depths of his memory of when he worked for Mary, Mikey was using their secret code so that Mary knew it was him calling.

"Ogs bogs hammer and tong… I hear you." Mary responded in her best baritone voice. She was, after all, Peter Pan, a lost boy of Neverland.

"Spirit of the forest, have you another name?"

Mary/Peter responded with excitement, "Yes."

"Is it vegetable? Mineral?"

Mikey was greeted with a grunt-like "no" for each question until he asked, "Animal?"

"Yes."

"Have you another voice?" Mikey finally asked.

"Yes!"

Suddenly Mary gave out with a wondrous soprano trill.

"It's a lady," Mikey practically sang in his best Cyril Ritchard voice. "A beautiful lady."

Suddenly Mary Martin's silvery bubble of a laugh spewed forth from the receiver all the way across continents and time zones.

"Michael! You caught us right before we crawled into bed. It's nine o'clock here. Bedtime for the Hallidays. How are you? How is that Merman treating my favorite boy?"

"I'm great and the last time I saw Ethel she was still at Sardi's celebrating with the rest of the *Dolly* cast. I don't want to disturb your imminent slumber, but I really need to talk to Richard."

In the next split second a man's voice spoke.

"I'm on the line already." Mikey recognized Halliday's cultured and slightly slurred speech. Had he been drinking? In any case, Mikey had the odd notion that this would be the last time he would ever speak to Halliday, whom he knew would die in just a few years.

"When the phone rings in this far away jungle at this hour," Halliday continued, "it's either another grandchild on the way or someone in Texas has given up the ghost and become one. But since you are bringing neither bit of cheery news, you are most welcome. What can I do for you, Michael?"

"I have an odd request. I need to get access to the star dressing room of the Imperial Theatre."

There was a short silence and Mikey wondered if one of Ma Bell's proteges had dropped the ball. Finally, he heard Halliday talking to Mary in a less slurred and more in control tone.

"Mother, you can go to bed now. I'll take it from here."

As Mikey approached the stage door of the Imperial Theatre, it almost magically opened. Although Halliday's power as a producer and president of Mary Martin, Inc. might have diminished these last few years of Brazilian exile, he was able to contact his oldest friends at the Shubert Organization and track down the night watchman (who did not usually show up this early), beg the favor and… voila! Mikey was in.

It took all of his faith to believe that this would work. He felt like the leading man of *Brigadoon* who, knowing that the magical Scottish village had disappeared into the Highland mist for the next hundred years, still came back looking for the town that used to be. Mikey had that much faith. He somehow knew that walking into the closet in the star dressing room (last occupied by Shelley Winters, but former home base of both Ethel and Mary) would bring him back to Ethel's apartment in 1983. For a boy who didn't have a bar mitzvah, he was filled with a religious fervor that almost frightened him.

The dressing room was spooky. A fallen star on the floor mingled with a feather and a bugle bead, surrounded by cobwebs lit by a single bulb over the dressing table. And there in the corner, the closet door stood half open, as if welcoming its next occupant.

Mikey approached the door slowly and as he touched it, a mouse came running out of the closet and scampered right across his left shoe. He stifled a scream, not wanting to bring the night watchman into the room. Then he began to laugh.

A mouse. That's what he had been when he first entered Ethel's closet. And now the mouse was out, and he needed to go back in so that he too could exit and be free.

Mikey touched the knob, pulled the door open and heard a distant single note of music being held that lured him deeper and deeper into the dark, until finally the note became a melody, a melody that Mikey had never heard before, but one that he longed to sing.

Epilogue

First You Have Me High… Then You Have Me Low
New York City, August 1983

"Mikey Marvin! Mikey Marvin Minkus!"

The music Mikey was hearing had mutated into the non-mellifluous voice of a cranky Mary2 calling to him from beyond the door at the end of the long dark closet. Mikey finally found his way through all the Merman clutter and pushed open the door. Vast amounts of artificial light hit him in the face, and he felt as if he were on a red carpet at some premiere as blinding flash bulbs popped in his face.

"There you are," Mary2 said, dressed once again in her nurse whites. "Finally, out of the closet."

The old Mikey would have looked at her with a blank stare, hiding his true horror at her words, but this Mikey broke out laughing at her double entendre.

Mary2 had an envelope in her hand and held it out for Mikey.

"What's that?"

"It's what I went looking for in Miss M's desk. It's a letter. Read it."

Mikey instantly recognized the familiar, prize-winning cursive writing style of the address – To Miss Ethel Merman. He carefully opened the fragile envelope and there, on a white-lined sheet of paper torn from a spiral notebook, was a hand-written note.

July 4, 1971

Dear Miss Merman,

I know that I should have written you a thank you note for the wonderful day you gave me and my dad when you asked us to come to your show and then to the party after. I mean that I should have written you sooner.

It was amazing and we had the best time. I was sad when the show closed in December and really mad when Fiddler on the Roof ran longer and became the longest-running musical. In my heart it will always be your show that holds the record.

My dad and me went to so many other shows, almost one every week, but Hello Dolly will always be my favorite and you are now my favorite star ever.

That's the good news.

The bad news is that my dad died. Wow! I really didn't want to have to write those words, but you were so nice to us that I thought you should know. I am going to be 13 soon but my mom said no bar mitzvah because it would be disrespectful. So, no gifts for me.

The other interesting news is that I have moved down into the room in the basement next to the washer and dryer and can decorate my room any way I want. I have a really neat poster of you on my wall now and hope to get more to put up and maybe even do a collage on the ceiling so I can see you when I sleep.

I hope, Miss Merman, that you might write me back sometime and that the next time you're in a show on Broadway I can come back and say hello and tell you how great you are. You really are my favorite Broadway star.

Very truly yours,
Michael Minkus

PS I saw you on TV the other night and you looked really young. It was an old movie with Eddie Cantor, and you sang a really wonderful song which I think was called "First You Have Me High and Then You Have Me Low." You sang it great. I think it was in black and white, but even if it was in color, I would have seen it in black and white since that's the kind of TV we have. You were really great in this movie and so pretty. Anyway, thanks again for the great show.

    Mikey carefully folded the note back up and returned it to its paper home. Now he knew that he really did change history, even if it was just a little bit. The Mikey who walked through the lobby of the Surrey Hotel to meet his idol had never gone to the historic performance of *Hello, Dolly!* and met Ethel Merman and written her that note. *That* Mikey never bonded with his Dad and went to show after show until there were no shows or days left for Morris. The rest of the world may have gone on as it always had, but Mikey Marvin Minkus had changed, both in the past and now, in the present. Before he could consider what else had changed, the door of Merman's room opened and a distraught Mary Martin emerged, dabbing at her eyes with a handkerchief.

    "She wants to see you."

    Mikey was scared. He had rushed here to see Ethel Merman, the star of stars. To save her from death. Or at least to comfort her. But now, after journeying back and getting to really know his idol as a human being, he was frightened to see the woman behind that door, what she had become. He looked first at Mary1 and then at Mary2, both of whom understood his trepidation. Their faces were encouraging and sympathetic.

    "Would you like me to be with you?" Mary Martin asked.

"Yes," replied Mikey.

Mikey and Mary entered the darkened room where a shrunken and diminished Ethel-who-was-no-longer-the-Merm sat in a chair propped up by pillows. Mikey thought this can't be her, this marionette without strings. It must be someone else, her mother perhaps. But he knew that Agnes Zimmermann had died a few years before. But then, who was this emaciated woman with the skinny legs and a face all puffed out as if she had been inflated like a Macy's balloon-version of Ethel? Who had made her up with redder than red lipstick and fake drawn-in eyebrows? Who had plopped that little red wig on the top of her shaved head, like a polyester cherry on top of a Halloween sundae?

"Ethel, you remember Michael."

Ethel looked at Mikey and then at Mary and muttered out of the side of her mouth, like a bus-and-truck Edward G. Robinson chomping on a stogie, "I'm not fucking senile."

Mikey almost laughed as Mary Martin blushed as pink as the fake plastic roses near the bed.

"I brought you roses, but I forgot you're allergic to them."

Ethel looked up at him with her ancient yet unlined face and sadly murmured, "Doesn't matter. No more singing."

Mikey could feel his heart breaking inside him, but he was determined to keep a cheerful conversation going. He asked about the sign on her TV that forbade any channel changing. He mentioned that he had just been playing the ten-inch Decca record of the *Ford 50th Anniversary* duet this morning and wondered why part of it was deleted on the record.

"Probably because of the lack of groove space on those old records," Mary chimed in.

Through all the forced, idle chit-chat, Ethel just stared straight ahead. It must have been a strain for her to even try to talk out of the one side of her mouth that still functioned. She looked like she might slide off the chair into a crumpled heap at any moment.

"You know what movie I got on VHS?" Mikey was pulling at straws. "*Strike Me Pink*. It's from 1936 and you co-star with Eddie Cantor? Remember?" He immediately felt stupid asking her if she remembered, but he went on anyway. "I watched it last night for the first time since I was twelve and marveled again at that torch song you sang. I think it was by Harold Arlen..."

At Mikey's mention of this movie, he could see a glimmer of recognition in Ethel's eyes, a spark of something that wasn't there when he and Mary walked into the room. Before he could finish his sentence and just as he mentioned Harold Arlen's name, the crisp, clear and very loud sound of a much younger Ethel Merman came out of her suddenly straightened out mouth.

"First you have me high… then you have me loooo-ooow!"

The woman in the polyester wig and painted eyebrows, whose brain tumor brought on a stroke that slurred her speech and gnarled her mouth, sang like it was 1936!

Mary Martin's mouth fell open. "Why, Ethel, you can sing!"

Even Ethel was shocked by the outpouring of sound coming out of her fully formed lips, so shocked that her painted-on eyebrows went up another inch. She sang those two lines of the song with such Mermanesque power that Mary2 came running into the room to see why the TV was on so loud. What she found was a miracle out of a fairy tale.

But as quickly as the miracle had occurred, it was over. Ethel's painted eyebrows returned to their usual abnormal place on her face and her mouth laid back on its side, as if it could do nothing more than lounge on a divan like an overly made-up Mae West.

Mikey and the Marys watched as a single tear slowly made its way down Ethel's round cheek.

"That's it!" Mary2 decreed as she turned on the TV that played day and night. "Miss M needs her rest, and this has been a more than full day."

Michael Minkus and Mary Martin both got up and gave Ethel a peck on her cheek.

"I will see you soon, Mighty Merm," Mary Martin whispered in Ethel's ear. "You keep on keeping on."

"Goodbye," said Mikey.

Merman stared straight ahead at the TV screen as the door shut, leaving her alone with her face illuminated by the glow of the Motorola TV. She never sang again.

Michael Marvin Minkus knew the history of Broadway and he especially knew the lives of his idols. But even he could not predict that Ethel Merman would live five more months, dying at 76 without ever singing another note, and that her friend and rival Mary Martin would live the same 76 years, but die six years later.

But in August of 1983, while the freak show was still running, while there were still Mermans and Martins and Channings living and breathing, Mr. Michael Minkus had options.

"Michael," Mary Martin said out of the blue, "my assistant Roger has disappeared. When I got up the other day he was just gone. I could hardly find the coffee. So… how about you move to Rancho Mirage and replace him? We could have such a good time. I'm considering going out on the road with a play and with Richard gone, I'll need lots of help knowing what the name of my theatres are. What do you say?"

Mikey suddenly had options in 1983. Mary2 acted as Mikey's agent and told Mary1 that Mikey needed some time. Time to think about it. Mary Martin, sure of her charms, smiled her warmest smile and gave Mikey her card with her Palm Springs address.

Mikey thanked Mary, took the card and put it in his pants pocket and held his hand over it as he exited Ethel Merman's apartment for the last time. He waited for the elevator for what seemed an eternity. As he waited, he imagined Ethel's gala funeral packed with all the friends and colleagues in her life. Mikey saw himself saying a warm hello to each of them, to all the people in Ethel's life he had met on the journey. Jerry Robbins would be there, older but still bearded and handsome. Leland Hayward and Josh Logan and Irving Berlin, but alas no Cole Porter or Richard Rodgers. And no Dorothy Fields to eulogize her Mermsie. They were gone. None of her living ex-husbands would be there either. Of that, he was sure. But there would be old friends like Josie Traeger and Benay Venuta and Maria Karnilova and, of course, Mary Martin. What a brilliantly melancholy tribute it would be to the Queen of Broadway.

Mikey had no way of foreseeing that not one of those "old friends" would be there for Ethel. That her funeral in January of 1984 would be a family-only affair without a hint of Broadway showmanship.

Mikey impatiently pushed the elevator button several times more. The elevator was never going to come, he thought, and he considered taking the stairs. But finally, a freight elevator arrived and when the door opened there was no uniformed elevator operator and the walls and ceiling were not burnished wood, but the kind of thick padding found on moving vans or trucks. Mikey was a little nervous to get in, but something compelled him. As he stepped inside, the doors closed quickly, and he pressed "L" for lobby. As the "L" button lit up, Mikey had an odd feeling that the elevator had another destination in mind for him.

As he descended, he wondered when and where he might be when the doors opened. Would he once again be in the past? The future? But when the doors finally parted after a rather rickety ride, Mikey saw a large calendar on the wall behind the concierge's desk of the Surrey Hotel that read August 1983. Mikey's flash of disappointment quickly turned to relief.

When he got home to Brooklyn after the long subway ride on the LL, he used his keys to unlock the triple lock, walked through his mother's empty apartment as he always did, and went down to his room in the basement. Rifka must be at the beauty parlor or one of her shady Mahjong games, he thought. As always, the door to his room was closed, but today he had to push a little harder than usual to enter his dark room.

When he finally got the door opened and put on the overhead light, he saw nothing but boxes; boxes of his record collection neatly marked alphabetically, A - C, D - F, and so on. Boxes of his rolled-up posters, which had been carefully taken down from the now bare walls. Boxes of his hundreds of *Playbills* and souvenir books. His few clothes were in brand new suitcases that he had never seen before. All the markings on the boxes were in his own hand.

Yes, Mikey thought, it was still August of 1983, but he had gone somewhere. He knew that now. He had entered his present on his way to his future. The boxes looked heavy, very heavy. But Mikey somehow knew, hard though they might be to move, he could do it. He knew he had the strength deep down to move every last box from that basement. It would just take time.

As Mikey started to lift the first box, he heard a rustling sound from his now-empty closet. He put the box down and cautiously approached the slightly ajar door and opened it, half thinking that a mouse might jump out, as it did at the Imperial Theatre thirteen years and a few hours ago. Instead, the light caught a slim young woman of about twenty or twenty-one dressed in a sleeveless, white flapper dress with a red-satin blouse and matching sash. On her feet were white ankle-strap shoes, and crowning her mid-length, curly brown hair was a cloche hat that screamed 1929. The young woman boldly strutted into the basement room. Masked by her self-confident air was a vulnerable little girl peeping out from behind her heavily made-up, big, brown eyes.

"Hi," she said in a booming Queens-accented voice. "My name is Ethel. Ethel Agnes Zimmermann. I'm the singer you hired. Now where the hell's the band?"

Mikey smiled. All he had to do now was find a band.

WHO'S WHO IN MARY & ETHEL LAND

A brief glossary of the "real" people in this novel, in order of appearance.

BENAY VENUTA Replacement to Merman (*Anything Goes*), co-star to Merman (*Annie Get Your Gun* revival), friend to Merman, and drinker of Campari.

SOPHIE TUCKER Star of nightclubs, vaudeville, film (with Garland), Broadway (*Leave it To Me*), and film; as in "Sophie Tucker will shit, I know, to see her name get billed below… Roxie Hart!"

WILLIAM GAXTON Broadway star of *Connecticut Yankee*, *Of Thee I Sing*, and *Anything Goes* (introducing "You're the Top" with Merman).

VICTOR MOORE Broadway star of *Oh Kay!* And, with Gaxton, *Of Thee I Sing*, *Let 'Em Eat Cake*, *Hollywood Pinafore*, and *Anything Goes*.

COLE PORTER Legendary songwriter who wrote five shows for Merman. Martin introduced his "My Heart Belongs to Daddy." Rich, married, gay. The epitome of class.

JIMMY DURANTE Large-nosed comic who co-starred with Merman in *Red Hot and Blue* and *Stars in Your Eyes*. She adored him.

JEROME KERN Classic composer of *Show Boat* and that's all you need to know.

EDDY DUCHIN Society bandleader. Accompanied Martin on her first record and played at the Rainbow Room.

NOEL COWARD The Master. Playwright, composer, lyricist, director, star. Wrote *Pacific 1860* for Martin, fought with her, made up, and co-starred with her on TV in *Together with Music*.

RICHARD HALLIDAY Martin's second husband, manager, and president of Mary Martin, Inc.

BERT LAHR Genius comic actor. Co-starred with Merman in *DuBarry Was a Lady* the same year in which he was Lion-ized in *The Wizard of Oz*.

HEDDA HOPPER One of two influential Hollywood gossip columnists (the other was Luella Parsons). Wore hats and was on *I Love Lucy*.

BILL SMITH Merman's first husband on rebound from Sherman Billingsley. Didn't last.

DOROTHY FIELDS Famed Lyricist and Book writer. Merman sang her in *Stars in Your Eyes*. She also wrote (with brother Herb) *Something For the Boys* and *Annie Get Your Gun* for Merman.

BING CROSBY Crooner of the 20th Century. Movies, records, and radio. Co-starred with Martin in movies and on radio.

JUANITA PRESLEY MARTIN Mary's mother.

BESSIE MAE ELLA SUE YAEGER Martin's best friend back in Texas. Martin made sure her name was always somewhere in her musicals.

HOWARD HUGHES Rich man who owned RKO Pictures and bedded lots of stars. Later an infamous recluse.

Y. FRANK FREEMAN Head of Paramount Pictures; Martin's boss for a while.

JEAN ARTHUR Movie star, best friend to Martin for a time. Rumors flew when they both went to parties dressed as *Peter Pan*. Both played Peter on Broadway.

RAY BOLGER Scarecrow, dancer, singer, and comic actor of stage and screen. Recorded with Merman in the 50s.

LEW FIELDS Father to Dorothy, Joe and Herb, and star, producer, and half of the vaudeville team Webber and Fields.

JOE FIELDS Playwright and Book writer. *Wonderful Town* and *Flower Drum Song* are his.

HERBERT FIELDS Book writer alone and then with his sister Dorothy. Happily unmarried.

SHERMAN BILLINGSLY Owner of the Stork Club. Married. Rough, tough and everything Merman loved.

RODGERS & HART Songwriting team of renown from the teens to the forties. Never wrote for Merman or Martin.

JOSIE TRAEGER Merman's best friend from "the real world." Fellow stenographer from before stardom. Stayed friends to the end.

HELLER HALLIDAY Mary's baby girl. Toured with her mom in *Annie Get Your Gun, Peter Pan,* and *Skin of Our Teeth* before retiring to go to school.

BERTHA BELLMORE Character actress; appeared with Bolger in *By Jupiter*.

GYPSY ROSE LEE Stripper, daughter of Rose, keeper of the stories that became Merman's greatest show, *Gypsy*.

KIT AND GUTHRIE Cornell and McClintock. Married show biz couple of the "marriage blanc" society.

BERNHARDT Sarah. One-legged French actress of note.

DUSE Eleanor. Famed two-legged French actress.

GERTRUDE NIESEN Radio singer; appeared in *Follow the Girls* with Gleason.

LARRY HAGMAN Martin's son from her first marriage. Birthing him at 17 made her proclaim "It's so hillbilly." Later a TV star who married a genie and was shot by Bing Crosby's daughter.

BEN HAGMAN Texas lawyer who married Martin when she was 16.

RODGERS & HAMMERSTEIN You know!

DOLORES GRAY Voluptuous, big velvety-voiced singer. Martin's protégé. Star of the London *Annie Get Your Gun* and Broadway's *Two on the Aisle*, *Carnival in Flanders* (won the Tony for doing 6 performances), and *Sherry*.

THE LUNTS Alfred and Lynn. Great acting couple of the 20th century. Loved to tour. Had a theatre named for them. Martin's friends.

JOSH LOGAN Director of hits: *Annie Get Your Gun, South Pacific,* and *Hot September*.

IRVING BERLIN Kern said, "he IS American music." Music and lyrics for *Annie Get Your Gun, Call Me Madam,* and *Mr. President* (with Anita Gillette).

ROBERT LEVITT Merman's second husband. Her love marriage. Father to Bobby and Ethel Jr. A reporter who aspired to lyric writing during the *Sadie Thompson* debacle. Committed suicide after their divorce.

LELAND HAYWARD Hollywood agent and Broadway producer of *South Pacific, Gypsy,* and *The Sound of Music*. Worked both sides of the Ethel Merman / Mary Martin fence.

MARY RODGERS Daughter of Richard and childhood friend of Sondheim. See *Shy*.

TALLULAH BANKHEAD Deep-voiced actress from Alabama with a potty mouth. Martin later played her role in a revival of *The Skin of Our Teeth*.

HELEN HAYES First Lady of the American Theatre. Appeared with Martin in *The Skin of Our Teeth*, both on stage and in a television production.

JEROME ROBBINS Dancer, choreographer, director, genius, and stool pigeon. Remembered for *On the Town, The King and I, Call Me Madam, West Side Story, Fiddler on the Roof,* and *A Pray by Blecht*.

ED SULLIVAN Influential right-wing columnist for *The Daily News* and host of a Sunday night TV show from 1948 - 1971.

SENATOR JOE MCCARTHY Hunted Commies. He had a little list. Gave the world Roy Cohn.

EARL WILSON Influential columnist for *The New York Post*.

JAY BLACKTON Broadway conductor and creator of the legendary Ethel Merman - Mary Martin medley for the *Ford 50th Anniversary Show*.

ROBERT SIX Merman's third husband because he resembled Sherman Billingsley. Head of Continental Airlines. Divorced in 1960.

CLARK JONES TV director of the Tony Awards and many variety shows.

PETE MARTIN Merman's ghost writer on her first memoir, *Who Could Ask for Anything More?*

EDWARD R. MURROW Famed reporter and star of *See it Now* and *Person to Person* on TV. Helped bring down Joe McCarthy.

BURR TILSTROM The hands inside Kukla and Ollie, but probably not Fran.

EDDIE ALBERT Broadway, film, and TV actor. Oliver on *Green Acres*.

CELESTE HOLM Haughty stage and screen star with an Oscar but no Tony.

JACKIE GLEASON Corpulent film and TV star. Ralph Kramden and Tony-winner for *Take Me Along*.

ANDY GRIFFITH Folksy actor remembered for being a small-town sheriff and Matlock on TV. Beloved by all who didn't know him.

JANE FONDA Daughter of Henry and star of stage, screen, television, and exercise videos. Best facelift in the biz.

JULE STYNE Brilliant composer of *Gypsy, Funny Girl,* and *Say, Darling*. Merman was hot for him after leaving Six.

SANDRA CHURCH Actress who played the title role in *Gypsy*. Rumored to be engaged to Styne. No nuptials ensued. Merman hated her.

JANET GAYNOR Oscar-winning movie star and Martin's best friend after Jean Arthur. Rumors flew when Janet and Mary both moved to Brazil.

DAVID MERRICK Fabled Broadway producer of *Gypsy, Hello, Dolly!* and *Breakfast at Tiffany's*. Friend to both Merman and Martin.

MARIA KARNILOVA Dancer, actress, and friend of Merman. Tessie Tura in *Gypsy* and Golde in *Fiddler on the Roof*. Married to actor George S. Irving.

GEORGE ABBOTT Legendary Broadway playwright and director who died at 107.

JUDY GARLAND Superstar of film, concerts, records, and TV. Merman duet-ed with her on Garland's CBS show. Almost starred in the film version of *Annie Get Your Gun*.

BETTY HUTTON Frenetic jitterbug movie star. Supported Merman in *Panama Hattie* and played Annie Oakley in the film version of Merman's hit.

BUDDY DESYLVA Songwriter, producer (*Panama Hattie, DuBarry Was a Lady* for Merman) and later head of Paramount studios.

LEE TRACY Stage and screen star, usually played fast-talking wisecrackers.

HOWARD LINDSEY Half of the writing team of Lindsey and Crouse, who wrote *Life with Father* and the book of *The Sound of Music*.

RUSSELL CROUSE See above.

MAINBOCHER Chicago-born fashion designer Main Rousseau Bocher. Martin wore him whenever she could. After she wore him in *The Sound of Music*, no other Maria ever did.

ADRIAN Fabled MGM costume designer, born Adrian Adolph Greenburg. Created Joan Crawford's look. Married to Janet Gaynor.

SLIM HAYWARD Salinas-born Mary Raye (Nancy) Gross became a model, socialite, and the wife of Howard Hawks and Leland Hayward.

PAMELA CHURCHILL Famed courtesan. Married for money. Always. Wife to Leland. A Churchill only by marriage and divorce.

JERRY HERMAN Songwriter of *Hello, Dolly!* (played by both Merman and Martin), *Mame* (Mary was the first star sought), and *La Cage Aux Folles*.

GROUCHO MARX Most famous of the Marx Brothers.

LAURETTE TAYLOR Actress. *Peg o' My Heart. The Glass Menagerie*. Admired Mary Martin. Martin played her in *Jennie*... sort of.

ARTHUR SCHWARTZ Composer with Dietz, Fields, Lerner, and others.

HOWARD DIETZ Lyricist with Schwartz, Kern, Duke, and the creator of Leo the Lion at MGM.

CAROL CHANNING Genius comic actress with a gravely baritone singing voice. The original Dolly after Merman turned it down.

ERNEST BORGNINE Ethel's fourth and last husband. The less said the better.

SHELLEY WINTERS Star of stage, screen and even musicals. See *Minnie's Boys*. A replacement Ado Annie in the original *Oklahoma!*

HAROLD ARLEN Brilliant composer of *The Wizard of Oz*. Look him up and listen to "Stormy Weather."

EDDIE CANTOR Star of Vaudeville, Broadway, movies, radio, and TV. He co-starred with Merman in the films *Kid Millions* and *Strike Me Pink*.

Stephen Cole

Stephen Cole is an award-winning musical theatre writer whose shows have been produced from New York City to London to the Middle East and Australia. His off-Broadway musical with Matthew Ward, *After the Fair*, was nominated for the Outer Critic's Circle Award for Best Musical and was subsequently produced in London to great acclaim.

The Night of the Hunter won the prestigious Edward Kleban Award and was produced in New York City, Dallas, and San Francisco, where it was nominated for several Bay Area Theatre Awards. The award-winning 1998 concept CD features Ron Raines, Sally Mayes, and Dorothy Loudon.

Saturday Night at Grossinger's has had successful runs in Texas (starring Gavin MacLeod), Los Angeles, and Florida. Broadway legend Chita Rivera toured in *Casper*, and Hal Linden and Dee Hoty starred in the world premiere of his musical adaptation of *Dodsworth*.

In 2005, Stephen was commissioned to write *Aspire*, the first American musical to premiere in the Middle East. This experience resulted in another musical about the creation of that show entitled *The Road to Qatar!*, produced to rave reviews and awards Off-Broadway, in London, and at the Edinburgh Festival, garnering a Best Musical nomination.

Among his other produced shows are *Rock Odyssey*, which played to hundreds of thousands of kids for ten seasons of productions at the Adrienne Arscht Center in Miami, and *Merman's Apprentice*, presented in concert at Birdland in New York City, followed by an all-star cast album on Jay Records, and an acclaimed premiere production in Sonoma, CA in 2019. Stephen's latest critically acclaimed musical is *Goin' Hollywood*.

Stephen's published books include *That Book About That Girl* and *I Could Have Sung All Night*, the Marni Nixon story, currently in development as a feature film from Amazon.

Stephen has also written several published stories and his real-life friendships with Ethel Merman and Mary Martin resulted in this, his first novel.

Visit www.stephencolewriter.org.

Printed in the USA
CPSIA information can be obtained
at www.ICGtesting.com
LVHW052105201223
766916LV00003B/3/J